RAVES FOR
REBEL OF THE SANDS

"You will cheer for Amani the whole way as she escapes the bonds of oppression and finds her own power, and you will mark your calendar for the sequel." —Rae Carson, bestselling author of the Fire and Thorns trilogy

"Buckle up for a wild ride! *Rebel of the Sands* is a stunning debut full of irresistible energy, heart-stopping action, and a new voice that sings." —Alison Goodman, *New York Times* bestselling author of *Eon* and *Eona*

★ "Romantic, thrilling, hilarious, and just plain great fun." —*Kirkus Reviews*, starred review

"Fans of Sarah Maas and Victoria Aveyard should give this one a try." —*VOYA*

★ "This atmospheric fantasy combines magic, mythology, and the Wild West to create a riveting tale . . . an exciting, romantic adventure that is unique and all its own." —*Booklist*, starred review

★ "If the best of the Old West and the coolest parts of Arabian Nights had a baby who then rebelled by going steampunk, the result would be this gem of a book." —*BCCB*, starred review

"Debut author Hamilton combines elements of Western and Middle Eastern civilization and lore with her own mythology, crafting an enticing, full-bodied story . . . successfully mingles romance with thrilling stakes, and hints at a welcome sequel." —*Publishers Weekly*

★ "Readers will be drawn into the story and won't want to put this book down." —*SLC*, starred review

OTHER BOOKS YOU MAY ENJOY

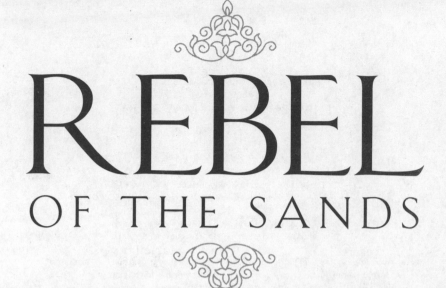

REBEL
OF THE SANDS

ALWYN HAMILTON

speak

SPEAK
An imprint of Penguin Random House LLC
375 Hudson Street
New York, New York 10014

First published in the United States of America by Viking,
an imprint of Penguin Random House LLC, 2016
Published by Speak, an imprint of Penguin Random House LLC, 2017

LIBRARY OF CONGRESS CATALOGING-IN-PUBLICATION DATA IS AVAILABLE
ISBN 9780451477538 (hardcover)

Speak ISBN 9780147517975

Printed in the United States of America

9   10

When I was fifteen, my parents pinned a cartoon to the kitchen corkboard of a girl angrily scribbling a letter that read, "Dear Mom and Dad: Thanks for the happy childhood. You've destroyed any chance I had of becoming a writer."

This book is dedicated to my parents.

Dear Mom and Dad: Thanks for the happy childhood. You made becoming a writer possible in an unquantifiable number of ways. Including the little, insignificant-seeming ones, like pinning a cartoon up on a corkboard and joking that you thought I could write a book anyway.

Now I have, and this first one is for you.

CAST OF CHARACTERS

Amani Sixteen-year-old sharpshooter, sometimes goes by the moniker of the Blue-Eyed Bandit.

Jin Foreigner from Xicha.

Tamid Amani's best friend, Holy Father in training, walks with a limp due to a deformity at birth.

Farrah Amani's aunt, eldest sister to her mother.

Asid Farrah's husband, a horse trader in Dustwalk.

Safiyah Amani's aunt, middle sister, left Dustwalk before Amani was born to seek her fortune in Izman.

Zahia Amani's mother, hanged for the murder of her husband.

Hiza Amani's mother's husband, not Amani's father by blood, killed by his wife.

Shira Amani's cousin, Farrah's only daughter.

Fazim Shira's lover.

Sultan Oman Ruler of Miraji.

Prince Kadir The Sultan's eldest son, Sultim, heir to the throne of Miraji.

Prince Naguib One of the Sultan's sons, army commander.

Prince Ahmed Al-Oman Bin Izman The Rebel Prince, leader of the Rebellion.

Nadira The Rebel Prince's mother by blood, killed by the Sultan for bearing the child of a Djinni.

Delila Half-Djinn sister of Prince Ahmed, marked by purple hair, able to cast illusions out of light in the air.

Shazad Al-Hamad Daughter of a Mirajin general, among the original members of the Rebellion, well-trained fighter, strategist.

Bahi Childhood friend of Shazad, disgraced Holy Man.

Hala Half Djinn marked by golden skin, able to twist people's minds into hallucinations.

Imin Half Djinn marked by golden eyes, able to shape-shift into any human form, Hala's sibling.

Izz and Maz Half-Djinn twins, marked by blue skin and blue hair respectively, able to shape-shift into any animal form.

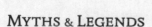

Myths & Legends

First Beings Immortal beings made by God, including Djinn, Buraqi, and Rocs.

The Destroyer of Worlds A being from the darkness of the earth who came to the surface of the world to bring death and darkness, defeated by humanity.

Ghouls Various servants of the Destroyer of Worlds, including Nightmares, Skinwalkers, and others.

The First Mortal The first mortal created by the Djinn to face the Destroyer of Worlds, made out of earth and water and air and brought to life with Djinni fire.

Princess Hawa Legendary princess who sang the sun into the sky.

The Hero Attallah Lover of Princess Hawa.

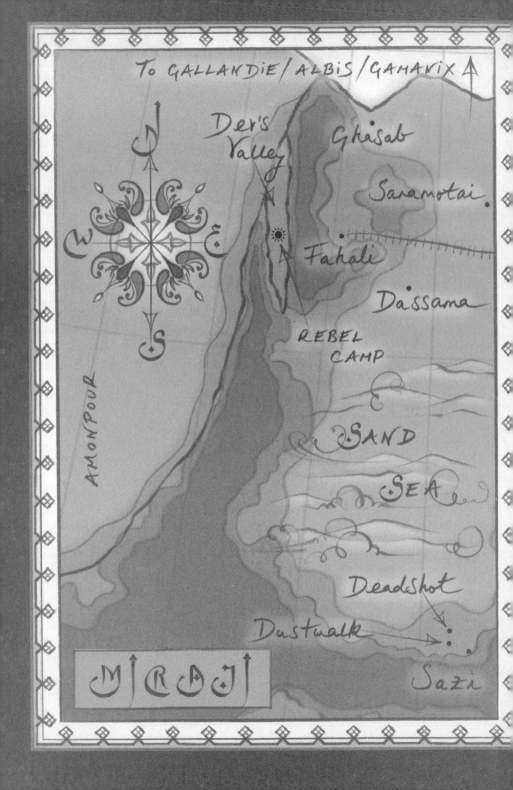

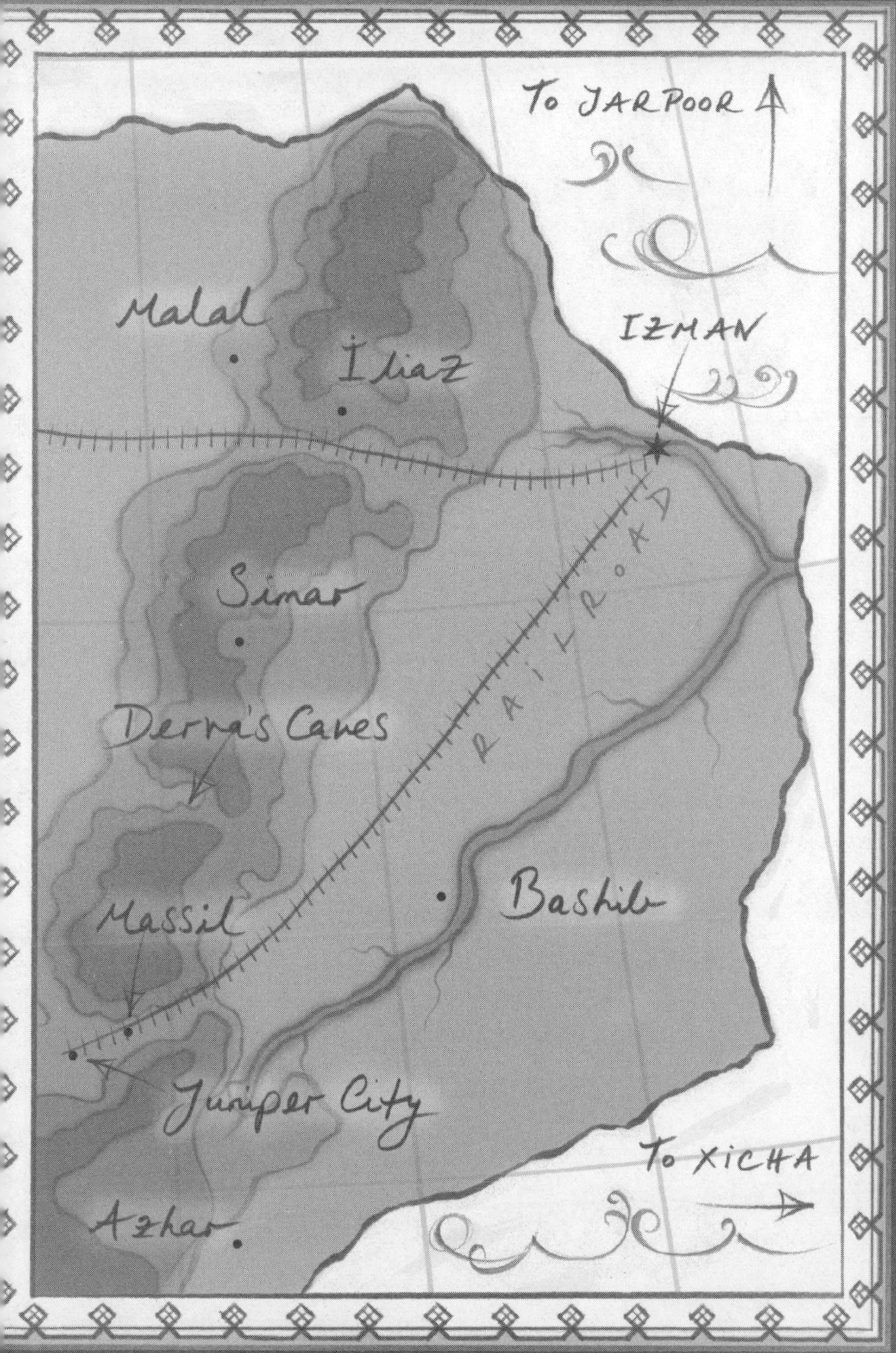

To JARPOOR
Malal
Iliaz
IZMAN
Simar
RAILROAD
Derra's Caves
Bashib
Massil
Juniper City
To XICHA
Azhar

ONE

They said the only folks who belonged in Deadshot after dark were the ones who were up to no good. I wasn't up to no good. Then again, I wasn't exactly up to no bad neither.

I slid from Blue's saddle and tethered her to a post behind some bar called the Dusty Mouth. The kid sitting against the fence was sizing me up suspiciously. Or maybe that was just his two black eyes. I tugged the wide brim of my hat lower as I stepped out of the yard. I'd stolen the hat from my uncle, along with the horse. Well, borrowed, more like. Everything I owned belonged to my uncle anyway, according to law, down to the clothes on my back.

The doors of the bar banged open, spilling out light and noise and a fat drunk with his arm around a pretty girl. My hand snapped to my sheema before I could think better of it, checking it was still tightly fastened so the better part of my face was covered. I was wrapped up to my eyes, and even hours after sunset I was sweating under the padding like a sinner at prayers. I figured I looked more like some lost nomad than a real sharpshooter, but so long as I didn't look like a girl it didn't much matter. Tonight I was getting out of here with at least my life. All the better if I got out with a few coins in my pocket, too.

It wasn't hard to spot the pistol pit on the other side of Deadshot. It was the noisiest building in town, and that wasn't saying nothing. A great big gutted-out barn at the end of the dusty street, it was swarming with bodies and blazing with light, propped up against a half-collapsed prayer house with a boarded-up door. Might be that once upon a time the barn had served some honest horse trader, but that was years ago by the looks of things.

The crowd thickened the closer I got. Like buzzards swarming to a fresh carcass.

A man with a bloody nose was pinned up against a wall by two others while another drove his fist into the man's face over and over. A girl called out from a window with words that'd make an iron dragger blush. A group of factory workers still in their uniforms huddled around a nomad in a busted-up wagon who was shouting about selling Djinni blood that'd grant good folks their hearts' desires. His wide grin looked desperate in the oily lamplight, and no wonder. It'd been years since anyone round these parts had seen a real live First Being, let alone a Djinni. Besides, he should've known better than to think desert dwellers would believe Djinn bled anything other than pure fire—or that anyone in Deadshot would believe themselves good folk. Everybody in the Last County went to prayers enough to know better on both counts.

I tried to keep my eyes forward, like I'd seen it all before.

If I climbed past the buildings, I'd be able to look across the sand and scrub all the way home to Dustwalk, though there'd be nothing but dark houses. Dustwalk got up and went down with the sun. Good honest behavior didn't belong to the dark hours of the night. If it were possible to die of boredom, everyone in Dustwalk would be corpses in the sand.

But Deadshot was alive and kicking.

No one paid me much mind as I slid into the barn. A big crowd was already gathered in the pistol pit. Lines of huge oil lamps hung from the eaves, giving the gawkers' faces a greasy glow. Scrawny kids were setting up targets and dodging a big man's blows as he shouted at them to move faster. Orphans, by the looks of them. Likely kids whose fathers had worked in the hulking weapons factory on the outskirts of Dustwalk until they'd gotten blown to bits by faulty machinery. Or until the day they'd gone to work drunk and burned themselves too badly to live. Gunpowder wasn't hardly safe work.

I was so busy staring that I nearly walked straight into the giant of a man at the door. "Front or back?" he demanded, his hands resting carelessly on a scimitar on his left hip and a gun on his right.

"What?" I remembered just in time to pitch my voice lower. I'd been practicing imitating my friend Tamid all week, but I still sounded like a boy instead of a man. The hired muscle at the door didn't seem to care.

"It's three fouza to stand at the back, five to stand at the front. Betting starts at ten."

"How much to stand in the middle?" Damn. I hadn't meant to say that. Aunt Farrah had been trying to smack the smart mouth off me for a year now with no luck. I got the feeling it would hurt more if this man tried.

But he just frowned like he thought I might be simple. "Front or back. There's no middle, boy."

"I'm not here to watch," I said before I could lose the last of my nerve. "I'm here to shoot."

"What are you doing wasting my time, then? You want Hasan." He shoved me toward a heavyset man with billowing, bright red trousers and a dark beard slicked to his chin, standing behind a low table piled with coins that bounced as he drummed his fingers.

I took a deep breath through my sheema and tried to look like my stomach wasn't trying to escape through my mouth. "How much to enter?"

The scar on Hasan's lip made it look like it curled up in a sneer. "Fifty fouza."

Fifty? That was almost everything I had. Everything I'd been saving up in the last year to escape to Izman, the capital of Miraji.

Even with my face covered from the nose down, Hasan must've seen the hesitation. His attention was already wandering past me, like he figured I was about to walk away.

That was what did it. I dropped the money on the table in a jangling handful of louzi and half-louzi that I'd scrimped one by one over the past three years. Aunt Farrah always said I didn't seem to mind proving myself dumb if it meant proving someone else wrong. So maybe Aunt Farrah was right.

Hasan eyed the coins skeptically, but when he counted them with the speed of a professional money-grubber he couldn't deny it was all there. For a brief moment the satisfaction tamped down on my nerves.

He shoved a piece of wood at me that dangled from a loop of string like a pendant. The number twenty-seven was painted in black on it. "Had much practice with a gun, twenty-seven?" Hasan asked as I put the string over my head. The tag bounced off the wraps I had forced over my chest to flatten it.

"Some," I hedged. We were wanting for almost everything in Dustwalk, in the whole Last County for that matter. Food. Water. Clothes. There were only two things we had too much of: sand and guns.

Hasan snorted. "Then you ought to know enough to keep your hands from shaking."

I pressed my hands close to my body to still them as I walked into the pit. If I couldn't hold a gun steady it wouldn't much matter that I learned to aim before I learned to read. I lined up in the sand next to a man who looked like he was mostly bones under his grubby factory uniform. Another man came to stand on my other side with a twenty-eight around his thick neck.

All around us the stands filled. The bet wranglers shouted out odds and numbers. If I were betting, I'd wager I didn't have any odds. No one in their right mind would put money on some skinny boy without the guts to even lower his sheema and show his face. Maybe I could win some crazy drunk a poor man's fortune by proving the right-minded ones wrong.

"Good evening, gents!" Hasan's voice carried over the crowd, quieting them down. Dozens of kids ran among us handing out the pistols. A girl with braids and bare feet passed me mine. The weight was instantly comforting in my palm. I quickly flicked open the chamber; there were six bullets neatly lined up. "Everyone knows the rules. So you'd better play by them or, God help me, I'll break your cheating faces myself." A laugh erupted from the stands, and a few whoops. Bottles were being passed around already and men were pointing at us in that way I knew from watching my uncle trade horses. "Round one: you got six bullets, six bottles. If you've got any bottles left at the end, you're out. First ten line up."

The rest of us stayed still as numbers one to ten shuffled into place, their toes on a painted white line in the dirt. I judged it about twelve feet between them and the bottles.

A kid could make that.

Two men still managed to miss with their very first

bullets. In the end only half the men hit all their marks.

One of them was twice the size of any other competitor. He was wearing what might once have been an army uniform, though it was too worn to tell for sure whether it used to be gleaming army gold or if it was just dirty with desert dust. He wore the number one painted in a bold slash across the piece of wood on his chest. He got the biggest cheer of all. There were cries of "Dahmad! Dahmad! Champion!" as he turned away, grabbing one of the kids scurrying around to collect broken glass. Dahmad spoke too low for me to hear, then shoved the child off. The kid came back with a bottle of brown liquor. Dahmad started chugging, lounging against the bars that separated the pit from the stands. He wouldn't stay champion long if he was going to wind up sloshed.

The next round was even more dismal. Just one of the shooters hit all his targets. As the losers shuffled off, I got a clear view of the winner's face. Whatever I'd been expecting, this boy wasn't it. He wasn't from around here, no doubt about it; that was the first thing I noticed. Everybody around here was from around here. Nobody in their right mind would chose to be in the Last County otherwise.

He was young, maybe a few years older than I was, and dressed like one of us, wearing a green sheema carelessly round his neck and desert clothes loose enough that it was hard to tell if he was really as broad as he seemed. His hair was as black as any Mirajin boy's; even his skin was dark enough that he might've passed for one of us. But he just wasn't. He had strange sharp features I'd never seen before, with high-angled cheek-bones, a straight square jaw, and eyebrows that made dark slashes above the uncanniest eyes I'd ever seen. He wasn't bad-looking either, at that. A few of the men he'd beat spat at his feet. The young foreigner's mouth pulled up in one corner like he was trying to keep from laughing. Then, as if sensing my eyes on him, he glanced at me. I looked away fast.

There were eleven of us left and we were jostling for space along the line with the extra body, even with me being half the size of every man here.

"Move, twenty-seven!" An elbow jammed into my side. My head shot up with a retort on my tongue. The retort died there as I recognized Fazim Al-Motem sidling up next to me.

I fought the urge to curse. Fazim had taught me every curse word I knew, back when he was eight and I was six. When we were caught using them, I got my mouth scrubbed out with sand and he blamed it all on me. Dustwalk was a small town. I'd known Fazim my whole life, hated him since I grew into some sense. These days he spent most of his time in my uncle's house, where I was stuck living, too, trying to get his hands under my cousin Shira's clothes. Every so often he'd make a grab at a piece of me, too, when Shira wasn't looking.

What the hell was he doing here? Actually, with the gun in his hand, I could sort of figure.

Damn him.

It was one thing if I got myself spotted as a girl. It was

a whole other thing if Fazim recognized me. I'd been in trouble plenty since I was caught cursing, but I'd only been beaten within an inch of my life once. It'd been right after my mother died, when I'd tried to borrow one of my uncle's horses all the way out of Dustwalk. I made it halfway to Juniper City before they caught me. I couldn't sit on a horse for a month when Aunt Farrah and her switch were done with me. If Aunt Farrah found out I was in Deadshot gambling stolen money, she'd beat me until that inch felt like it had been a mile.

The smart thing would be to turn around and get out of here. Except that would mean I'd be fifty fouza poorer. And money was in shorter supply than smarts.

I realized I was standing like a girl and straightened up before facing the targets. The kids were still racing around, lining up the bottles. Fazim tracked their movements with the barrel of his gun, calling out, "Bang, bang, bang!" and laughing as they flinched. I wished his gun would backfire on him and shoot that smile off his face.

The kids cleared out fast, and it was just us shooters and our bottles. We were the last group before the end of the first round. Guns were already going off all around me. I focused on my six bottles straight ahead. I could make a shot like this blindfolded. But I was being careful. I checked my distance, lined up the barrel, checked my sight. When I was satisfied, I pulled the trigger. The bottle farthest to the right exploded and my shoulders eased a little. The next three bottles went down in quick succession.

My finger pressed down on the trigger for the fifth time. A shout punctured my focus. I had no other warning before a body rammed into me.

My shot went wide.

Fazim had been shoved sideways by another shooter, ramming into me on his way to the ground, another one of the shooters on top of him. A boo went up from the crowd as Fazim scuffled in the sand with the other man. The big man from the door was already breaking up the fight. Fazim was dragged to the side by the scruff of his neck. Hasan watched them go, looking bored, then turned back to the crowd. "Winners from this round—"

"Hey!" I shouted without thinking. "I want another bullet."

A laugh went up around me. So much for not drawing attention to myself. My neck was burning with all the eyes on me. But this was too important. Too important not to ask. Scorn was written all over Hasan's face, and I felt the mix of humiliation and anger rise up in my throat in answer. "That's not how it works, twenty-seven. Six bullets, six bottles. No second chances."

"But that's not fair! He pushed me." I gestured at Fazim, who was nursing his jaw up against the wall.

"And this isn't a school yard, little boy. We don't need to be fair. Now you can use your last bullet and lose or get out of line and forfeit."

I was the only one with any bullets left. The crowd started jeering at me to get out of the way, and an angry flush rose in my hidden face.

Standing alone on the line, I raised my gun. I could feel the weight of the single bullet in the chamber. I let out one long breath that moved my sheema from where it was sticking to my lips.

One bullet. Two bottles.

I took two steps to my right and then half a step back. I twisted my body and tried to see it all in my mind. Dead center and I'd never hit the second one. Clip it too far off and neither would break.

Fifty fouza.

I shut out the shouting and taunts around me. I ignored the fact that every eye in here was on me and that I'd blown all chances of being inconspicuous. Fear crept in in its place. The same fear that had crouched in my stomach for the past three days. Since the night I'd been crawling around my uncle's house after dark, on my way to Tamid's, and overheard Aunt Farrah say my name.

"—Amani?"

I hadn't caught whatever had come before my name, but it was enough to make me stop.

"She's needing of a husband." My uncle Asid's voice carried more than his first wife's. "A man could finally beat some sense into her. In less than a month, Zahia will have been dead a year, and Amani will be clean and allowed to wed." Since my mother was hanged, folks had slowly stopped saying her name like a curse. Now my uncle mentioned her death more like a matter of business.

"It's hard enough to find a husband for your daughters." Aunt Farrah sounded irritated. "Now you want me to find one for my sister's brat, too?" Aunt Farrah never said my mother's name. Not since she'd been hanged.

"I'll take her as a wife, then." Uncle Asid said it like he was talking about trading a horse. My arms nearly buckled into the sand.

Aunt Farrah made a disdainful hissing noise at the back of her throat. "She's too young." There was an impatient tone in her voice that normally ended a conversation.

"No younger than Nida was. She is living in my house anyway. Eating my food." Aunt Farrah normally ruled the house as first wife, but every so often her husband would root his feet, and just now Uncle Asid was warming to this idea unnervingly fast. "She can either stay here as my wife or leave as someone else's. I choose her to stay."

I didn't choose to stay.

I chose to get out or die trying.

And just like that, everything came into focus. Me and my target. Nothing mattered but the aim.

I pulled the trigger.

The first bottle broke instantly. The second teetered for a moment on the edge of the wooden bar. I could see the chip in the thick glass where I'd hit it. I held my breath as the bottle rocked back and forth.

Fifty fouza I might never see again.

Fifty fouza to lose and my only way out.

The bottle hit the ground and shattered.

The crowd roared. I let out a long breath.

When I turned around Hasan was looking like I was a snake who'd dodged a snare. Behind him the foreigner was watching me, eyebrows up. I couldn't stop grinning behind my sheema. "How'd I do?"

Hasan's lip curled. "Line up for round two."

two

I didn't know how long we'd been shooting.

Long enough for sweat to start pooling in the small of my back. Long enough for Dahmad the Champion to slosh down three whole bottles of booze between rounds. And long enough for one man after another to get knocked out of the game. But I still had a gun.

The target faced me at the end of the room, bottles moving on a slow rotating board some kid was turning with a crank. I slammed my finger down six times. I didn't hear the glass shatter over the roar of the crowd.

A hand dropped onto my shoulder. "Your final competitors tonight!" Hasan shouted near my ear. "Our own champion, Dahmad!" The man stumbled from the drink and raised his arms high. "Our returning challenger, the

Eastern Snake." The foreigner barely acknowledged the taunts and hoots; his mouth just pulled up at one side and he didn't look up. "And a newcomer on this fine evening." He yanked my arm up hard and the crowd went wild, hollering and stomping their feet until the barn shook. "The Blue-Eyed Bandit."

The nickname killed my excitement in one panicked jolt. I searched the pistol pit for Fazim. No matter if I could pass for a boy, my eyes weren't something I could hide. Everything else about me was as dark as any desert girl was supposed to be, but my pale eyes made me stick out. Stupid as he was, if Fazim was still here he might just be smart enough to put two and two together and not come out with three. But I grinned behind my sheema all the same and let the cheers wash over me. Hasan dropped my arm. "Ten minutes to get your last bets in, folks. Our final round is coming up."

There was a rush for the bet wranglers. With nothing else to do, I sank down in the sand in an empty corner of the pit, leaning against the railings. My legs still felt a little unsteady from leftover nerves, my shirt was sticking to my stomach with sweat, and my face felt flushed behind the cloth of my sheema.

But I was winning.

I closed my eyes. I might actually leave with the cash pot.

I worked it out quick in my head. The prize money came to over a thousand fouza. I'd have to scrimp till I was dead to steal and save a thousand fouza. Especially with the mines in Sazi collapsing a few weeks back. An accident. Badly placed explosives. That was the official story. It'd happened before, though maybe not so bad. Only I'd heard whispers of sabotage, too. That someone had planted a bomb. Or the wilder rumors claimed it was a First Being. A Djinni striking Sazi down for its sins.

But no matter what happened, no metal coming down from the mines meant no guns, which meant no money. Everyone was tightening belts lately. And I didn't even have enough to buy a belt.

But with a thousand fouza I could do a hell of a lot more than that. Get out of this dead-end desert that ran on factory smoke. I could run straight for Izman. All I'd have to do was get to Juniper City on the next caravan. Then there'd be trains from there to Izman.

Izman.

I couldn't think of the city without hearing it whispered like a hopeful prayer in my mother's voice. A promise of a bigger world. A better life. One that didn't end in a short drop and a sudden stop.

"So, 'Blue-Eyed Bandit.'" I opened my eyes as the foreigner sank down next to me, propping his arms on his knees. He didn't look at me when he spoke. "It's better than 'Eastern Snake,' at least." He was holding a skin of water. I hadn't realized how thirsty I was until that moment, and my eyes tracked it as he took a long drink. "Still, it has a certain dishonest bent to it." He glanced at me out of the corner of his eye. There was a skew to his words that would make even the most trusting fool think he was trouble. "You got a real name?"

"Sure. But you can call me Oman if you've got to call me something." My eyes might betray me to some, but telling him my name was Amani Al-Hiza would betray a lot more.

The foreigner snorted. "Funny, Oman's my name, too."

"Funny," I agreed drily, a smile pulling at my mouth all the same. I reckoned half the men born in Miraji were called Oman, after our exalted Sultan. I didn't know if their parents figured it would win them favor with our ruler—not that they'd ever get so much as spitting distance from him—or if they thought God might give them favor by mistake. But I did know that the stranger wasn't named Oman any more than I was. Everything about him was foreign, from his eyes to the angles in his face and the way he wore his desert clothes like they didn't belong against his skin. Even his words were tinged with an accent, though he spoke cleaner Mirajin than most folks around here.

"Where you from, anyhow?" I asked before I could stop myself. Every time I opened my mouth it was another chance to get found out for a girl. But I couldn't help myself.

The foreigner took a swig of water. "Nowhere in particular. You?"

"Nowhere interesting." I could play that game, too.

"Thirsty?" He offered me the skin, his attention a little too sharp. I was parched, but I didn't dare lift my sheema, not even a little. Besides, this was the desert. You got used to being thirsty.

"I'll live," I said, trying not to run my tongue over my dried lips.

"Suit yourself." He took a long drink. I watched his throat rise and fall greedily. "Our friend certainly seems to be. Thirsty, that is."

I followed his gaze to Dahmad. He was draining another bottle, his face red.

"So much the better for you." I shrugged. "I was going to beat you both anyhow. At least you're bound to come in second now."

The foreigner broke into easy laughter. I felt stupidly pleased with myself for being the one to drag it out of him. One of the men pushing to the front of the bet wranglers looked over at us, frowning. Like we might be conspiring. "I like you, kid," the foreigner said. "And you're talented, so I'm going to give you some advice. Throw the game."

"You really suppose that's going to work on me?" I tried for bravado, straightening up as much as I could.

"You see our friend over there?" He nodded to Dahmad. "He plays for the house. Hasan gets rich off Dahmad's winning. They don't like it when strangers beat him."

"And how do you know so much? Not being from around these parts."

The foreigner leaned over conspiratorially. "Because I beat him last week." We both watched Dahmad sway on his feet, grabbing the wall for support.

"Doesn't seem all that hard."

"It's not. The two men Hasan sent to corner me in an alley and get the money back were more of a challenge, though." He opened and closed his hand, and I saw healing bruises on his knuckles. He caught me looking. "Don't worry." He winked at me. "You ought to see the other guys."

I wiped away whatever he'd seen in my face that he thought was worry. "And here you are, back to give them a second chance at you."

He turned his full attention on me, all joking gone. "How old are you? Thirteen?" Sixteen, near seventeen, as a girl, but as a boy I looked young. "Someone who can shoot like you, you'll go far in a few more years if you don't get killed tonight. There'd be no shame in quitting. We all know you can shoot. Don't need to die proving it."

I eyed him. "Why are you back if it's so dangerous, then?"

"Because I need the money." He took a swig from the waterskin before getting to his feet. "And I always make it out of trouble alive." I felt a twinge at that. I knew what it was like to be desperate. He offered me a hand up. I didn't take it.

"You can't have more need than I do," I said quietly. And for a moment I felt like we understood each other. We were on the same side. But we were still against each other.

The foreigner dropped his hand. "Suit yourself, Bandit." He walked off. I sat there a moment longer, convincing myself that he was just trying to intimidate me into quitting. I knew we could both beat Dahmad. But the foreigner was a decent shot.

I was better. I had to be better.

The bet wranglers were fending off the last of their customers as the three of us stepped back up to the line. This time when the little barefoot girl ran up, she only brought one bullet with her. In her other hand was a strip of black cloth.

"Our final round tonight!" Hasan declared. "Blind man's bluff."

I reached for the blindfold, but the sound of gunshots stopped me.

I ducked before I realized the sound was coming from outside. Someone screamed. Half our audience were on their feet, craning over one another to get a look outside at this new entertainment. I couldn't see, but I heard the shout clear enough.

"In the name of the Rebel Prince Ahmed! A new dawn, a new desert!"

Pinpricks raced to every bit of skin I had.

"Damn." The foreigner rubbed his knuckles across his chin. "That wasn't smart."

A new dawn. A new desert. Everybody had heard the rallying cry of the Rebel Prince, but only in whispers. You'd have to be an idiot to shout your support of the Sultan's rogue son. There were too many men with old ideas and new guns to say a word against the Sultan in the Last County.

Snatches of voices rose from the babble. "The Rebel Prince was killed in Simar weeks ago." "I heard he's hiding in the Derva's caves with his demon sister." "—should be hanged straightaway." "He's marching on Izman as we speak!"

I'd heard half those stories, too. And a half dozen more. Ever since the day of the Sultim trials, when Prince Ahmed reappeared after disappearing fifteen years earlier, to compete for his father's throne, the stories about him walked the line between news and myth. They said that he'd won the Sultim trials outright and the Sultan tried to have him killed instead of naming him heir. That he'd cheated using magic and lost all the same. The only part that stayed the same in every version was that after failing to win the throne at the trials, he'd disappeared into the desert to start a rebellion to win the country back.

A new dawn. A new desert.

A spark of excitement struck inside me. Most stories I knew were about things that happened long ago to people long dead. The Rebel Prince was a story we were all still living. Even if he was likely to get killed any day now.

The scuffle outside was short, and then the lug from the door was dragging in a kid by the collar. He was probably as young as I looked in my disguise. Drunken *boos* went through the crowd as he passed.

"Well, well!" Hasan's voice carried over the din as he tried to get the crowd's attention back. The boy stumbled to stay on his feet, blood pouring from his face. He looked like he'd taken some bad hits to the face but nothing worse. No bullet holes or stab wounds yet. "It looks like we have a volunteer!"

The lug dragged the boy forward and shoved him

against the target. He put the bottle on top of the kid's head. My heart went down like a stone into my stomach.

"We have a new game, then! *Traitor's bluff*," Hasan crowed, his arms wide. The crowd answered in a roar.

I could make that shot without hurting the kid. The foreigner could, too. But the champion was swaying on his feet and downing another drink. I wasn't sure he could hit the ground if he tripped, never mind anything else.

The kid swayed on his feet, and the bottle clunked dully into the sand. The crowd answered with heckles. He looked like he might cry as Hasan's lug rammed his shoulder back until he stood straight, putting the bottle back on his head.

"The kid is too hurt to stand up straight, let alone keep the bottle steady." I caught the foreigner's words. He was talking to Hasan. "You can't shoot a target that won't stay put."

"Then don't shoot." Hasan waved a hand. "If you and the Bandit are too cowardly, then you can just walk away. Let my man win." So that's what Hasan was counting on. That the foreigner and I would go yellow-bellied and let Dahmad win. Just to keep some kid alive.

Just some kid who was younger than I was and already had arms marked with scars from factory work.

No.

It was him or me.

This kid wasn't going to survive long in the desert with rebellion on his tongue anyway. Not when half the Last County would rip him to shreds for treason. What would it matter if I took the shot and someone else killed him? Wouldn't make it my fault if he died.

"Or shoot him in the head and we'll call it close enough," Hasan joked. My hand tightened. "I don't care." Of course he did. He was counting on us walking away. We both knew it.

"You don't think it will look a little bit suspicious if we both drop out and let your man win?" I asked, cutting off whatever the foreigner had been about to say.

Hasan spun a bullet between his fingers. "I think that my pockets will be heavy with gold and yours won't."

"Sure," I flung over my shoulder without taking my eyes off the pathetic young rebel standing with his back against the target. He didn't deserve to be a victim of the desert any more than I did. "And you'll have more trouble than gold when your customers figure they've been duped." Hasan's face changed. He hadn't thought of that. I scanned the crowd, trying to look bored, like I didn't need this. Like I wasn't trying to play him just like he was trying to play us. "You've got a room full of drunks here who've put up some hard-earned money on this. And times are tight lately, what with no raw metals coming in from Sazi. It's making everyone mighty irritable, I've noticed. Don't you feel it in your bones?"

I didn't need to check if Hasan was following my gaze; a blind man could see the mass of broke factory workers and underfed boys and men with already-raw knuckles aching for a release. Even the kid with his split lip lined up as a target was one of the restless. Only he was drunk on the prince's rebellion instead of two-louzi liquor. Hell, I knew the feeling. I was counting on it to carry me all the way to Izman.

"Living under our sun doesn't exactly give men a cool head. Especially, say, if an Eastern Snake and a Blue-Eyed Bandit were to start talking out there." I looked at Hasan out of the corner of my eye, praying that he wasn't about to have me shot. "I'll tell you what, though. I can help you out."

"Can you, now?" Hasan scoffed, but he was still listening.

"Sure. I'll forfeit and take the kid's place. For a thousand fouza."

The foreigner rounded on me, saying something in a language I didn't know but that sounded like cursing. "Are you crazy, kid?" He switched back to Mirajin. "You want to get shot instead of him?"

"If I'm lucky, he'll miss me." I felt my chest rising and falling with each shallow breath. The kid was rocking back and forth on the sand that I was sure was filled with glass. He had bare feet, but he didn't whimper.

"Are we shooting or what?" Dahmad bellowed, chucking his empty bottle at the kid, missing him by a foot.

I was still watching Hasan; the sale wasn't made yet.

"If I'm not lucky, you don't have to pay me a thing and your crowd gets blood."

Hasan's lip curled up nasty-like. "And everybody goes home happy."

"Except the dead Bandit," the foreigner said, low enough that I was the only one who heard. He raised his voice. "We'll throw the game." The foreigner's eyes hadn't left me, though he was talking to Hasan. I opened my mouth to argue, but something in his gaze made me stop. We were on the same side now. "If the Blue-Eyed Bandit here is so determined to get up there as a target, I'll shoot first. I'll miss the bottle without shooting him in the head. Then you let the Bandit shoot. With me as the target. He'll miss, too." My shoulders felt tight, like my arms knew I couldn't bear to miss a shot. But he was trusting me. So I nodded ever so slightly. "Your champion wins by default. We all get out of here without a bullet hole in us."

"And with the money," I piped up before the foreigner could make us both honorable and poor. "We leave with a thousand from the house winnings. Each."

"I'll give you a hundred each," Hasan said.

"Eight," I retorted.

"Five and you're grateful I don't send someone after you to break your fingers and bring me my money back."

"Done." Five hundred wasn't a thousand, but it was better than nothing. And I might still be able to get to Izman on that.

The crowd was beginning to get rowdy. A cry went up from the stands. "Are you yellow-bellied fools going to shoot? The kid's about to piss himself!"

Hasan tore away from us. "Gents! Who really wants to see this rebel brat get shot at? He's too short by half anyway." Hasan snatched the bottle off the kid's head. "Scram!" The kid stared at him like he was the hangman who'd just cut the noose. *Go*, I urged silently. Then he was stumbling away.

The pressure on my chest eased even as a murmur of discontent rose. Hasan silenced them with a raised hand. "Wouldn't you rather see these three men with a score to settle take aim at *each other*?" The uproar from the stands was deafening, feet stamping so hard the whole building shook, down to the nails. "Step up, Bandit!"

I took one long, shuddering breath. Maybe I ought to have thought this through. Or at least held firmer at a thousand. "Come on, kid," a voice by my ear said. "You trust me, don't you?"

I eyed the foreigner's cocksure grin. "I don't even know you."

He reached out and pulled my hat off my head. I was glad I'd thought to shove my hair back under the sheema that was pulled low as my eyebrows, but still I felt bare without the hat. "All the more reason to trust me."

The walk across the barn seemed too long.

Hasan grinned as he balanced the bottle on top of my head. "Better earn your money and not shake, kid. Or everyone'll see the bottle trembling like a girl on her wedding night."

My anger rooted me; the bottle didn't move. Not when the foreigner stepped to the line. Not when he slotted his single bullet into the chamber. Not even when he raised the gun and pointed it straight at my head. Except I couldn't breathe. He took careful aim, adjusting the shot. He was taking his time, and my nerves were fraying by the second.

"Just fire, you coward!" The shout burst from my lips the same second the gun went off.

I didn't have time to flinch.

A boo went up from the crowd. And I was still alive to hear it.

I tipped my head and the bottle tumbled unbroken into my hands. I looked, and a bullet was embedded in the wall a hair to the left of my skull. Only then did I start to shake. I wasn't sure if it was from nerves or from excitement. I wrapped my hands around the bottle to hide it either way.

In a blur of boos I walked back to the line. The foreigner passed me halfway across the pit as he walked out to the target. He paused for a second, placing my hat back on my head. "You all right?" he asked.

"Cut it a little fine there." I tugged my hat back down.

"What's the matter, Bandit?" Like he thought something was too damn funny. "Feeling a little less immortal?"

I shoved the bottle at him. "I wouldn't taunt someone who's about to aim a gun at your head."

He laughed and kept walking.

And then I was the one standing behind the white painted line and he was the target. I could hit the bottle no problem if I wanted to. What were the chances Dahmad would actually hit the foreigner anywhere fatal? And even if he did, what was the foreigner to me? Not a thousand fouza in prize money.

I fired. The bottle stayed in one piece.

"The game is over!" Hasan cried over the shouts. "Dahmad reclaims his spot as your champion!" Some cheered, likely those holding slips with his number on them.

And slowly a new chant started to go up from the crowd. "Shoot! Shoot! Shoot!"

The champion was weaving unsteadily. "Yeah! I want a shot at the Snake, too."

The foreigner had pulled the bottle off his head, but now the champion was swaggering over to the line, taking aim and gesturing at him to step back into place.

"They're right!" Hasan crowed. "We can't have a winner if Dahmad doesn't shoot." He cut his gaze toward me. I understood what he meant clear enough. No winner meant no winnings for the house. And that meant no money for us. "What do you say, Eastern Snake?"

My eyes met the foreigner's and I shook my head. He held my stare for a long moment, all hints of joking gone. Then he stepped back and set the bottle on his head.

The champion stumbled up to the line. He could barely stand. He squinted at the foreigner, as if trying to make out where he was exactly. My father had been this drunk most days when he came home from factory work. He got his hands on a gun one of those times. My mother and I would've both been dead if he'd been able to shoot straight.

Dahmad raised the gun. From where I was standing I could see he was aiming straight at the foreigner's chest.

The foreigner had beaten the champion last time. Dahmad was drunk enough to think revenge was a better idea than winning. And a man was a big enough target for even a drunk to hit.

As the champion's hand squeezed down on the trigger,

Hasan's earlier words crashed down around me. There were no second shots in this game. I flung my body sideways without thinking and crashed into Dahmad.

The shove sent the bullet three feet to the left. The liquor sent Dahmad down into the sand while I staggered to find my footing, clutching my arm.

The crowd went up like a powder keg that had been waiting for the right spark.

They knew they'd been tricked, but no one seemed to know how. Some were screaming that the foreigner and I were in it together; others were shouting that Hasan had scammed them. In an instant they were rushing the bet wranglers.

"Son of a whore!" A pair of hands grabbed me by the front of my shirt. Dahmad was back on his feet and he had me clear off the ground, my toes dragging in the sand. I started to thrash, but he shoved me back against the wall of the pistol pit, knocking the air out of my lungs. And then there was a knife in his hand. Dahmad's face was close to mine, his teeth bared, his breath reeking of spirits hot against my cheek. "I'm going to gut you from navel to nose and leave you here picking your insides up off the ground, boy."

The foreigner's hand clamped over the champion's wrist, moving too fast for me to see. But I heard the sickening snap. I dropped to the sand in a heap as the champion fell onto his side roaring in pain, the knife clattering away. I saw bone sticking out of his arm. The foreigner swiped the knife from the ground. "Run," he ordered.

The whole place had gone to hell.

A drunk smashed into a lantern as he careened; it dropped into the stands, shattering in oil and flames.

I turned to make for the entrance, but the brawl was too far gone already. There was no escape that way. The foreigner and I stood, backs against the wall. We were forgotten—the chaos wasn't even about us anymore. The whole barn was filling with smoke. We were going to be choking in seconds.

"I don't suppose you can fly?" he shouted over the noise, pointing his chin straight above us. A window just out of reach, above the stands.

I grinned at him even though he couldn't see it. "I can't fly, but I don't weigh so much."

He understood me perfectly. Linking his fingers together, he created a foothold. I shoved the pistol I was still carrying into my belt. Damned if I'd leave a decent weapon here.

I took a few short steps back and ran. My third step landed my right boot in the foreigner's interlaced fingers and he launched me upward. My arms banged into the ledge with a jolt that was going to leave bruises. His hands were there under me, holding me steady as I dragged myself up the windowsill. The prayer house's roof was an easy drop below, and in a few seconds I was out in the night air. I was dying to make a run for it.

Instead I turned back, bracing my feet against the roof as I pulled him up, until he was out of the window and on the roof beside me.

We jumped down from the old prayer house, rolling as we hit the sand below. A bullet bounced off the wood near my head. "All right, Bandit," he gasped. "Where to?"

Where to? he asked me, in the town with the sky smelling of smoke and fiery chaos blooming in the dark.

I had to get back to my uncle's house. I had to lose him. My little cousin Nasima once got slapped silly for bringing home a mouse she found under the schoolhouse. I could only guess what'd happen to me if I brought a stray foreigner anywhere near home. And that wasn't even banking on what the foreigner would do if he found out I was a girl. "Nah, I'll be all right."

He looked over his shoulder. "Got somewhere to be?"

I was already backing away, eyeing the bar where I'd left Blue, hoping to God the horse was still there. "Thanks for everything." I forced a grin at him even though he couldn't see it. "But I've got to go see a bar about a horse."

And before he could say another word, I bolted.

three

"Get your useless self up and to the store, or don't expect to eat today." My blanket came off me with a violent rip. I groaned, squeezing my eyes shut against the sunlight and my aunt's face. "And don't expect to eat tomorrow either."

I counted her footsteps as she stomped away. Ten steps and she was clear to the kitchen. I cracked an eyelid. How much sleep had I had? A few hours, maybe. I wanted sleep more than I did food. But burnt dawn light was leaking in and calls to prayer were starting.

I rolled from the mat to the wooden floor, pulling my blanket over my head as I dug around for some clothes. Around me, the six cousins I shared the cramped room with were stirring. Little Nasima sat bolt upright before flopping back down and stuffing the corner of her blanket into her mouth.

You could barely see the floorboards between our mats. Our room looked like a battlefield, clothes strewn everywhere like fallen bodies, schoolwork, mending needles, and the odd book scattered throughout like shrapnel. Only Olia's corner had a clear floor. She'd even tried to hang a horse blanket from the ceiling to separate herself from her sisters. It took some getting used to, this room.

There'd been only two rooms in my father's house. The one he and my mother slept in and the big room where we ate and where I slept for almost sixteen years. That room was gone now, with the rest of the house I grew up in.

It took some searching, but I found my good blue khalat shoved in a ball under my mat. It was wrinkled, so I did my best to smooth out the creases with my hands before tugging it quickly on over the plain brown shalvar I wore on the bottom.

Shira sighed into her pillow. "Can you stop crashing around like a dying goat? Some of us are trying to sleep." In her corner, Olia pulled her blanket back over her head.

I found a boot and dropped it from as high as I could so it hit the floor with a loud thud. Shira flinched. She was the only one of my female cousins I shared blood with. The others belonged to my uncle's other wives. Aunt Farrah had given her husband three boys, then Shira.

She simpered at me through heavy-lidded eyes. "You look terrible, cousin. Didn't sleep well?" My fingers faltered on the sash I was knotting around my waist. Shira smirked pointedly. "Looks like you must've been tossing and turning, too." I resisted the impulse to tug my sleeve down over my bruised elbow. Of course Shira knew I'd snuck out. She slept two feet away.

Not that she could've guessed where I'd gone. But that wouldn't stop her from telling if she thought it'd get her something, even if it was just the satisfaction of seeing me get a beating.

"How could I sleep?" I went back to tying my sash with sluggish fingers. "Did you know that you snore?"

Olia snorted under her covers. "See, I told you," she shot at her half sister. Sometimes I almost liked my next youngest cousin. We used to get along just fine before I lived under my uncle's roof and hating me became one of Aunt Farrah's household rules.

"Though maybe that wasn't you last night," I jabbed at Shira. "Hard for a pile of blankets to snore."

Shira's bed had been as empty as mine when I'd clambered back through the window after using some of our precious water to scrub the smell of smoke and gunpowder from myself. Judging by the sickly sweet smell of oils on her, she'd been out to see Fazim. He'd probably told her he was going to the pistol pit and coming back rich.

I tried not to smile at the memory of him getting pitched from the competition. I wasn't even sure Fazim had made it out alive.

We were at a stalemate. I wouldn't tell so long as she didn't. After a moment, Shira flopped back onto her bed and started pulling a comb through her hair, ignoring me.

I was running my fingers through my own mess of black hair as I made my way into the kitchen. The boy cousins were already starting to mill around on their way to work, shouting to one another over the prayer bells. No one who worked in the factory had time for prayers except on the holy days. I snaked around my cousin Jiraz, whose uniform was half on, half knotted around his waist as he scratched at a healing burn across his chest. He'd gotten it from one of the machines a few months ago when it belched fire at him unexpectedly. He was lucky he'd lost only a month of work instead of his life.

I grabbed the tin of coffee off the top shelf. It was mighty light. There was sawdust mixed in to thin it out, too. My stomach tightened. Things always got bad when food was low. Actually, things were always bad. They just got worse.

"Farrah." Uncle Asid walked into the kitchen, rubbing his hand across his face. Nida, his youngest wife, trailed behind, eyes on the ground, hands over her pregnant belly. I turned my attention away just in time to pretend I didn't notice my uncle's eyes drag along me. "Is there coffee yet?"

Desperate restlessness filled me. I wasn't staying here. No matter how light the coin purse I wore tied against my middle felt after last night.

"Give me that." Aunt Farrah snatched the tin with one hand, the other smacking me sharply across the back of the head. I winced. "I told you to go open the store, you hear me?"

"I couldn't *not* hear you." I stepped out of her reach, not that it'd save me from a beating later. I was glad to get the hell out of this house and out of my uncle's sights, but I couldn't stop my smart mouth. "Any louder and the whole town could hear you screeching." I let the door clatter shut behind me as I dashed down the steps and into the street, Aunt Farrah's threats of a switch to my back fading with every step.

My uncle's shop and his house were at opposite ends of Dustwalk, which was a whole two hundred and fifty paces to walk. Dustwalk's single street was as crowded as it ever got, what with the men trudging to the factory and women and old folks rushing to the prayer house before the sun burned away the last of the cooler night air. The familiarity weighed on me. Lately I'd been thinking someone just ought to kill this town out of mercy. No steel was coming down from the mountains. It'd been years since the last Buraqi was spotted. There were a few regular horses left to sell, but they weren't worth a whole lot.

There was only one thing I'd ever liked about Dustwalk, and that was all the space outside of it. Beyond the flat-faced, dead-eyed wooden houses, you could run for hours and still find nothing but scrub and sand. I resented it now, how far it was from everywhere else. But when I was younger it'd been enough just to get away. Far enough that I couldn't hear my father slurring that my mother was nothing but a used-up foreigner's whore who couldn't give him a son. Far enough that no one could see me, a girl with a stolen gun, shooting until my fingers were sore and my aim was good enough that I could've knocked a shot glass out of a drunk's shaky fingers.

The furthest away I could ever get was when my mother used to tell me bedtime stories of Izman. Only when my father couldn't hear. The city of a thousand golden domes, with towers that'd scratch the blue off the sky, and as many stories as there were people. Where a girl could belong to herself and the whole city was so rich with possibilities that you almost tripped over adventures in the street. She read me the stories of Princess Hawa, who sang the dawn into the sky early when Izman was attacked by Nightmares in the night. Of the nameless merchant's daughter who tricked the Sultan out of his jewels when her father lost his fortune. And she read me the letters from her sister Safiyah.

Safiyah was the only person I'd ever heard of who'd gotten out of Dustwalk. She ran away the night before she was meant to be married and made it all the way to Izman. Letters came from her in the capital to my mother with a caravan every once in a blue moon. They talked about the wonders of the city, a bigger world and a better life. Those were the times my mother would talk most about Izman. How we were going to leave and go and join Safiyah someday.

She stopped talking about it on the hottest desert day anyone remembered in a long time. Or maybe just one of those days that folks remembered so well after because of what happened. I was as far into the desert as I could get without losing sight of the house. The sun was glaring so hard off the six empty glass bottles I had lined up that it was making me squint, even with my sheema pulled up to my nose and my hat low over my eyes as I took aim. I remembered swatting at a fly on my neck as I heard three gunshots. I stopped. But I didn't wonder much. This was the Last County. Then the smoke started to come up.

That was when I ran back into town.

My father's house was on fire. Later, I'd find out my mother shot my father in the stomach three times and then dropped a match to the house. But all I remembered understanding then was relief when they dragged my father's body out of the house. He wasn't even my real father. I remembered my mother trying to run to me before they dragged her off. And my throat going raw from screaming when they put the noose around her neck.

Dreaming about the places my mother talked about stopped being enough when the trapdoor dropped open below her feet.

•••

I WAS JUST about halfway across town when I noticed the crowd forming in the big gap next to the prayer house, where the house I grew up in used to be. I spotted Tamid's too-neatly parted dark hair through the crowd. I shoved through bodies until I was next to him. People tended to stand clear of Tamid. Like they thought they might catch a limp from him. It left that much more room for me.

"What are we staring at?" I moved to take the place of the wooden crutch under his left arm. It worked fine and all, but the stupid boy kept getting taller, and every time somebody bothered to build him a new crutch, he'd go and grow again. He flashed me a smile that I returned with a stuck-out tongue.

"What's it look like?" He passed the crutch back to Hayfa. She was the only servant in town, on account of Tamid's family being the only one that could afford both to buy food and to pay someone to cook it. He rested his weight against me. Tamid was pale as sin for desert folk. But at least his tall, skinny frame looked less hunched today.

At first, in the glare of sunrise, all I saw was the familiar blackened brick of the Sultan's weapons factory on the edge of town. The only reason the hellholes around here were allowed to exist was to serve the factory. Then I caught the glint of the sun on polished metal.

The Sultan's army was coming.

They marched in lines of three abreast, down from the hills. Their gold sheemas covered them from the sun, and their sabers hung from one hip, guns from the other, white zouave tucked neatly into their boots, and gold shirts cinched at their hips. Their march was slow but inevitable. It was always inevitable.

At least there were no blue uniforms dotted among the white and gold. Blue uniforms meant the Gallan army. The Sultan's army might not make life easy, but they were still Mirajin, and we were their people.

The Gallan were foreigners. Occupiers. They were dangerous.

Politics and history weren't exactly what folks talked

about in our end of the world, but the way I heard it, our most exalted Sultan Oman had figured two decades back that he was better suited to rule Miraji than his father. So he made an alliance with the Gallan army. The foreigners killed his father and anybody else who refused to bow to him as Sultan. And in return he let the Gallan army set up camp in Miraji and take the guns we made, to go off and win their wars on far-off shores.

"Aren't they back from Sazi a bit soon?" I squinted into the dawn, trying to count them. Seemed like there weren't as many as usual.

"You didn't hear? The pistol pit in Deadshot burned to the ground last night." I stiffened, hoping Tamid didn't notice. "There was some riot. My father heard this morning; something to do with the Rebel Prince. He says the army's coming down from the mountains to sort it out."

"To hang drunks and gamblers, you mean." The Sultan's army had passed through on their way to Sazi only a few days ago. They'd gone to see the mines, probably to find out if they were worth salvaging. It was unsettling to have them back so soon. Normally the Mirajin Fifteenth Command came through every three months to collect the weapons the factory churned out and take them for the Gallan.

"Deadshot was always a bed of sin; they had it coming. I was meditating this morning on the golden city of Habadden." Tamid's voice took on a righteous tone. He had a tendency to read the Holy Books until the spines were worn, and I swore he'd started preaching at me more than the Holy Father did lately. "Their people were so corrupted by wealth, they turned their backs on God. So God sent the warrior Djinn to cleanse it with their smokeless fire."

Sure, then there were the less holy stories of Djinn seducing women, stealing them from fathers and husbands, and carrying them off to hidden towers.

Those were the good old days. Nobody had seen a Djinni in decades. Now all it took to burn down a den of sin was a girl, a foreigner, and a whole mess of drunks.

"See," Tamid went on, sounding more like my chiding friend again. "I bet you're glad you listened to me about going to the pistol pit." I screwed up my face. It was as good as admitting guilt. His expression dropped. "You *didn't*."

"Shut up, will you?" I looked at Hayfa, who seemed a little too interested in staring at Tamid's crutch while pretending not to listen. "You want to get me hanged?"

When he sighed, I felt his disappointment. "So that's why you look like an exhausted wreck this morning."

"And folks say you're not much of a charmer." But I scrubbed a hand over my face all the same, like I might be able to rub away evidence of last night. "I could've won." I leaned in close to Tamid so nobody would overhear. "If they'd played halfway fair."

"Didn't say you couldn't, Amani." He didn't share my excitement. "I said you shouldn't."

It was an old argument. We used to have it back when my mother was still alive. When she used to talk about Izman. We stopped having it after she died. I didn't bother telling Tamid I was still planning on going. Not until the night I overheard my uncle.

After scrambling away from where I had been crouched below the window, I headed straight for Tamid's house. I'd climbed through his window like I'd done since I was old enough to be able to jump to the windowsill. And just like always Tamid greeted me, trying to look exasperated and failing. I told Tamid I was running out of time, that I needed to get out now or never. While I talked his expression turned less joking.

Tamid had never really understood my need to get out of Dustwalk. Of all folks in this godforsaken town, he should have.

That night he said the same thing he always did. No matter where we went, nothing could change what we were: a cripple and a girl. If we were worthless here, why would it be different anywhere else? I'd tried to tell him different. About the letters from Aunt Safiyah. About a better life. About bigger things than living and dying in this dead-end desert town. But for someone so filled with holy zeal, Tamid wasn't really the blind faith sort. So I let him figure he'd converted me and didn't tell him I was planning on strapping my chest down and making a run for it, one way or another. I wasn't like him; I had to believe Izman was better than here, or there wasn't much point living anywhere at all.

Now Hayfa cleared her throat. "It's not my place and all, but you're about to be late for prayers, sir."

Tamid and I traded a look, both of us stifling our laughs

like we were kids in a classroom again. "Lateness is a sin, you know," Tamid said with mock sternness.

In school, Tamid and I were late all the time. We used to try to blame his leg, and our schoolteacher used to scold us that lateness was a sin. We might've been frightened, except he told us everything was a sin. Tamid had read the Holy Books three times over, and as far as he could find, neither lateness nor talking in lessons nor falling asleep in school was a sin.

Still, Tamid took the crutch back from Hayfa as she tried to usher him toward the prayer house and away from me.

"We're not done talking about this," Tamid called as I turned to walk in the opposite direction. I spun long enough to give him a mocking salute before I dashed across the scorching sand toward the shop.

I tossed open the iron grates on the storefront before kicking the door open to get as much sunlight inside as I could before going in. I checked around the bags of salt and shelves stacked with tinned things swimming in thick juices that made them last unnaturally long, watching for any shadow that might move. The doors and windows of the store were edged in iron, just like every house in the Last County, but that didn't always stop things from crawling through in the dead of night. In the desert you learned to look out for ghouls in the shadows. Ghouls came in a thousand different forms. Tall faceless Skinwalkers, who'd eat a man's flesh and take his shape so they could feast on his family, too. Small leathery Nightmares, who sunk their teeth into sleeping men's chests and fed off their fear until the soul was sucked out.

Iron was the only thing that'd keep them out. It was the only thing that'd kill them, too. They hid from the sunlight, but the only thing that would really do the trick was a bullet to the skull or an iron knife through the ribs. Iron turned all immortal things mortal. Powerless. That was how the Destroyer of Worlds killed the first First Beings. And that was how humans, in turn, killed the Destroyer of Worlds' ghouls.

There weren't so many ghouls as there used to be. The last person to get killed by one round these parts was a decade ago. But every once in a while, one would crawl over some break in the iron and into the corner shadows of a house and get a bullet to the head for its troubles.

Once I was satisfied that the shop was as empty as a drunk's bottle, I propped open the door to get whatever breeze there was before dumping out what was left of my money on the counter. It came to six fouza and three louzi, no matter how many times I counted it. That wasn't enough to make it out of sight of Dustwalk, let alone to Izman. Even if I emptied the shop till and didn't get caught I wouldn't make it that far.

I needed a new plan. And I needed one soon.

The iron bell on the door rattled, giving me just enough warning to swipe up my pathetic collection of coins before Pama Al-Yamin came in, herding her three boys.

The day wore on with painful slowness while I tried to

think my way out of Dustwalk. By late afternoon my chin was dipping to my chest as the heat tried to drag me down into sleep.

The sound of hoofbeats made me look up just in time to see a handful of soldiers clatter past. I scrambled up, my mouth dry. Tamid said the army was coming to deal with Deadshot. So what were they doing here? Had somebody told them about the Blue-Eyed Bandit and pointed them the way of the only girl in the desert who could've played the part?

A shape dove into the shop as fast as a shadow, plastering itself in the blind spot between the door and the window. I felt for the rifle Aunt Farrah kept below the counter. The man didn't come for me, though. He stayed so still, I thought he might have stopped breathing. Another horse rode past without looking in the direction of the shop.

I waited until it was clear before speaking. "Fine day for hiding."

He spun around. His badly wrapped sheema fell away from his face and I saw him clearly in the late afternoon light that leaked through the window. My heart did a strange little jump. The foreigner.

I schooled my face to look impassive. He gave me a smile that didn't match the tension in his shoulders. "Just needed to get out of the sun on a day like this." His voice was sure and smooth, like I remembered from last night. There was no hint of recognition there, and I felt a flicker of disappointment.

"It's not a big town, you know. They're bound to look here sooner or later. I'd guess sooner." Another horse clattered past, then slowed, looping around. It came to a halt outside the shop, and the mounted soldier called something out. Two more horses came into view. A muscle in the foreigner's jaw twitched. The knife at his side was the same one he'd taken off Dahmad last night. When he'd saved me, and I'd left him to fend for himself. "You might want to find a better hiding place."

His hand was still playing with the hilt of the knife when he looked up, questioningly.

I stepped back, nodding to the gap below the counter. The soldier was dismounting now. In the second that his back was turned, the foreigner dashed across the short space between the door and the counter.

He vaulted over the counter and landed so close to me, I felt his shoulder brush mine before he ducked down below. I quickly adjusted myself so I was standing square in front of him a second before the soldiers entered. The first one stood in the doorway for a long moment, looking in every corner of the tiny place, the other two flanking him. Finally his scrutiny landed on me.

He was young. His hair was combed back more carefully than most soldiers, and he had a round face that made him look soft. But the gold sash across his uniform told me he was in command.

"Afternoon, sir," I said in my best shopgirl voice. I was keenly aware of the foreigner below the counter, trying to quiet his breathing.

"Commander to you." His hand twitched, and he turned the gesture into a straightening of his cuffs.

"Can I help you, *Commander*?" I'd learned young to give the army false respect.

The two soldiers who'd followed their commander took up position by the door. Like I might make a run for it. One of them was older and looked every inch a career soldier: stiff back, dark eyes straight ahead. The second one was younger than his commander, maybe even younger than me. He slumped in a uniform that didn't quite fit, with a glazed look on his face. I'd bet that he wasn't going to live long enough to ever look like a soldier.

"I'm looking for a man." The commander's accent was sharp and northern and expensive. I felt the foreigner's arm brush my leg as he tensed. I didn't know if it was the soldier's voice or because he thought I was about to sell him out.

I gave the commander my best guileless blink. "Funny, most men round here are looking for a woman." The words were out of my mouth before I remembered that he could shoot me in the head and call it justice. The older of the two soldiers coughed, covering a laugh.

The commander just frowned, like he thought I didn't understand him. "A criminal. Have you seen him?"

I shrugged. "Seen a few people today. Fat Pama and her sons were in a few hours ago, and the Holy Father, too."

"This man's not from around here." His head twitched from side to side, peering around the small store. He started pacing evenly. His steps made the glass bottles of liquor on the shelf behind me clink together.

"Is that right?" My eyes tracked him as he walked to the door of the storeroom and squinted through into the dwindling stacks of tinned food. Our supplies were too sparse to hide anyone there.

As the commander turned back toward me, I noticed a fresh speck of red on the counter. Like a drop of blood. I laid my hand across the stain as casual as I could.

"You'd know if you'd seen him," the young commander was saying in his tightly coiled accent.

I smiled like my heart wasn't racing in my chest, telling me to run for the hills. "Like I said, not many folks round here today. Not many foreigners, neither."

"You sure about that?"

"Well, I've been here all day. It's quiet on account of the heat and all."

"You'd be clever not to lie to me, *girl*."

I bit my tongue. He was barely older than I was. Eighteen. Nineteen at most. Probably the same age as the foreigner.

I crossed my arms, careful to hide the bloodstain, and leaned over the counter with a smile. "Oh, I don't lie, Commander. Lying is a sin after all, isn't it?" Where was Tamid when I needed him to share a joke?

But to my surprise the younger of the two soldiers spoke up. "This desert is full of sin."

The commander looked toward his soldier in the same moment I did. I expected him to get a sharp reprimand for speaking out of turn. But the commander didn't say a word. No wonder the older soldier didn't work too hard to hide his laugh. No commander who wanted respect would let a soldier talk out of line like that.

The young soldier met my gaze and I realized with a start that his eyes were as blue as mine.

I'd never met another Mirajin with light eyes. Desert dwellers had dark hair, dark skin, and dark eyes. It was the Gallan who had pale features.

Just because they were entitled to our weapons, the Gallan army seemed to think they were entitled to everything else in the desert. A couple of years back the men of Dustwalk hanged pretty young Dalala Al-Yimin after a Gallan soldier took a bit too much of a shine to her. All the women in town comforted Dalala's mother by saying how it was the best thing to do, considering she wasn't any good to anyone now he was done with her. That night I'd looked at my own blue eyes and thought of the Gallan with their pale eyes and light hair. For years I hadn't really understood what my father meant when he'd get into one of his drunken rages and call my mother a foreigner's whore. But I was fourteen then, old enough to understand that folks didn't actually believe the dark-eyed desert man my dark-eyed mother was married to was really my father. I figured my mother had just been smarter than Dalala. She'd gotten herself married to Hiza in time to pretend the reason she was swelling up with child was him, and not some foreign soldier who'd caught her alone and against her will on some dark desert night. And by the time I came along with my contrary eyes, there was no admitting I was anything but Hiza's daughter, not in this town.

Seemed the scrawny soldier had a smart mama like mine. Just not smart enough to keep him out of the army. His mother's husband would've wanted to get rid of him, I reckoned. That's why he was in uniform too young and too underfed and too smart-mouthed to last all that long.

As his blue gaze met mine, the desert heat suddenly seemed to become stifling. The shop closing in around us, the air getting thick with nervous heat. I felt a bead of sweat roll down the back of my neck.

"Quite so, Noorsham." The commander's voice pulled my attention back to him abruptly, as he gave another nervous tug at his sleeves. He gestured to his two soldiers, a sign. The older soldier leaned toward the younger soldier and said something to him before leading him outside, gripping him tightly by the elbow. It struck me as a strange gesture from one soldier to the other.

I didn't have any time to consider it though. Because just like that I was alone with the commander. And the foreigner I was hiding. And it occurred to me, he might've just been getting rid of anyone who might interfere. I touched my hand to the rifle under the counter

The commander planted his arms on either side of me so he could stare straight down at me. "This man, he's dangerous. He's a mercenary, and his ilk turn on a coin. There is a war going on." Like he thought I could have lived sixteen years without noticing the Gallan soldiers in our desert. "Miraji has more enemies than you can understand. And any one of them could be paying him. If it suited his purposes, he'd slit a girl's throat wide open.

Except he'd do other things to her first, if you catch my meaning." My mind went back to last night, to the stranger who'd stepped in front of a gun to save a kid. "If you do see him, you'd better tell your husband."

I frowned, faking confusion. "I don't have a husband."

"Your father, then." He pulled away from me, straightening his cuffs with a twitch.

"Don't have one of them around, neither." I kept playing dumb. "I could tell my uncle, though, if that'd do?"

The commander nodded, seeming satisfied that I was just duller than a bag of rocks instead of a liar. I watched him all the way to the door.

But I was never good at keeping my mouth shut. "Sir— Commander!" I called out, keeping my eyes down, like a good respectful girl in the presence of an officer. With my head down, I was staring straight into the foreigner's eyes. Something darted across his face, and for a moment I wondered if he recognized me from last night after all. "This mercenary. What's he wanted for, anyhow?"

The commander paused on the porch. "Treason."

I raised my eyebrows at the foreigner, a question. Below the counter, he winked at me and I couldn't stop myself from smiling back. "Well, then, I'll keep an eye out for him, sir."

I waited until I couldn't hear the commander's horse anymore before reaching down to pull the foreigner to his feet. "Treason?"

"You're a good liar." A small smile still played over his face. "For someone who doesn't lie."

"I've had a lot of practice." His hand was lingering on mine, fingers against my pulse. I dropped my arm and looked up. That was when I noticed the red staining his white shirt, same as the blood on the counter.

"Turn around." I sucked air through my teeth. The whole back of his shirt was a mess of red. "I don't mean to worry you and all," I said, trying to keep my voice calm, "but have you noticed that you've been shot?"

"Ah." Looking at him closer now, I could see he was clutching the counter to stay upright. "I'd almost forgotten about that."

four

We sat on the floor behind the counter so that the foreigner could hide if someone came in. The blood was mostly dry, and his shirt was sticking to his skin. I had to cut it off him with his knife. His shoulders were broad and all hard muscles; they rose and fell with shallow breaths as I peeled away the ruined fabric. I was close enough to smell the smoke of last night's fire on him.

I'd grabbed a bottle of liquor off the shelf. The foreigner sat perfectly still as I doused a clean corner of his shirt in the spirit and wiped it across his skin. We had more liquor to spare than water.

"You shouldn't be helping me, you know," he said after a moment. "Didn't you hear the righteous Commander Naguib? I'm dangerous."

I snorted. "Yeah, well, so is he." It was as much truth as I could give without telling him the Blue-Eyed Bandit owed him a favor. "Besides"—my hand darted up—"I've got the knife." He froze, feeling the blade against his neck. The hairs on the back of his neck stood up. And then he laughed.

"So you do." When he spoke, his skin scraped across the edge of the knife like a dangerously close shave. "I'm not going to hurt you."

"I know you won't." I tried to make it sound like a warning as I went back to work on his shoulder. I dug the tip of the knife into his skin. His muscles bunched under my hand, but he didn't cry out.

As I tried to get under the bullet, I noticed a tattoo inked on his ribs. I traced the edge with the tips of my fingers. His muscles tensed under my hand, sending shivers all the way through my arm.

"It's a seagull." When he spoke, the inked bird moved under my fingertips. "It was the name of the first ship I ever served on. The *Black Seagull*. It seemed like a grand idea at the time."

"What were you doing on a ship?"

"Sailing." I could feel the restlessness building below my fingers. He let out a long breath that seemed to make the bird fly. I pulled my hand away and felt him ease.

"I don't think the bullet tore any muscles in your shoulder," I said, moving the knife. "Hold still." I leaned my elbows into his sides for support. He had a tattoo of a compass across his other shoulder; it rose and fell against me as he breathed heavily. The bullet pinged to the ground and blood started to gush freely. I pressed the ruined shirt over it quickly with one hand. "You need stitches."

"I'll be fine."

"Maybe, but you'll be better with stitches."

He laughed, but it didn't sound easy. "You've had medical training, then?"

"No," I said, pressing the rag soaked in liquor against his back harder than I needed to. I grabbed a spool of ugly yellow thread and a needle off the shelf. "But you don't grow up round these parts without seeing a few dozen people get shot."

"I didn't think there were more than a few dozen people in this town."

"Exactly," I said, and though I couldn't see his face, I knew he was smiling. His fingernails dug into the floor as the needle slid into his skin. A question was building like an itch, and I had to ask. "So how did you commit treason against the Sultan when you're not even from Miraji?"

"I was born here," he said after a moment. He knew that wasn't what I'd been asking. *What kind of treason can a mercenary possibly commit?* The question was on the tip of my tongue.

"You don't look it," I said instead.

"Not here. In Izman." Mention of the capital struck too close to the bone just now, when I'd been so close to getting there last night. "Though my mother was from a country called Xicha. That's where I lived most of my life."

"What's it like there?"

He was silent, and I was sure he wasn't going to tell me.

"I don't suppose you've ever seen a rainstorm," he said, "so you don't know that kind of heavy air that clings to your skin and gets its fingers under your clothes." My eyes went to my own fingers against his naked back; his shoulders rose and fell as he spoke. "The air in Xicha is like that all the time. And everything is as green and alive as this country is dry and dead. The bamboo grows so fast, it might uproot houses someday. Even in the city. Like it's trying to take the ground we've built on back from us. And it's so hot, the women walk around with paper fans colorful enough to make the spirits jealous. We used to cool off by jumping in the sea fully clothed and trying not to get hit by any ships. Ships from all over the world. Albish ones with naked sea maids carved into them, and Sves ones built against the cold. And Xichian ones that looked like dragons, carved out of a single tree. Some of the trees in Xicha are taller than the towers in Izman."

"Don't suppose you're going to tell me what you're doing here?" I asked. "If Xicha is so wonderful?"

"Don't suppose I am," he replied, wincing as the needle went through his skin. "Don't suppose you're going to tell me what made you lie to our friend Commander Naguib Al-Oman for me?"

"Don't suppose so." My needle paused in his skin. "Naguib Al-Oman?" They were both common names, but all the same. "He's the Sultan's son?"

"How is it you know that?" His head dipped a little, breath deepening as I pushed the last stitch in.

"Everybody knows the story of the Rebel Prince. And the other princes who competed in the Sultim trials."

The story went that when Sultan Oman was still new to the throne, one of his prettiest wives gave him a son, Ahmed. A strong and clever boy, and even as the Sultan's harem grew and more wives gave him more sons, Ahmed was much in the favor of his father. Three years later, the same wife gave birth to a daughter, but not to an infant, to a monster half human and half Djinni, with scales instead of skin and claws instead of fingers and horns growing from its purple head. Seeing that his wife had betrayed him by lying with an immortal Djinni, the Sultan beat her until she died. The same night the monster child and Ahmed disappeared.

Fourteen years later, the time for the trials came. It was the way the Sultim, the successor to the throne, had been chosen since Miraji began. As per tradition, the twelve eldest princes were to compete for the crown.

That was just over a year ago. My mother was still alive. And when news of the trials reached Dustwalk, even men who'd tell you gambling was a sin started placing bets on which of the young princes would win the throne.

On the day of the contest, the twelve sons lined up and the whole city gathered to watch. Then a thirteenth man joined the princes. When he pulled back his hood, he was the picture of Sultan Oman as a younger man and no one could deny his claim that he was Prince Ahmed, returned. No matter what suspicions surrounded the sudden return of the prince, the law of tradition was upheld.

Prince Ahmed would compete, and the youngest of the twelve princes was expelled from the contest. That prince was named Naguib. I knew the name because when folks were betting on the Sultim trials, before the news about the Rebel Prince came, odds were that Naguib would get killed first in the trial. His prodigal brother might've saved Naguib's life by getting him expelled.

Ahmed beat the other eleven princes in the test of intelligence, a huge maze full of traps built in the palace grounds, and the test of wisdom, a riddle posed by the wisest of the Sultan's advisors. When he came to the test of strength, trial by single combat, Ahmed won every fight until only he and Prince Kadir, the firstborn of the Sultan's sons, were left standing. They fought all day, until Kadir surrendered. Instead of executing his eldest brother Ahmed spared his life. He turned his back on him to face their father, to claim the title of Sultim. Behind Ahmed's back Kadir raised his sword in a blow that would have killed his brother. At that moment Ahmed's sister, the Djinni's monster daughter, stepped from the crowd, throwing away her human disguise, and used unnatural powers inherited from her father to deflect Kadir's blade so that he missed. Furious at this intervention, the Sultan declared Kadir Sultim and ordered Ahmed's execution. But the young prince escaped into the desert with his monster sister, to raise a rebellion for his throne. *A new dawn, a new desert.*

I tied the thread and sliced off the excess with the knife. The foreigner turned around, giving me my first view of his bare chest. I suddenly felt like I needed to look any-where but at him. Which was stupid, because this was the desert and I'd seen every man I'd ever known without a shirt. But this man I didn't know. And usually I didn't no-tice the muscles in their arms or the way their stomachs rose and fell or the tattoo of a sun over their hearts.

He was looking at me in the fast-fading sunlight. "I don't even know your name," he said.

"I don't know yours." I looked up, shoving dark hair off my face with my knuckles so I didn't get blood all over myself. I started to rub them on one of the rags that was still soaked with alcohol.

"Jin." He'd given me a false name last night, though he didn't know it. I wasn't so sure he was giving me a real name now. It didn't sound like any I'd ever heard.

"You sure about that?" I pressed.

"About my name?" His mouth quirked up as he rolled his injured shoulder. It pulled the bare skin of his stom-ach so I could just see the edge of another tattoo pull up above his belt. Suddenly I wanted to know what it was. The thought made my neck feel hot. "Fairly sure."

My eyes flicked up to his face. "Sure you're not lying to me?"

His grin spread. "Lying's a sin, don't you know?"

"So I've heard."

Jin's eyes danced across my face in a way that made me restless. "You know I'd be dead without your help."

So would I.

But I didn't tell him that. I didn't joke that he should

call me Oman like I wanted to. Or the Blue-Eyed Bandit, or anything else I wanted to say. "It's Amani," I said. "My name, that is. Amani Al-Hiza."

It was damn hard to trust a boy with a smile like that. A smile that made me want to follow him straight to the places he'd told me about and made me sure I shouldn't at the same time.

"I can get you a clean shirt," I managed. I was having a hard time keeping my eyes on his face when there was so much else of him on show. "If you can wait here."

"The army will be back for me." He scratched the back of his neck, inching the tattoo on his hip higher still. It looked like an animal I didn't recognize. "I should probably move on."

"I reckon you should." I tore my eyes away. I couldn't trust him, I reminded myself. I didn't really know this foreign boy with a strange name. No matter that we'd saved each other's lives. I'd known him all of two days. But hell, I still liked him twice as much as the men in this town I'd known my whole life. And my life was what was at stake here. One way or another. "And you should take me with you."

"No." Jin's answer came so quick, I knew he'd been expecting me to ask, maybe even before I'd decided to. He didn't meet my eyes as he spoke next. "You saved my life and I'm returning the favor."

"I didn't ask you to do that." I tried to check the desperation in my voice. "I'm just asking you to get me out."

His eyes were fixed on mine, trapping me there. "You don't even know where I'm going."

"I don't care." I caught myself leaning closer, too close when there was already nothing between us. "I just need help getting anywhere that's not here. Somewhere with a train, or a decent road. Then we can call it quits and I can find my own way to Izman. There's nothing for me here, any more than there is for you."

"And who says there's anything for you out there?"

The words stung. "There's got to be more than here." He laughed, and for that split second, I had the advantage. I took it. "Please." I was as close to him as I could get without touching him. "Haven't you ever wanted something so bad that it becomes more than a want? I *need* to get out of this town. I need it like I need to breathe."

His breath came out in one hard exhale. I saw his resolve teetering. I didn't dare say another word in case I pushed it the wrong way.

Then the bells started and the moment toppled. I looked round so fast, I near split my skull on the counter.

"Isn't it a bit early for evening prayers?" Jin said what I'd been thinking.

"Those aren't prayer bells." My heart felt like it might've stopped, but I was still breathing. Listening long enough to be sure.

"If the army—"

"It's not," I interrupted. We didn't ring bells for the army.

"You should—"

"Shut up." I held up a hand to silence him. To listen. And sure enough, I knew that frantic ringing, though it'd been years since we'd heard it last. A few seconds later it was echoed by others. Bells on porches, from open windows. Iron clanging against iron. The sound sent shivers down my back. "It's a hunt."

And then I was running for the door.

five

I barreled out of the store full tilt and near knocked straight into Tamid.

"I was coming to find you." He was out of breath and resting heavily on his crutch. "You should go back inside."

"Is it—" I started.

"A Buraqi." He nodded. My heart jumped in excitement.

A desert horse. A First Being made in the days before us mortal things, from sand and wind. That could run past the end of the world without tiring. And worth its weight in gold if you could catch one. Like hell I was going back inside.

I squinted past the edge of town. Sure enough, I could see the cloud of dust and men getting closer, herding the thing in with iron bars. It must've sprung one of the old traps.

"It'll be on account of the fire in Deadshot," Tamid said in his preacher's voice. "First Beings are fond of fire."

I saw a crooked nail sticking out of the porch and yanked it out. Used to be, folks in this desert made their whole living gathering the metals from the mountains and sending daughters out into the sands with iron gloves to trap and tame the Buraqi. To turn them from sand and wind to flesh and blood so that the men could take them into the cities to sell. Then the Sultan built the factory. The sand filled up with iron dust. Even the water tasted of it. Buraqi got scarcer, tents turned to houses, and horse traders turned into factory workers.

Iron could hold First Beings. Or kill them, same as it could a ghoul. Bind them to mortality. But the only thing that could turn them to flesh and blood long enough to bind them was us.

Tamid had read in some holy text that there were no females among First Beings. They didn't need any sons. They could just live forever, unlike mortal things. They didn't need us.

But if knowledge was power, then the unknown was the greatest weakness of immortal things. We all knew the stories. Djinn who fell in love with worthy princesses and gave them all of their hearts' wishes. Pretty girls who lured Nightmares straight onto men's blades. Brave merchants' daughters who caught Buraqi and rode them to the ends of the earth.

They were drawn to us, but also vulnerable to us. We could turn them into flesh and blood.

Folks were pouring out onto their porches all around now, a nervous glint of excitement shivering through them. A Buraqi meant either a whole lot of gold for who-ever caught it or a whole lot of blood. Or both.

The Buraqi surged into view at the edge of town.

Someone screamed. A few doors slammed. But most folks leaned forward, trying to get a better look. I hung off the edge of the shop, craning in with the rest.

It was putting up one hell of a fight.

For a second it looked like a mortal horse. The next it was pure sand. Shifting from bright gold to violent red, fire and sun in a windswept desert. A trill of ex-citement that belonged to a long desert bloodline went through me. The factory had changed our ways. We weren't desert tribes hunting the Buraqi any longer. But we still filled the desert with iron traps. When one of the traps was sprung, everyone knew what to do.

A rattle of chains made me pay attention. The young widow Saira was hooking one end under the box of za'atar in her window while the other got anchored to the prayer house by the Holy Father. Half the town was throw-ing iron dust out of their windows, the same dust every household kept handy in case of attack by desert ghouls. It mixed with the sand and air until the whole town was a prison for a First Being.

The Buraqi reared with a cry. The men hemmed it in with iron bars, fighting to keep it from plunging back into the sand. The Buraqi's hooves came down hard. There was a cry cut off by the crunch of hoof meeting skull. Blood splattered across the sand.

Gold and red like its coat.

Uncle Asid jabbed the Buraqi with the wicked point of his iron bar. The Buraqi reared back, the wound shifting to flesh just long enough to bleed. Long enough for the men to retreat behind the iron chains with everybody else. Their job was done.

The men got the Buraqi into town as one. But from there it was every woman for herself. If you caught the Buraqi and managed to hold it long enough to trap it in its mortal form, then it belonged to you, or rather to your husband or father. Or uncle, in my case. And the money from selling it belonged to him, too.

Not that I was planning on handing it over if I caught it. Hell, I'd needed a new way out of here. Well, here I had one. I'd just have to catch it.

The other women lingered on the edge of the iron chains. The widow Saira's tongue flicked out across her cracked lips. Even Shira had come out of my uncle's house. She seemed to be praying, her fingers laced through the iron chain. My heart was thumping through my whole body at once—stomach, throat, anywhere but where it belonged.

Two steps took me to the edge of the iron chain. This was my shot. My way out. "Amani—" Tamid called me. I turned to answer. A flash of pink khalat caught my eye. Aunt Farrah yelped Shira's name as my cousin dodged under the chain and ran toward the Buraqi.

Damn her. Of all the times for her to decide to do something other than laze around. The Buraqi, which had been tossing itself frantically between sand and skin, turned and charged her.

She wasn't going to win this one.

I dropped to the ground and rolled under the iron chain toward her. I was on my feet and running before Tamid could finish whatever warning he was shouting.

I crashed into Shira and we collided with the ground. A hoof clipped my head, sending a spiderweb of blinding pain across my vision.

I started to get up, but Shira's hand clamped over my ankle, wrenching me down. Her eyes were almost as frantic as the Buraqi's.

"Mama's going to tan your hide for this," she hissed, her fingernails digging into the soft skin of my wrists.

"She's gonna have to catch me first." I drove my knee into her stomach before she could get us both killed. I untangled myself from her coughing shape and rushed to my feet.

A half dozen more women had entered the iron ring while we'd been scuffling like this was the school yard. They were keeping their distance. The Buraqi's hooves were starting to sink back down in the sand. Much longer and it'd manage to go back to its immortal form and become part of the desert.

I whistled. It spun.

For a few long heartbeats we faced each other. I took one step. Then another. Two more. It still hadn't moved.

All at once, Shira dove for it, gripping a fistful of iron. The Buraqi darted out of her way. And then it charged me.

I made myself hold my ground. Like I was facing down Jin's bullet again. I wasn't going to die today, not even now with the Buraqi's hooves cutting through the sand and its weight bearing down on me.

I danced out of the way a moment before it reached me. I put out my hand, holding the nail; my skin skimmed its hide, then went flat against its flank. Iron and skin.

The Buraqi's scream was the sound of something being torn, and I felt it deep in my gut. I moved with the immortal beast as it furiously struggled. I moved with it, fighting to keep skin against spirit. I saw the anguish in its face. It didn't want to be trapped. I understood that. Neither did I. The nail dropped from my hand, but it didn't matter.

My hands wrapped around its neck as it turned to muscle. The world seemed to drop away as the Buraqi panted against my chest. Sun and sand became flesh and blood below my fingers. I felt the strength of it below me, old as the world, older than death and darkness and sin. All I'd have to do was climb on its back and let it carry me to the end of the desert.

The Buraqi cried out and my thoughts scattered as the scream made something tear loose inside me.

Someone shoved me back as men swarmed the beast with my uncle at the forefront. My chance to run was gone. The Buraqi whinnied weakly as an iron bit was shoved between its teeth and nails and horseshoes were hammered to its feet. Three iron shoes, enough iron to anchor it to its physical form permanently, and one bronze, to make it obedient.

Men were shouting to send word that we had a Buraqi. Onlookers were whooping and laughing. Kids were clapping their hands. I was already forgotten. The beast tossed its head, looking at me like I'd betrayed it.

I had blood in my hair and on my clothes. No. I wasn't letting it get taken away that easily. I started pushing through the crowd before I could think better of it.

Someone grabbed my arm and wrenched me sideways between two houses. A hand covered my mouth, keeping in my shout.

"Well, hello there," a nasty voice slithered into my ear, "Little Miss Bandit."

six

"Goddamnit, Fazim." I shoved him away. I guess he made it out alive from the pistol pit after all. And he'd called me Bandit. He knew. "What the hell is wrong with you?"

Fazim let me go, stuffing his hands into his pockets. He took two steps away from me, to the edge of the shadows between the two houses. He didn't need to guard me all that close. We both knew I didn't have anywhere to run.

"Do you always drag girls behind your house to beat them up for putting a knee in your sweetheart's gut?" I leaned back against the weak wooden frame.

"Marry me." He said it so suddenly, for a second I just stared at him with my jaw still moving.

Then I burst out laughing.

I couldn't help it. He looked so damn pleased with himself. Like he really expected me to say yes. "Well, paint me purple and call me a Djinni, if that isn't the dumbest thing I've heard all day." I shoved bloody hair off my face.

He was still grinning. "You've got nice eyes, you know. There was someone else with eyes like yours out in Deadshot last night. Blue-Eyed Bandit, they called him. Got me thinking, not many people in this desert with eyes like that."

Of all the times for him to grow some brains. "You saying I've got a long-lost brother?"

"You know what I'm saying, Amani." He stepped toward me, and I fought everything in me telling me to step back. Only a few feet away the commotion over the Buraqi was still making a racket, but just then it felt like the world had narrowed to Fazim and me. "And you're going to marry me so that no one else finds out."

"And what's the next part?" My eyes darted to the opening between the two houses. I saw a flash of colorful khalat as someone rushed by. I willed the next person to look our way. "You tell me you're in love with me and these months with Shira have been a big ruse while you were waiting for my mother to be dead a year?"

Fazim grinned. Like he'd just been waiting for me to ask. "Well, until you caught that Buraqi, Shira was my best shot in town to get me on the way to rich."

"And she'll get you even further that way once my uncle sells it." Was that why Shira had flung herself into the fray? To get this idiot to marry her, for love or money?

"See, I've thought it all out, though." He tapped his head. He was pretty dumb to be acting like he was the smartest man ever born. "Sure, if I marry Shira I'd get a little bit of that money. But seeing as you caught it, if you were to get married, the Buraqi wouldn't belong to your uncle no more."

It would belong to my husband.

Damn him. He wasn't clever, but he was right. And worse, he was serious. Here was the moment I'd been trying to outrun, only it wasn't coming at my uncle's hand.

Anger burned my fear straight out of me. "I'd rather shoot myself." *I'd rather shoot you.*

"You wouldn't have to." He was still smiling, his teeth looking too big for his handsome face. "The army will probably do it for you once I tell them you were with that foreigner they're after." His gaze stripped me all the way from my blue eyes to my boots. "Of course, they'll probably torture you first."

I smiled at him sweetly instead of knocking his teeth in. "Still sounds better than a lifetime married to you."

Fazim's hand slammed into the wall behind my head, scaring the smirk straight off me. "You know, I don't have to wed you first." His voice was low, his smile still fixed, like he thought he was charming me. "I can make you worthless. Then you'd have no choice. You could marry me or hang. If you're anything like your mama, you've got a fine neck for hanging." His free hand traced a line along my throat. I could best just about any man in this desert if I had a gun. But now I was unarmed and helpless.

"Fazim." Shira's voice saved me. "What are you doing?"

Fazim pulled away, just far enough for me to see Shira standing in the narrow opening between the two houses. Her mouth was pressed together in that way I remembered from when we were little, when she was trying not to cry. I pulled away from him and scrambled back toward the street. My pace slowed just as I passed Shira. I thought she might stop me, stick an arm out and demand to know what I was doing between a wall and her lover. But she stepped aside at the last moment, her eyes firmly fixed on the ground.

I bolted for home.

• • •

I HAD TO leave. Bluffing took more brains than Fazim had. He'd go to the army and tell them I knew about their traitor. I wasn't going to beg Jin. I was going to *make* him take me with him.

I paused in the doorway into my uncle's house, listening for any noise that might mean I wasn't the first one to get back to the house. When I was sure, I stepped inside, letting the floorboards creak below my boots, praying this would be the last time I ever walked over that threshold.

I snatched up everything I could find that I thought might belong to me from the chaos of the bedroom floor, and a few things I knew didn't.

I dashed into the boys' room. It was even worse than ours, with clothes piled halfway up the walls; I grabbed a shirt that seemed as clean as anything got around there. Across the house the front door banged open. I heard Aunt Farrah call my name.

I slung the shirt around my neck as I eased myself through the window, dropping to the sand below before she could think to check the boys' room.

The main street was busy with folks hanging lanterns, setting out tables of food to sell, and tuning their instruments in the last dredges of daylight. We'd had nothing to celebrate since Shihabian, the longest night of the year, when we remembered the time the Destroyer of Worlds brought darkness and celebrated the returning of the light. That'd been near a year ago now. The Last County was thirsty for celebration. There would be plenty tonight. I just wouldn't be here for it.

Nobody noticed when I slipped into the store, shutting the door on the noise of the street. As soon as I did, I knew it was too quiet. The floorboards creaked under my feet as I took a step into the shop. Dust motes danced between the shelves.

"Jin?" I whispered into the shop. I felt stupid just for saying it.

I was too late.

He'd gone.

I didn't know why I'd figured he would stay.

The shirt hung loose in my fingers. It was stupid of me to think he would help me anyway; he didn't owe me anything. Besides, this was the desert; everybody looked out for himself.

For one wild moment I considered running to the young commander. I could sell Jin out to them before Fazim sold me out. No. I shook the thought off as soon as it came. I'd never be traitor enough to go to the army.

I shoved the shirt in my bag. I'd just have to find another way out of town before they got to me.

The sun had finished setting by the time I made my way back out of the store, and Dustwalk was lit for celebration. Small oil lanterns strung between houses and torches burning in the street lit up the sorry spectacle. What was left of our food was laid on tables to sell, but liquor was flowing freely as folks wove through the music and sang along. I gave it another few drinks before someone got into a fight.

Half of the Last County was here by now, come to see the Buraqi, which was tethered in the center of town, tossing its head angrily. Uncle Asid was trying to soothe it, but the immortal beast was getting more and more worked up with the crush of bodies jostling to touch it. Finally my uncle started to lead it away from where it might kick a person's head in. I kept one eye on it and the other out for Fazim as I pushed through the crowd, dodging dancers and drunks.

Something whacked hard into my ankles, shooting pain up my leg. I kicked back without thinking and turned to see Tamid standing just out of reach in the crush of people, propped on his crutch and looking all innocent, like he hadn't just hit me with it.

"Come on now, you're not going to kick a cripple, are

you?" he joked. I wanted to smile back, but I felt like someone had wrung me out. Tamid's own good mood flickered uncertainly. "Well, um, I've been looking for you." He stumbled over his words, making my heart swell. I was going to miss him like fire. I'd always known at the back of my mind there'd come a day when I'd leave and he'd stay behind, but I hadn't expected it to rush in on us so quickly. "Here." He pressed something into my hand. "Seemed like you took a bit of a beating capturing that Buraqi." It was a small glass bottle with white powder pills bumping in the bottom. Pain pills. The kind his father made his money from, selling them to factory workers who got hurt on the job. Or when they shot each other to settle a fight.

"It's the kind that knocks you out, isn't it?" I knew the medicines better than I'd like. I'd had enough lashings for my smart tongue in the last year. "I can't take it." I tried to hand the pills back. I took a deep shuddering breath. "I'm going to make a run for it on the Buraqi. Want to come?"

Tamid smiled gamely. "Sure, where are we going?" He figured I was joking. I didn't answer. I just held up my bag for him to see. It registered on his face slowly. "Amani . . ." There was an edge to the way he said my name, like he needed to have enough fear for the pair of us. "You're likely to get yourself hanged."

"I'm just as likely to die here." I pulled him aside, out of the crowd, next to the schoolhouse so we were out of the way. Wild recklessness had been building in my bones for hours. Days. Weeks. Years. And it filled up too much of me to let in anything else just now. "And they could do a lot worse than hang me." The truth came out in a rush as the celebrations carried on around us. Everything—about my uncle, Jin, and Fazim, and how Jin left without taking me with him, and how Fazim blackmailed me to wind up wed or dead if I stayed. And I sure as hell wasn't going to wed anyone. Not him. Not my uncle.

"And in what part of this brilliantly thought-out plan were you going to tell me you were leaving?" He looked wounded.

"I didn't think . . ." I swallowed hard against the guilt welling up. I hadn't really thought. That was the truth of it. There'd been no time to think. No room to think about anything other than Fazim and getting away. "You weren't ever going to come, Tamid," I said softly. "You're only going to try to make me stay, and I'm in too much trouble to stay."

"You wouldn't *be* in trouble if you'd just stayed put instead of running off to the pistol pit in the first place. Why didn't you talk to me? We could've figured something out together, you and I. Why do you always—" Tamid bit off his words in a breathy huff. "You always have to make things so difficult." A long silence stretched out between us in place of the argument we'd had a hundred times. "I know what to do." Tamid wasn't looking at me. In the shadow of the house cast by the swinging lamplight, it was hard to read his expression. I cast my eyes around nervously, keeping my eyes out for any sign of Fazim. "You could—you could marry me."

That pulled my attention back. "What?"

"Fazim can't do anything if you're already wed." He looked so terribly earnest, it made me want to reach out to him. "I could keep you safe. From him. From the army. From your family. You wouldn't even have to live under Farrah's roof anymore. I'd been figuring I'd ask your uncle anyway." He couldn't quite meet my eyes, he looked faintly embarrassed. "Once you were a bit older. I didn't want to pounce as soon as your mother had been dead a year. I wanted to give you time. But I'd never let him wed you, Amani, if you'd told me. This would just mean asking him for you a bit sooner."

He'd been planning on asking to marry me? For how long? The notion had never crossed my mind. I'd figured he'd always understood that I was planning on leaving. Or maybe he'd just thought I'd never make it.

"Tamid." I lowered my voice, unsure of what to say. I didn't know how to explain what I wanted. Not when our ideas were so at odds.

Fazim appeared through the crowd. He wasn't alone. Gold-and-white army uniforms trailed behind him, parting the crowd.

My stomach leapt into my mouth as I plastered myself into the shadows. Tamid glanced over his shoulder. He saw what I did. When he turned back he must've read my answer all over my face. I couldn't stay. He couldn't keep me safe. "Go."

"Tamid . . ." I didn't want to leave with him angry at me. But he wasn't angry enough to want me dead.

"Go!"

For once I did as I was told.

The street was thick with the crowds. I dodged around Old Rafaat leaning heavily on his granddaughter's arm and shoved past a stranger who was playing a sitar out of tune before colliding with the side of my uncle's house. I was steps from the stables. If I could get to the Buraqi—

"There you are!" Aunt Farrah yanked me around to face her. For the first time the cold fury in her face didn't reach me. She was going to scream at me for my smart mouth, for knocking over her daughter, for not helping with dinner for all I knew. It might've mattered this morning, but I was long past caring now.

"Let me go." I tried to tug my arm free, but her grip tightened.

"Where do you think you're going?"

"Away." I stopped struggling, facing her head-on. "Out of this town and away from you. You don't want me here. You don't want your husband wanting me." Her fingers dug in. "And I don't want your husband or anyone else having me." I darted a look over my shoulder, couldn't see anyone through the crowd. But it was a damn small town. Fazim would find me. "Just let me go and I'll leave." I turned back to Aunt Farrah. The hatred that she usually wore had slipped. I was right and she knew it. In this we were allies. "Please."

Her fingers loosened.

Too late. Uniform-clad arms clamped around me and I was lifted off my feet with an involuntary cry. I was half dragged back around the house into the street. The celebrations had quieted, revelry turning to panic as the army penned folks back against houses in a line. Soldiers marched down the street, lanterns held high, checking every man's face.

"Search all the houses and see if he's there." I recognized the clipped, careful accent of young Commander Naguib. He walked through our town like he owned the whole damn place.

Jin was wanted for treason. As a mercenary, they claimed. They didn't send so many men to bring in traitors for pay. So either they weren't here for Jin or he was a lot more than a mercenary.

The soldier holding me dropped me in front of the young commander, who gave me a once-over before turning to Fazim over his shoulder. "This is her?"

"Yes. She was with the foreigner in Deadshot." The swinging lamplight made Fazim ugly as he hovered over the commander's shoulder. I'd been afraid before, but this was a new sort of terror. "She was working with him. She's the Blue-Eyed Bandit."

A soldier snorted from the edge of the lamplight. "From the pistol pit? This girl?"

"He's an idiot." I found my voice. I was trying to be brave. But it was Fazim's word against mine. They were going to believe a man over a girl any day.

The commander grabbed my chin and held the lantern so close to my head, I figured he was going to burn me. "You have lovely eyes." It was no use pretending anymore.

I'd been betrayed by my own face. "Now, where is our foreign friend?"

"If I knew that, I wouldn't be here answering stupid questions." His hand connected with my cheek so hard, I was afraid that he'd snapped my neck, only I was too surprised to die. Pain echoed in my teeth and bones.

"Where is he?" The commander's voice wormed its way through the ringing in my ears. I was only still standing because a soldier was holding me up. I struggled to find the ground again. The commander grabbed my chin. "Tell me." There was a gun at my temple. "Or I will shoot you in the head."

My jaw hurt, but I made it work. "Well, that wouldn't be real clever, because then you'd never get to hear what I've got to say." The click of a bullet slotting into the chamber of a gun was a noise I knew like my own voice. I'd just never heard it so close to my ear.

"That's not going to work on her." Fazim spoke up. "If you really want to frighten her, you need her cripple."

Anger rushed in, pushing out my fear. I lunged at him so fast that the grip holding me slipped. I got my hands on his throat, but arms wrenched me off him before I could do much damage. Someone slapped me again. When my vision cleared, Tamid was kneeling on the sand in the circle of lamps. His bad leg was sprawled out crookedly, and a gun rested against the back of his neck.

I hated Fazim, but I hated myself more. Tamid had warned me I'd get in trouble. I just hadn't figured on getting anyone in trouble with me.

"Now," the commander said in his fine accent. "Would you care to tell us whether or not you were with our friend from the east in Deadshot?"

I swallowed angry words that rose up automatically. Mouthing off wasn't worth Tamid's life. "I wasn't with him." I spoke through clenched teeth. "We were both there."

"And where is he now?"

"I don't know." I thought he would hit me again. But the commander just pursed his mouth like he was disappointed in a bad student. He moved around to Tamid. I was suddenly afraid again.

"What happened to your leg?"

"Leave him alone!"

Tamid and the commander both ignored me. "It was twisted when I was born," Tamid answered cautiously. We had an audience of about two dozen soldiers and a few hundred Last County folks. All of them were watching us with a mix of horror and fascination.

"Well, then." The commander circled behind Tamid. "It's hardly much good to you, is it?"

The bullet went straight through his knee. I screamed so loud, I couldn't even hear Tamid's cry as he crumpled to the ground. A single shriek pierced through the sudden uproar. Tamid's mother. Two soldiers were holding her back.

"What do you think, Bandit?" Commander Naguib cried to me over the noise from the crowd. "A man with one leg might as well have none for all the good he is." He aimed his gun at Tamid's good leg.

"No!" The cry ripped through me.

"Then tell me the truth. And tell me fast. Where is he?"

"I don't know!"

Tamid's mother screamed.

"No! No! I don't! He was here. He came here. Then he left."

"When?" The commander came at me full stride, the simmering rage that lived under the cool face rising up again.

"Dusk. A few hours ago."

"Where did he go?"

"I don't know!" I cried out. The gun smashed across my head. Blood erupted across my vision. I saw a burst of red and light before it cleared and I could see the lanterns swinging above my head again.

"Where is he?" the commander asked.

"I don't know," I repeated, because the truth was all I had now, as weak as it was.

"I will shoot him again, and this time it might not be in the leg."

"I'm not lying! He didn't tell me. Why would he tell me?" I was shouting now.

"Which way did he go?"

"I don't know!"

"Lying is a sin, you know." The gun pressed against my cheek, hot metal in my face.

And then the world exploded into noise and light.

• ● •

RINGING.

Everything was ringing.

My first thought was that someone had been shot.

Tamid?

I was facedown on the ground. I pushed myself to my elbows.

In the dark all I could see was fire where I knew a cliff of black brick was supposed to be.

The entire weapons factory was ablaze.

Sound rushed back in. Screaming came first. The folks of Dustwalk had flung themselves to the ground in prayer, or just covered their heads; some staggered to their feet, others just stared. Commander Naguib was already shouting instructions, Tamid and I forgotten. Soldiers were leaping onto their horses, riding full tilt toward the blaze.

Tamid.

He was crumpled on the sand, not moving, but as I called his name he looked up at me. At the same moment I heard his name again. His mother was cowering and weeping in the sand, trying to crawl toward him.

Then I heard the unmistakable scream of a Buraqi. The desert horse was barreling down the street toward us. On its back was Jin, riding straight toward me. Guns swiveled uncertainly in Jin's direction. He fired a shot and a soldier went down.

I turned back to where Tamid was crumpled.

The Buraqi was almost on top of me.

I had seconds to decide. My legs were trapped, my gut tugging me recklessly toward Tamid. To near certain death. My heart tugging me to Jin and escape and the unknown.

Jin leaned over the horse, reaching down. A gunshot went off at my feet.

It wasn't a decision. More than a want.

It was an instinct. A need. Staying alive.

Jin's hand came into reach. I clasped it tight and swung my body as Jin pulled me up behind him. I saw Aunt Farrah's ashen face. I saw Tamid crumpled in the sand. I saw Commander Naguib, reloading his weapon. Defenseless. Young.

It would be a clean shot. And Jin was armed. One shot and the commander would be dead. Jin knew it, too; I felt it in the tension of his shoulders. Instead he pulled the horse around, lowering his gun, and my hands twisted into Jin's shirt a second before the Buraqi burst into the speed of a beast of wind and sand.

seven

"Tell me you drink."

I woke to rough cloth against my face and the smell of gunpowder in my nose. I'd dozed off with my head against Jin's back as we rode. His words vibrated through his shoulder blades and into my skull, jangling loosely until I put them together.

"You've seen where I grew up." My voice sounded scratchy. When I opened my eyes all I could see was the weave of his shirt, but I could already tell we weren't anywhere near Dustwalk. The air tasted different, of cooler mornings and grit instead of heat and dust and gunpowder. "Of course I drink." My body ached and my chest felt like something was clattering around it. God knew I could use a drink or five right about now.

Sometime while we rode I'd wound my arms around Jin's waist to hang on. I let him go and wiped the sweat of my palms onto my own shirt as Jin slid from the saddle. I tried to line up my thoughts along with my spine as I forced myself straight.

Wherever we were, it looked like most desert towns. Slapped together wooden houses and dusty ground. Only it was rockier than Dustwalk, and the horizon loomed close and high around us in the predawn haze. We must've gone up into the mountains.

I squinted up at a swinging signpost with a picture of a crudely drawn blue man with closed eyes. The lettering announced it as the Drunk Djinni. I knew that story, but I couldn't remember it just now.

The town was dead quiet.

"Where are we?" I asked, only to realize Jin was gone. I twisted atop the Buraqi and spotted him two houses down, hopping over a flaking white fence. A line of laundry was strung between the house and a crooked post, and Jin snatched a piece of crimson cloth straight off it. My eyes traveled past him, up the mountain, beyond the houses. I answered my own question.

Sazi was a full day's ride from Dustwalk. Or a few hours as the Buraqi ran. I'd heard so much about the mining town, but I'd never seen it. They said it was bad here after the mines collapsed a few weeks ago. But I still couldn't have imagined this.

An explosion. An accident. Gunpowder gone wrong was the word in Dustwalk, and I'd figured I knew what they meant. I'd blown up bottles and tin cans along with all the other kids in the desert. I'd seen them shatter as we ran hollering for cover. Sometimes a kid would get a burned finger that needed to be sawed off, or a scarred chin, but most of the time we just wound up with a mess of metal and glass and sand all melted up together.

The collapsed mines looked a lot worse than a melted hunk of old tin. It reminded me of my father's body when they dragged him out of our house, his skin still smoldering. The mountain itself was disfigured, like the earth had rebelled from within its very soul and closed the mountain's ancient mouth, swallowing the mines whole.

No wonder the army hadn't stayed long in Sazi. There wasn't a whole lot to be done. Hundreds of prayer cloths were tied around rocks and stakes all the way up the mountain, but God had failed here.

"Here." Jin's hand on my knee pulled me back. He was holding the strip of red cloth up to me. I realized it was a sheema. "Better if no one sees your face."

"Is that how you got a shirt?" I asked. "You took it off someone's clothesline on your way out of town?"

He nodded ever so slightly. "While you were putting on one hell of a show with the Buraqi. I needed to get out of there before the army came looking. You were too good a distraction to waste."

I was a distraction.

I riffled around in the bag that was still strapped over my shoulder. The shirt I'd grabbed off the floor of the boys' bedroom was at the top. The one I'd meant to give him when I stupidly thought he'd need my help. I balled it up and flung it at him. Jin caught it deftly with his free hand.

"Stealing's a sin, you know." I snatched the sheema from him and started tying it, wincing as my fingers brushed the spot where Naguib's gun had smashed across my cheek. "And that shirt doesn't fit you well."

Jin paused for a moment before peeling off the shirt he'd been wearing. "Is drinking yourself under the table one, too?" He tugged on the new shirt as I busied myself wrapping my face against the sun that was still rising.

"If I say no," I said, tucking the fabric into place, "will you be buying?"

• • •

MY SECOND DRINK burned less than the first one on the way down, but it still wasn't close to burning out the aching hollow space in my chest.

"Tamid." I blurted out the name I'd been biting back since we sat down. "My friend. He got shot through the leg. What do you reckon will happen to him?"

"Not a clue." It was dark in the Drunk Djinni. Busy, too. Full of men with no mines to go to and nothing to do but drink and tell their stories to painted girls. It wasn't even noon and this whole town was drunk, or well on its way. And I was helping. Jin's hat was tugged low over his face, concealing as much of it as he could manage. "Could be they'll leave him alive. Could be they'll shoot him in the head to finish the job. You never know with your Sultan's army. But there's nothing you can do about it now—you already left him." I wanted to tell him that I didn't—that he took me away—but we both knew that wasn't true. "Only way to find out for sure would be to ride back into town and get matching bullets straight through our heads. I hear that's the latest style in Izman."

"Well, it's the last thing they'd expect," I joked lamely.

But I knew I wasn't going back. I'd spent near seventeen years planning on leaving. With my mother. And then on my own. And now I'd finally made it out. After all that time scraping and saving, and fighting, dragging the horizon closer by my fingernails one louzi at a time, I was on my way. The warm rush I was feeling wasn't all from the drink.

"So where to now?" My foot started tapping on the ground. I'd spent years in one place, and now that I'd finally started moving, it was hard to stop.

The bar girl came over. Jin stopped her as she started to slosh liquor into his glass. "Leave the bottle." He slid a coin across the table to her.

She held the coin up to the faint light before tossing it back on the table. "This isn't real money."

I picked it up. Sure enough, the round piece of metal was about the same size as a louzi, but it was too thin, and printed with a sun instead of the profile of the Sultan.

"My mistake." Jin kept his head low, so the brim of his hat hid his foreign features, as he gave her a new coin. The girl bit it before sauntering back to the bar.

Jin propped his elbows on the table and filled my glass

back up to the brim. He was favoring the shoulder he hadn't taken a bullet to. I watched the strain across his back, his shirt pulling so I could see the tattoo of the sun rising over his collar. I glanced down to the coin in my palm, the same image staring up at me.

"What's the sun?" I asked.

"That might be a bit of an existential question four drinks in," Jin said, putting the bottle down, his shirt shifting again to eclipse the tattoo.

"Three drinks. And I meant that one." I reached across the table and tugged his collar down so I could see the tattoo on his chest. My knuckles grazed his heartbeat. I let go quickly, realizing I was too close to start undressing him.

"It's a symbol for luck," Jin said. He pulled his collar back up, but I could still see the edge of the ink over his heart.

"It's on your foreign coin." He raised his eyebrows at the accusation in my tone. But I figured he knew what I meant. The sun was printed on what I figured was a Xichian coin, which meant it was a national symbol. Jin might have been born here, but he'd told me he was raised in Xicha. It seemed awfully patriotic for a mercenary to have his country's sun tattooed over his heart.

"Why did you come back for me?" I leaned toward him, trying to unravel him. "You could've made a clean getaway."

There was a tug at his mouth as he leaned in to whisper conspiratorially, "I needed a fast horse." He was so close I could smell the alcohol on him. So close he might've kissed me. He seemed to realize that at the same moment I did and pulled away. "Besides, I owe you. When you caught the Buraqi, it drew every person in the Last County away from that goddamn factory just long enough for me to get in and send it up. I've been trying to do that for weeks now. I was getting mighty low on money."

So that was why he'd been in the pistol pit that night.

"And all of it just to blow up some factory in the dead end to nowhere?"

"The biggest weapons factory in the country. And by extension, the world."

"The world?" I'd never known that. It didn't seem possible.

"It's not hard when you can't build something half the size of it anywhere else without it getting torn down by First Beings."

My head was feeling light from the alcohol, and in the dark of the bar I was struggling to put his words together. "What do you mean, torn down?"

Jin paused, drink halfway to his mouth. "Come on, desert girl. How long had it been since you'd seen a First Being before the Buraqi came into town? Magic and metal don't mix well. We're killing it. But it's fighting back." The Buraqi's screams lit up my memories. "Most other countries can make anything on a small scale, including weapons. But a few tried to build factories just like yours hundreds of years ago. The living earth itself rebelled. There's a valley in Xicha that's called Fool's Grave. It used to be a town. They'd built a cannery there. Legend says they were open about a month before the First Beings who lived in the earth had enough and tore apart the ground under the town and flooded the ruins. The same thing happened everywhere. So after a while folks stopped building factories. Except in Miraji. Your First Beings are the only ones who seem to put up with it."

"And what makes us so special?"

Jin shrugged. "Maybe it's because the desert's magic already comes out of fire and smoke instead of growing, living things. Or because the earth here is already dead. But the fact is, your country is at the crossroads between the East, where guns were born, and the West, where they're waging a war of empires. And it's the only one in the world that can build weapons on a massive scale. This desert is valuable. Why do you think the Gallan are here?"

"So we're just one giant weapons factory to them?" The notion was unsettling.

Jin poured himself another drink. "And there are a lot of countries who aren't very pleased by your Sultan providing the Gallan with weapons to invade them if they got it into their heads to try."

"So which one of those countries are you blowing up factories for?" I prodded the sun on his chest. The Xichian symbol.

Jin raised his glass in a mock toast. "Maybe I'm just a pacifist."

I clinked my glass to his. "You have an awful lot of guns for a pacifist."

The words were met by a wry turn of his mouth. "And

you're too smart for someone who doesn't know nearly enough about her own country."

We drank. As my empty glass hit the table, something crashed in the corner of the room. I jumped. A chair had knocked to the ground. Its owner, a man in a dirty green sheema, was on his feet, facing another man who was lounging back, both feet propped up, a game of cards spread out on the table. A pretty girl was between them, molding herself up against the standing man, whispering in his ear until he folded back into his chair. The sitar player started up again in his corner, and someone laughed high and clear, breaking the tension.

The thought hit me all of a sudden. "Did you blow up the mines, too?"

If Xicha wanted to cut off our weapons, then it made sense to cut off the supply of metal, too. Factories could be rebuilt. Collapsed mines were harder. "Here?" He actually looked surprised. "No. I heard it was an accident."

"Why should I believe you? Is Jin even your real name?"

"Well, around here they call me the Eastern Snake. But you know that"—he looked up at me from under the brim of his hat—"Blue-Eyed Bandit." The shock made me pull back. Jin's face split into a grin at my surprise.

"You knew who I was?" I asked, sounding a little breathless. "In Dustwalk?"

"Your eyes aren't exactly inconspicuous," Jin said.

"You knew who I was and you wouldn't take me with you?" The frightened, humiliated feeling of returning to the empty store rushed back in. "Why?"

"Because you shouldn't go to Izman." He settled back in his chair. "No matter how well you can take care of yourself with a gun out here, the city'll tear you apart."

"I wouldn't be alone," I said. "My mother's sister lives in Izman. That's where I'm headed."

"Do you even know how to get there?"

I shrugged. "How are you getting there?"

"I'm not," he said simply, catching me by surprise. I reached back, trying to remember if he'd ever said he was. It just seemed like he must've been.

There was another crash and I reached for a gun that wasn't there as Jin turned around, already tensing for a fight. The card table across the room was overturned, and the man in the green sheema was on the ground, clutching a bloody nose.

I had a moment of distraction to decide.

If I stayed with Jin, I wasn't getting to Izman. He'd left me behind once already and he could just as easily do it again.

Besides, we only had one Buraqi.

I fished out the bottle Tamid had given me. The pills crushed up easily in my fingers and I put them straight into Jin's drink. My fingers were back around my own glass by the time the fight got broken up and Jin faced me again.

I watched him drain his drink.

eight

'd never seen so many people in my whole life as there
were outside the train station in Juniper City. On my
left, a man with a gray beard shouted through the steam
rising from his stall as he shoved more skewers of meat
into the fire; on the other side, a woman dressed in gold
and bells sang with every step. The sound of someone
preaching carried over the ruckus. A Holy Father stood
on a small platform, his hands raised, the twin circular
tattoos on each palm facing the crowd. The rise and fall of
his voice as he preached reminded me of Tamid. A shot of
guilt went through me thinking of my friend. I'd left him
bleeding in the sand to keep myself alive.

The Holy Father dipped his hands at the end of each
prayer, blessing the crowd huddled around his feet.
Forgiving us our sins.

The stream of bodies pushed me past him through the tail end of the souk, under the soot-stained archway. Women carrying bundles on their heads slipped by me; men dragging trunks twice their size crowded me forward.

I moved with the crush of bodies into the shade of the station, stumbling as I took in the sight before me. I'd heard about trains, but I hadn't imagined this. The huge black-and-gold beast stretched out across the station like some monster out of the old stories, breathing black smoke into the dirty glass dome. The crowd jostled toward it.

"Ticket?" A man in a pale yellow vest and cap reached out his hand, looking bored.

I tried to keep my fingers from clinging to the ticket as I handed it over. It had taken me two days to get from Sazi to Juniper City, even on the Buraqi. It hadn't exactly helped that the compass I'd stolen from Jin while he was unconscious, along with half his supplies, was broken and steered me the wrong way, making me wait for sunrise to find my way again.

I'd reached the city in time to get ripped off selling the Buraqi for half of what it was worth. But half was better than nothing. And more importantly, it was enough to buy a ticket straight to Izman. Seeing the name printed in black ink on yellow paper made it seem like just another story in my fingers, ready to slip away at any second. I'd hidden the ticket under the mattress of the room I'd rented and checked it over and over again until I decided it was easier to just keep it against my skin.

The ticket man frowned at me, and I ran my palms over

my new clothes self-consciously. I didn't pass for a boy quite so easily in daylight, but I had to try anyhow. The ugly bruise on my cheek had gone down to a yellow-green that just peeked over the red sheema, and my new clothes were loose in the right places—what was left of my money and some spare Xichian coins and the battered compass that Jin had left jangling around the saddlebags were stuffed into the wraps around my middle that hid my waist. All it'd take was someone looking for too long to see through my disguise. But even a poor imitation of a boy was better than a girl traveling on her own.

I tugged the edge of the shirt where it covered the new gun I'd bought with the Buraqi money. I wouldn't be able to fight my way onto the train, but I might be able to outrun men in yellow caps if I needed to.

I could be about to find out.

"This ticket is first class." He shook it at me like a mother wagging a finger.

"Oh," I said, because I didn't know what he was talking about. I made my fingers go still. "Yes?"

For a second I was sure he was going to accuse me of stealing the ticket. Whatever first class was, I was guessing I didn't look it. Especially with my busted-up cheek and the cut above my eyebrow. "You need to head to the front of the train for first class." He shoved the ticket back at me and pointed farther up the metal beast, somewhere past the churning crowds.

"Oh," I said again. I took the ticket back and pressed through the crush of people, narrowly dodging a man wheeling a covered cage from which I could hear squawking, even over the din.

The man who'd sold me the ticket had asked if I wanted a compartment to myself and I'd said yes. It'd seemed safer, and I didn't think anything of handing over the money he asked. Now I wondered if I might have more than twenty fouza to my name if I'd been smarter.

I saw a roped-off area where folks in fine-spun khalats and colorful sheemas waited, holding yellow tickets like mine. My own clothes were new, but they were just desert clothes. My whole life was in a bag slung over my shoulder. Not even much of a life. Extra bullets, a change of clothes. More like survival. Everybody else looked like they could be carrying a dozen lives in their heavily loaded trunks.

I caught a man with a braided beard giving me a once-over out of the corner of his eye and I got the feeling I knew what the pair of girls behind me were stifling laughs over. I wasn't sure if the man who took my ticket was raising his eyebrows at my appearance or if that was just where they sat on his forehead. He took the ticket all the same, tearing it neatly before handing it back. My neck burning, I climbed the metal steps as fast as I could manage without looking like I was getting away with something.

I'd never seen anything like the inside of the train either. A long corridor with carpets the color of new blood shot in a straight line through the carriage, polished metal doors opening off it, each with glass windows hung with red curtains.

And I thought Tamid's family had money.

The giggling girls pushed past me with a huff of air through their muslin veils. The man trailing behind them spat a sharp-tongued "Excuse me" that made me think he wasn't excusing anyone at all. I ducked my head and wound up looking at the colorful hems of their khalats sweeping across the thick carpet and down the hall.

I stayed a few feet behind the group until I found a compartment whose number matched the one inked onto my ticket. I opened the door as carefully as the time I got dared to find out if the snake behind the school was dead or just sleeping. Turned out my mother knew how to get out snake poison. But this, this wasn't something she would've known anything about.

I locked the compartment door safely shut and folded myself into the bed, pulling off my sheema. I reached a hand out to run across the impossibly clean pillow, but my fingers curled back without my meaning them to. I'd bathed that morning. At proper baths, too. I'd poured oil into my hair and dragged a comb through it with my head under water until it wasn't matted anymore. The steam had wound its way around the swirling tiled patterns of the bath, making my hair curl out. But I still felt like I was going to track the whole desert in with me, like the sand was too deep in my skin after nearly seventeen years.

A whistle split my ears. An alarm? I scrambled to my feet and backed to the other side of the room, gun already in my hand, pointing at the door. I waited for it to fly open.

For two long heartbeats nothing happened, though

there was a lot of commotion outside. And then the whole room lurched sideways. I pitched so hard to the right that I sat down hard on the bed, narrowly keeping my finger from hitting the trigger. I clutched the bed while the train stammered a few more times and then started to move, smoother now.

I hadn't really thought about what riding a train would feel like—the same as riding a horse, I'd figured. I was sure wrong on that count. I sat on the bed, feeling the train pick up speed for a few moments before I got to my feet. All I could see out of the window was black smoke filling the station.

Then, in a violent heave, we broke free. Smoke rushed up, sucked toward the desert sky. My window cleared.

I rested my forehead against the glass. For once the desert didn't seem like it went on forever. The horizon was racing up. A grin stretched the bruise on my cheek painfully.

I was on my way to Izman.

• • •

I LAY ON the soft bed, being rocked pleasantly by the motion of the train. The room darkened as the sun made its way from one side of the carriage to the other. Eventually my stomach started to growl hungrily.

I ignored it as long as I could. But it was a week's journey to Izman. I'd have to leave my compartment sooner or later.

The train was bustling when I stepped outside. Women in fine clothes brushed by me in the corridors and men stood laughing and slapping one another on the back with hands so heavy with rings, it was a wonder they could hold them up. I caught myself dragging my hand across the thick red wallpaper as I made my way down the train. I shoved my hand in my pocket. That wasn't the gesture of someone who belonged in first class.

I passed out of the sleeping area and into a carriage that seemed to be a bar. Nothing like the dark dusty one in Sazi, this one was blazing with light, the ceiling stained dark with thick pipe smoke. Laughter exploded among a group of men over a card table as I passed. Beyond it was a dining carriage. I hovered uncertainly in the doorway for a moment before a man in a uniform came and ushered me to a table.

Dark leather gave way under my back as I settled uneasily in a chair by the window. The chair squeaked below me every time I shifted. A woman at the next table looked up at the noise as I tried to make myself comfortable, sitting as still as I could. Being by myself, surrounded by strangers instead of the folks I'd known my whole life—I was still getting used to it. Best not to draw attention. If anyone looked my way they might wonder why there was a scruffy boy still wrapped in his sheema eating among their glittering clothes.

Colorfully painted plates piled high with food were laid out for me. I eased my sheema away from my mouth, keeping an eye on anyone who might be watching too closely.

But everybody else was looking at their own food. I kept my head down as I shoveled a forkful into my mouth. I almost gagged with surprise on the huge bite. Spices like these were worth a month's wages in Dustwalk. I chewed and swallowed before downing the glass of arak that'd been set out for me.

The second, smaller bite was better, since I was expecting it. Soon I was shoveling mouthfuls in fast. I was scraping the fork along the pattern of the plate when they came and took it away.

One plate followed another. By the time I licked the last of the honey from the baklava off my fingers, I was full to bursting. And tired.

Sleeping away the afternoon heat wasn't a luxury we could afford in Dustwalk. But I'd seen it done in Sazi, when the streets emptied of the wealthy, who drew in behind their cool walls. It looked like they honored the tradition here. Folks were slipping back to their own compartments or settling back on the cushions in the dining carriage to close their eyes.

I retreated to my own compartment, kicking the door shut behind me. I tugged off my boots and collapsed on top of the clean linens. In a week we'd be in Izman. By then, I'd have to figure out how to eat and dress and act like I was supposed to in the big city. Until then, though, I could do whatever the hell I wanted.

nine

I woke in the dark. The thin light that still lingered out-side the curtains of my compartment told me the sun had only just set. The full weight of the desert night hadn't descended yet. Folks would just be waking up again to eat dinner.

The meal was still resting heavy in my stomach, and the jolting of the train wasn't helping. The compartment felt close and hot, even after the sun set. I needed clean air. I tried the window but it was sealed shut, as best I could figure from scrabbling at the edges.

I'd bought a few changes of clothes in Juniper City. I pulled on a fresh shirt, reveling in the cool against my skin, before venturing out into the hall. It was quiet, the carriage still heavy with the afternoon's sleep. Though some of the stifled noises through doors suggested a few folks doing something other than resting. I pulled the nearest window open as far as it would give and let the cooling desert air rush in.

Since the hallway was empty, I pulled my sheema free so my face was exposed as I leaned my forehead against the glass pane. I stayed there, taking deep breaths, settling the rich food in my stomach. The rush of the air, like I was running toward Izman, toward adventure, faster than ever, made me feel that I was finally moving.

A door clattered open behind me. My hand was halfway to pulling my sheema up when I caught sight of a familiar face.

I froze like a fox caught in the henhouse.

Stepping through the door, head tipped forward as she fastened the top button of a new pink-and-yellow khalat, tousled black hair tumbling over her shoulders, was Shira. The sight of her was so familiar that it stuck out like a rusty barb here in this new place.

She didn't see me. She took another step without looking, expecting the world to get out of her way as usual. Her step took her nearly straight into me. Only then did she look up. She was close enough that I could see the biting comment shaping in her mouth. Her lips parted in a surprised O and then split into a jackal's smile.

"Cousin."

I had my gun pointed at her face before the end of the word left her mouth. "Don't scream." I was already looking for an escape.

"Why would I?" There was mocking in her voice as she clasped her hands behind her back, leaning idly against the wall. "You're not going to shoot me."

"How do you figure?" I shifted my finger on the trigger.

"It's a sin to kill your own flesh and blood." She made a pouting face. "See, I paid attention in prayers."

"What are you doing here, Shira?" I checked over my shoulder as quick as I could without taking my eyes off her long enough for her to get up to anything. Somebody might stumble through any moment and see us.

She rolled her eyes skyward. "Did you honestly think you were the only one who wanted a life outside that useless little town?" Truth be told, I'd never given a moment of thought to what Shira might want. I'd reckoned she was the same as anyone, stupidly content to stay in Dustwalk. "Fazim and I used to talk about a future where we were rich and we had all the things we wanted in the world. Only it seems Fazim didn't much care about who got him rich in the end." There was still a mark on my wrist where Fazim had grabbed me. "So I'm making my fortune without him. And that charming young commander who busted up your face was nice enough to take me with him. I knew you'd be here, cousin."

"How could you know that?"

She raised one shoulder coyly. "Well, you don't sleep three feet from someone and not know a thing or two." That was true. I knew Shira liked wearing yellow, hated the taste of pickled lemons, and played with her hair when she was lying. And Shira knew I'd head for Izman if I ever

106

got out of Dustwalk. But there was no way in hell or earth she could know I'd be on this train.

Even if there was only one train a month.

"So what does that get you?" I asked. "Knowing that?"

"I'll show you, cousin." She smiled like we were both in on some big joke. And then she took a deep lungful of air and screamed.

Before I could run, the door of the nearest compartment crashed open in answer, spilling Naguib out. It was the same one Shira had just tiptoed out of. Naguib looked younger with his uniform jacket missing, his shirt unbuttoned at the throat. His eyes went wide when he saw me.

"Help! I found her!" Shira screeched. "The traitor can't be far. Help!" I wasted a precious second wishing a good lie would come.

My tongue failed me.

My legs couldn't afford to.

I grabbed Shira and moved at the same moment the train pitched sideways. The force sent Shira careening backward into the young commander with a cry. He caught her clumsily.

I flung myself through the carriage door, ignoring the shouts behind me. I ran the length of the carriage, shoved past the passengers who'd started to emerge into the corridor, and through the next door, fumbling for a lock behind me. Anything to slow them down.

Nothing.

Cursing, I turned and kept running, down and down until I was halfway through second class. I could still hear my pursuers. I was going to run out of train any minute now. I needed to figure out where I was going before I wound up in the sand.

I'd worry about that when it happened.

I flung myself against the door at the end of the carriage. It jammed.

I rattled the handle, looking behind me for uniforms. I rammed my shoulder against the door again and again. Shouts were getting closer, though it was hard to tell over the rattling of the train.

The door gave. Night air, rails, and sand rushed up to meet me as I pitched forward. I grabbed the door frame, catching myself just in time.

Where there'd been a walkway between the other carriages, here there was only a yawning gap with a narrow metal coupling linking the two cars. In the light from the carriage behind me I could make out the rails whipping below my feet. The air lashed my clothes around me, invisible fingers trying to snatch me back to the sands where I belonged.

There was another door across the way. I could make it through that.

Probably.

Only one way to find out.

I leapt and hit the door full force. It gave way with a dull thud that sent me sprawling, battered and breathless, but alive, across the carriage floor.

I pulled my dangling feet up behind me in a graceless scramble. The door swung shut, narrowly missing my toes. There was a lock this time, and I shoved the bolt into place and hurried to stand up.

There were no more compartments here, just rows of bunks, stacked one atop another all the way back. Dozens of passengers craned around the metal frames to stare at me. They looked like prisoners pressing desperate faces through iron bars. At least one of them was bound to give me up as soon as the soldiers got through the door.

I dodged between beds. A game of dice and drink was under way between some men. They were sitting on the floor, using a bunk like a table. Stained cards were spread out across the sheets, between handfuls of coins. I wove my way through the mass, looking for a place to hide. Four women huddled together on a single bunk, combing one another's hair and eating dates. A little boy with bare feet ran up and tried to grab one. He got a hairbrush to the knuckles and started to wail.

I realized my sheema was loose around my neck, my hair tumbling free, making me a girl again. A girl in boys' clothes. I went to wrap it back around my face. Even as I did, an arm latched around my waist, a hand over my mouth. My attacker pulled me free from the crowd and pushed me up against the train wall between two bunks.

I looked up straight into a pair of familiar foreign eyes.

"You," Jin said, pinning me in place, "are really something else."

The panic dropped away. Jin might not look all that happy with me, but it was better than being caught by a soldier. I shoved him so his hand fell away from my mouth. "I'm going to go ahead and take that as a compliment. What are you doing here?"

"Searching this whole damn train for you," he said, sounding relieved.

"Well, you didn't make it to the front," I said.

"The front?" He cocked an eyebrow questioningly and then it hit him "You bought a first-class ticket? Why? How?"

Like hell I was going to admit it was a mistake. "I sold Iksander," I said instead.

"Iksander?" Jin's grip loosened a little.

"The Buraqi," I explained, looking over his shoulder. It was just a matter of time until I'd see the flash of gold-and-white uniform.

"You named him Iksander?" There was something in his face, like he was trying to figure me out.

"I had to call him something, and it's as good a name as any other. My uncle had a horse he named Blue. I don't know about you, but I've never seen a blue horse." I didn't know why I was getting defensive.

"So you named him after a prince who got himself turned into a horse by a Djinni two hundred years ago?"

"Why does it matter how long ago it was?" I asked in exasperation. "It won't stick anyhow. I sold him. To this trader who called himself Oman Slick Hands, even though his palms just seemed sweaty to me. Only he wasn't exactly honest, because an honest trader would've turned me in for a girl."

"Or a blue-eyed thief." Jin looked amused. "I ought to turn you in."

"Well, you're going to have your chance soon enough, because the army is on this train, and they're after me just now. Or probably after *you*, but I'm in their way."

Jin's head darted up, looking back the way I came.

"Fine," Jin said. "Give me the compass and I'll get us out of here."

"The *compass*?" I wasn't sure what I'd been expecting after he'd tracked me three days across the desert, but it wasn't this.

"You're too smart to play dumb, Bandit." Jin's eyes searched me, like I might be hiding his compass in plain sight.

"You're mistaking my playing dumb for my thinking you're an idiot for wanting a beat-up compass."

His hand was clamped firmly over my pulse. "So we both know you took it. Give it back and we'll call it quits for poisoning me. I won't even ask you to pay me back half of the money for the Buraqi you stole."

"I didn't poison you. I drugged you. And that Buraqi was mine." I tried to pull my arm free, but he was stronger than I was. "You stole it first. If you hadn't set such a bad example, maybe I would've never stolen your broken compass."

"Broken?" His hand tightened until it hurt.

"Yeah." I struggled not to wince. He wasn't smiling anymore. "I rode all night in the wrong direction following the needle on that compass, until the sun came up and straightened me out."

I felt him relax against me. "If it's no good to you, then you won't miss it."

"Seeing as it's no good to me, why would I have kept it?"

"Amani." He leaned toward me until I could feel the heat of him in the small space. "Where is it?"

I tightened my jaw. "Soldiers are coming."

"Then you'd better tell me fast, Bandit."

I didn't speak right away. Our wills locked against each other. I wanted to lie to him. Tell him it was gone with the Buraqi. Keep making him suffer for refusing to take me with him in Dustwalk, for saying I wasn't going to get to Izman in Sazi. For trying to keep me where I was when I was fighting so hard to break away.

"Amani," he lowered his voice. A real note of desperation in my name. "Please." My anger came apart with a tug of his words.

"It's under my clothes," I admitted finally. He let go of me.

I tugged my shirt up, too conscious of his eyes on me as I bared the skin of my hips to reach the cloth wrapped around my waist to pad it out. My hand slipped between cloth and skin and closed around the cool metal and glass. I let my shirt fall back into place as I pulled it out. The compass was a battered brass thing. The glass was scratched and chipped on one edge. The needle swung back and forth over a background of a blue sky the same color as my eyes, dotted with painted yellow stars. I'd figured it might be of value.

His expression shifted as his hand closed over the compass, locking it between our hands. The tension fled his body and he leaned his forehead into mine, catching me off guard. I could smell the desert on him. "Thank you," he said.

His eyes were closed, but mine were wide open. This close I could make out the smallest scar on his upper lip. I was keenly aware of our breathing mixing in the closeness. It would take almost nothing to lean forward and press my mouth to that scar.

There was a crash and a shout from the other end of the carriage. Jin's eyes flew open. What I'd been saying about the soldiers seemed to register on his face at last. "Come on." He started to lead me out from between the bunks. "Let's—"

White and gold flashed across the carriage, out of place among the dingy third-class passengers.

Too late.

There was no time to run and even less time to think. We needed to hide. Only there was nowhere to hide— except exactly where we were standing. I yanked Jin back toward me. My knuckles skimmed over the edges of the sun tattooed over his heart. That was the last thing I noticed before I kissed him.

His jaw tensed in surprise for a moment; his hand gripped my arm hard enough to hurt. And then his body was flush against mine, pushing my back against the wall of the train.

I was a desert girl. I thought I knew heat.

I was wrong.

The contact sent a rush through me so sudden, I

started to pull away before I caught fire. But Jin trapped my face in his hands. There was nowhere to run to. Nowhere to go.

Nowhere I wanted to go.

I hadn't really thought this through, but now I didn't have any thoughts left. Only the strength of his fingers against my neck.

His breath vibrated through me until I couldn't feel anything anymore except want.

More than want.

Need.

His thumb struck the place where Naguib's gun had hit me. An involuntary hiss escaped my lips.

Jin broke away and the moment cracked. Cold air rushed into the gap between our bodies, filling the place his hands had been on my skin a moment before. Now they were planted flat against the wall on either side of me.

His eyes weren't on me anymore. They were on the gun at my hip. I saw a flash of a uniform through the space under his arm. His body wasn't pressed to me. Wasn't wanting me, I reminded myself, only hiding me.

I was breathing like someone who'd never had enough air. Somewhere at the bottom of my lungs I found words again. "They're not out of sight yet."

Jin didn't look at me. "No." His arms were planted on either side of my head, against the rattling carriage wall. He bent toward me just a little, and my body tugged toward him. "They're not."

Someone slapped him on the back and the world careened back in. "How much is she charging, friend?" One bunk over someone laughed.

At the other end of the carriage, a head that might've belonged to a soldier turned at the sound. Jin grabbed my hand. "Let's get out of here."

The door I'd come through was still open. I was about to tell him it was no good heading back that way, that we didn't have anywhere to hide. Then his arms were around my waist.

I didn't have time to say a thing before he jumped.

ten

For a sliver of an instant I was flying.

Then rails flashed in the edge of my vision, narrowly missing a chance to get better acquainted with my skull. My ribs and the ground weren't so shy.

We hit the sand hard. Air burst out of my lungs. We rolled one over the other, Jin's grip tight around me, the train screaming in my ears, drowning out everything I wanted to shout back. Finally we stopped in a bank of sand.

I shoved Jin off me, an ache spreading from my shoulder to my hips. He cursed, clutching his side, but I was ready to run as fast as the train until I caught up. I was on my feet just in time for night and black smoke to swallow the last of the gleaming metal carriages.

For one crazy second I thought about running behind and grabbing hold. Riding for days hooked onto the back of a train.

But the train was gone. Carrying hundreds of people away to Izman. Without me. And I felt something rupture inside. I wrapped my arms around my ribs to keep it in.

"You all right?" Jin was watching me, clutching his side. "Amani?"

The way he said my name on a long exhale set me off like a spark in a powder keg. I swung my fist, straight for his face.

Jin grabbed my wrist before my knuckles could get flirting distance from his nose. He pulled me into him, knocking me off balance.

"Here's a tip for you." He was close to me now, close as he had been when he kissed me, or when I kissed him. "Don't try to hit a man in the face when he's looking straight into your eyes. You've got traitor eyes, Bandit."

I drove my other fist into his gut hard enough that my knuckles popped. Jin doubled over, coughing. "Thanks for the tip." I wished victory didn't feel so much like I'd sprained my hand.

"Any time." He clutched his stomach where I'd hit him, but it looked like he was laughing. I had the wild urge to hit him again while he was down. Instead I drew my shirt up, pulling the gun out of where it was tied against my hip.

"We should start walking," Jin said. "We're probably less than a day out of Massil. We'll have to follow the rails. We could be there before the sun gets too high if we start now."

"What makes you think I'm going anywhere with you?" If it weren't for his having an army on his tail, I'd still be on the way to Izman. Of course, if it weren't for him I'd also still be in Dustwalk. But I wasn't going to get into that just now. I shoved my gun back in my belt; no need to hide it here. Better for folks to know I was armed.

"You got a better plan?" Jin waved his arm at the empty desert like he was offering me a feast for fools. "Would you rather strike off across the desert and wind up food for buzzards than walk another day with me?"

He wasn't wrong. It was open nothingness as far as the eye could see all around us. Except for the rails that ran like an iron scar through the sand. There were only two ways to go if I wanted to stay alive. Forward with him. Back to Juniper City.

I wasn't going back.

"Don't flatter yourself." I riffled my fingers through my hair, pulling it loose from where it was trapped under my sheema as I started to walk. "You're not near worth dying over."

●●●

WE WALKED IN silence as night crept its way across the sky. My anger kept me three steps ahead of Jin as we walked. But even that fire started to dim as the night wore on. I told myself over and over again there'd been another way. We could've stayed on the train. Found somewhere to hide. Something.

After a few hours of turning it over and over in my head, though, I couldn't think of anything else that we could've done except jump.

It was hard to stay angry at someone who'd saved your life.

We'd been walking near all night when I noticed the other figure.

I thought it was a trick of the hazy gray predawn light. The uncertain times between day and night, where neither God nor the Destroyer of Worlds had true dominion, were the most dangerous. But no, down the rails, someone was walking toward us.

I dropped to the sand on instinct, flattening myself into the landscape. Jin was down next to me in a second without question. "What is it?" He had the sense to keep his voice low as he crawled up next to me on his elbows.

"Someone is coming." I nodded ahead. All I could make out was a silhouette on foot, coming in our direction. It could just be a lone desert nomad, leaving Massil as we were going in. Or it could be that someone in the third-class carriage had told the soldiers they'd seen a girl dressed as a boy and a foreigner jump off the train.

The same thought clearly occurred to Jin. "Come on." He started to push himself forward on his elbows to stay close to the sand, moving away from the rails. We'd been walking between them, from one wooden slat to the next, so there'd be no tracks. I crawled behind Jin, kicking any marks from our bodies away with my boot. We crested a sand dune. I rolled over to the other side, flattening myself on my front so we were hidden from the rails.

I loosened my gun just in case. Jin already had a knife in his hand.

We lay in the sand in silence, side by side. I could feel the desert shifting below my stomach with every breath. I listened for the sound of passing footsteps. That was the trouble with sand—it muffled most noises. We'd never hear him climbing up the dune until he was on top of us. We outnumbered him, but surprise made a single man dangerous.

It probably wasn't a soldier, I realized. Soldiers didn't tend to travel alone. But that still left a hundred dangerous possibilities. A hungry Skinwalker. A greedy desert bandit. A Djinni.

No. That was ridiculous. It couldn't be a ghoul—the iron ought to keep them away. And no one had seen a Djinni for decades. They didn't live among us like they used to anymore.

But they were immortal. And this was the desert. The true open desert. Legend said things were out here that hadn't been seen by civilizations in decades.

The unknown made me itch to clamber over the dune and take a look. I shifted ever so slightly, inching my way up the dune. Jin hissed a warning under his breath. I pressed the gun to my lips, to silence him. And remind him I was armed, and likely a better shot than whoever was on the rails. He didn't reach out to stop me as I pulled myself the rest of the way up.

The rails were as empty as a drunk's liquor bottle on prayer day.

"There's no one there. They've gone past." Or they'd vanished in a column of smokeless fire like the Djinn in the stories.

"Do you have a death wish?" Jin sounded almost impressed, his voice returning to a normal volume as he sat up.

"If I did, I wouldn't be very good at it, seeing as I'm still alive," I said, holstering my pistol.

"God knows how." Jin scrubbed his hands over his face, tiredly. I was dead tired, too. It hit me all at once. "Didn't anyone ever tell you the story of Impulsive Atiyah and the Djinni Sakhr when you were a child?"

"You mean the Djinni Ziyah," I corrected him absently.

"What?"

"It's Atiyah and Ziyah, it rhymes. Who's ever heard of Sakhr?" I argued. Everybody knew the story of Atiyah, the impulsive girl who was always getting herself into trouble and her Djinni lover Ziyah, who feared so much for her life that he gave her his name. His true name. Which she could speak and he would be summoned to her rescue. That she could use to bind him to her will. The name that she could whisper to the lock of any door and it would open into his secret kingdom.

"You think the point of the story is the Djinni's name?"

"No, but I reckon you ought to get it right. She died because she said his name wrong in the story, not because she was impulsive, and why are we arguing about this?" I snapped. We both went silent.

"Is your aunt in Izman really worth your life?" he asked finally.

"I don't know, I've never met her."

Jin stopped, hands caught midway through his hair. He'd shoved his shirt up to his elbows and I saw the tension in the muscles in his forearms as he scrutinized me. "You're going to Izman to find someone you've never met?"

"I'm going to Izman because it's got to be a better life than out here."

"No, it doesn't," Jin said. "Cities are worse, if anything. It's not like Dustwalk, where everybody knows your name and kills you for a good reason. They'll kill you for no reason at all. And that'd be a crying shame. You're too remarkable to waste as a corpse in a gutter." He got to his feet and offered me a hand. I ignored it. I ignored what he'd said about me being remarkable, too.

"You sound like my father," I said, standing up without his help.

"Your father?" He dropped his hand.

"He used to say the city was for thieves and whores and politicians." I mocked my father's slurred tones with a wave of an imaginary drink. "I was better off staying where my family was going to keep me safe. Do you want to know how safe my father kept me?"

"What happened to him?" Jin asked. There was a tense note in his voice that I couldn't read.

"My mother killed him." He opened his mouth. "And

don't bother to say you're sorry. He was an ass and he wasn't my real father anyway." I thought back to the blue-eyed soldier who'd been working for Commander Naguib and wondered how many half-Gallan children there were in the desert. No others that I knew of, but I hadn't exactly traveled far. Until now.

"I was going to say that it sounds like he deserved it." Jin said. "And your mother?" His voice said he already knew.

"What normally happens to murderers?" Sometimes in my nightmares I still saw her swinging from a rope. I squared my shoulders. Let him tell me she deserved it, like everybody else had.

"That I am sorry for," he said. "A mother is a hard thing to lose." I got the feeling he might know something about dead mothers.

"I've got nothing to go back to," I admitted. "My aunt Safiyah in Izman is all I've got. So why not Izman?"

He didn't answer me right away. There was some kind of war behind his eyes. "Fine," he said on a long resigned exhale. "Here's what we do." He dropped to his knees and started sketching a lopsided triangle in the sand that I gathered was meant to be Miraji. "We walk to Massil. Here." He jabbed at a point at the bottom of the triangle. "Trains are the only way to get through the mountains this time of year. And I don't suppose you have enough money left to wait around for the next one." He looked to me for confirmation as he drew a jagged line across Massil, cutting us off from Izman.

"First class tickets are expensive," I admitted.

"But," he went on, "there'll be caravans preparing for the journey across the Sand Sea. Toward the port cities on the northwest coast."

"That's where your compass was pointing," I prodded. His hat tipped over his face hid any answer from me.

"And they'll be hiring."

"Hiring what?" I asked.

"Muscle." He shrugged. "Guns. Your desert's not all that safe, you know. The crossing is nothing but sand from Massil to Dassama." He pointed at another dot he'd made in the top left of the triangle. North and west. "It's a month of walking."

"It's also the wrong direction from Izman." I scuffed the top right corner with my toe, give or take where I knew the capital was.

He gave me an exasperated look that told me to shut up and let him finish. "From Dassama it's another ten days of walking across the plains; the caravans do some trading on the way, so it can take longer. Then you get to the sea. It's two days' sailing to Izman. You can buy your way across with wages from the caravan. What do you say, Bandit?"

"You sure didn't miss your calling as a mapmaker." I looked at the muddled lines in the sand on which he'd sketched out our path. It seemed easy drawn out like that. But I knew better than to underestimate the desert. "It's a lot harder than a train." It came out as an accusation.

"Yes, but with fewer soldiers who want to kill you." Jin

stood up, brushing the sand off his hands onto his clothes. It was such a foreign thing to do. The gesture of somebody who wasn't used to sand getting into everything. Who was still trying to fight it.

"They want *you*," I reminded him. "I'm just trying to get to Izman in one piece." I had to admit, it was the best plan I had. He seemed to know Miraji better than I did. And I'd be lying if I said I didn't want to carry on with him. And lying was a sin.

But something was nagging at me all the same. "I suppose you want me to think it's a coincidence that the best way across the desert is the way your compass is pointing."

"I want a lot of things, Bandit. To get out of this goddamn country of yours, a cold bath, a decent meal . . ." Jin trailed off, and for just a moment I could've sworn his eyes drifted to me. "But what we *need* is to start walking if we want to be in Massil before we die of thirst. So what do you say, Bandit." He stuck his hand out. "Stick together?"

My hand fit well in his.

eleven

Jin was standing motionless in the middle of the ring, the muscles across his bare back glistening with sweat as they rose and fell. He let his opponent circle him. The other man dove at Jin, who caught him and slammed him to the ground. I heard the crack of the man's nose just before the cheers drowned anything else out.

"He can throw a hit as well as take one, I'll give him that." Parviz of the Camel's Knees Caravan ran his knuckles along his jaw as he watched Jin's opponent wipe his bloody nose.

I snorted, pitching my voice low to go with my disguise. I was a boy again tonight. No matter how many noses Jin turned bloody, no one was going to take us on as hired muscle so long as I was a girl. And we needed a caravan to get across the Sand Sea without dying of thirst.

It had taken us a day of walking and all our supplies to get to Massil. What was left of our money we spent getting into the city. It was five fouza for every camel to enter the ancient walls and three fouza for every person. The cost of a life told you all you needed to know about a place, especially in the Trader City, where everything was a commodity. Here, human life was the cheapest thing going. Those were Jin's words as we passed beneath a huge stone arch into the once glorious city.

Even I knew the story of Massil. A wise and powerful Djinni once ruled there, back when it was the greatest city on the edge of the Small Sea. The Djinni fell in love with the daughter of one of the traders and offered him the whole city in exchange for her hand. The girl was already promised to another trader from far across the Small Sea, but the greedy father wanted the city. So he fashioned a living doll of wax and magic to trick the Djinni while marrying his daughter to the trader. When the Djinni discovered the trick, he had already given the man the city. And Djinn were only able to tell the truth, which meant they were bound by their word. Unable to take the city back, he raised a sandstorm so great that the sea filled up and up and up until the water was swallowed and there was nothing but sand as far as the eye could see. And then he vanished, leaving the worthless city on the edge of the desert to the greedy merchant.

Massil, the last bastion of civilization before the Sand Sea crossing.

The crowd roared as Jin landed a punch on his opponent's face with a crunch and sent him down to the ground again.

No more civilized than anywhere else, best I could see.

"You ought to see him in a real tight spot," I said to Parviz. "I've seen him break a man's hand like that." I clicked my fingers, thinking of the noise Dahmad's wrist made when it cracked. Just then Jin's opponent dove at him again. Jin sidestepped him, his leg lashing out, catching the man's knee and flipping him over to land flat in the sand. Parviz had a trader's face, even better than a gambler's. But I reckoned he was impressed.

"He'd have to be able to fight if he's always got to be rescuing scrawny little brothers," a voice chimed in from a few bodies over. I knew before I made the mistake of raising my head that the comment was meant for me. A boy with crooked front teeth had been trying to get a rise out of me all night. I reckoned he wanted me to take a swing at him so he could beat me up and impress some caravan leader without having to step into the ring and fight someone his own size. Jin might be able to hit him hard enough to straighten out his teeth, but I wasn't fixing to get my arm broke.

Parviz turned to me and eyed me up against Jin. "He's your brother?"

"We had different mothers." Our charade was rickety as an old henhouse, but it was the only thing we had that was likely to get us hired and across the desert without being picked apart by buzzards two days out. "We'll work for half of what the others are asking for," I said instead of answering the question. We'd been turned down twice already tonight, maybe on account of Jin's foreignness or my size. But the Camel's Knees clan had a reputation for being cheapskates.

"I've been trading since I was high as a camel's knee." Parviz chuckled at his own joke. "I can count well enough to know that with two of you it works out the same fee as a single man, and then there's an extra mouth to feed. I don't need dead weight, Alidad." He called me by the fake name I'd given. "Even if you don't hardly weigh nothing."

Parviz turned away, and already my heckler was stepping out to meet him. "You've a fine eye for business, my friend. Now I could take any of these fellows any time of the day." He gestured in a wide arc with a glass of dark liquor dangling from his fingers.

My gun was in my hand in a flash, ready to execute some half-formed plan.

I squeezed the trigger.

The glass in the heckler's hand shattered before the bullet sank into the wall behind him.

The pit fell silent. The heckler stared dumbly at his handful of glass, blood, and liquor. Someone in the crowd burst out laughing, and then the roar of conversation went up again.

"You son of a bitch!" The heckler had a piece of glass sticking out from his thumb. "You shot me!"

"No, I shot your glass. Don't worry, the liquor'll wash the blood off." I holstered my pistol, hoping I wasn't about to get shot back. "Like I was about to say before getting interrupted, it's a modern age. I don't need a lot of muscle to pull a trigger."

Parviz's eyes swept the heckler, then me. Traders knew the worth of things. And they knew when they were getting a bargain, too. "We're leaving from the West Gate at dawn. Don't be late."

Jin was at my side, pulling his shirt on over his head, as Parviz disappeared. "Did you just shoot someone?"

"I got us hired, if that's what you're asking." I scratched the back of my head and tried to look sheepish. I was sure I wasn't successful judging by the look Jin was giving me. "And I only shot his glass."

Jin hooked one arm around my shoulder, leaning on me. "I knew I liked you, Bandit."

And then came that grin. I might have traitor eyes, but Jin had the sort of smile that would turn over whole empires to the enemy—that made me feel like suddenly I understood him exactly, even though I knew nothing about him. The kind that made me feel like if I was on the right side of it, we could do anything together. I had the next six weeks to find out if that was true.

twelve

We left at dawn with the Camel's Knees as promised. I thought I knew the desert, but as I watched the sun rise in a perfect clear sky over an unbroken stretch of gold, I knew this was something else. The Sand Sea was huge and restless. The Camel's Knees treated it like something between a beast to be broken and a tyrant to cower in front of. I felt at home instantly.

The landscape shifted from one moment to the next, the moving sands dragging me irresistibly down a dune one moment and trapping me in place the next. Some of the dunes seemed infinite—no matter how long we walked we never seemed to crest them. The wind sliced its path through the land, scattering sand like shrapnel into my eyes and my mouth, in spite of my sheema. In the middle of the day the whole desert shifted and a huge wooden structure appeared out of the sand, red and blue paint flaking off of it with the wind.

"What's that?" I asked Jin, shielding my eyes from the sun.

"It's a shipwreck," Jin told me. And just as quickly as it had appeared, the sand swallowed it up again.

When we pitched camp on the first evening, my skin was raw, my whole body ached from walking, and I was happy.

There were sixty-odd people in the Camel's Knees, plus two dozen camels heavy with supplies and goods for trade. The years of travel between them were obvious; they moved as one when they made camp.

"Is this what the real sea is like?" I asked Jin, taking my food to sit next to him on a darkened dune just away from the fire. Jin had started a rumor that I was in a fire as a kid so I was ashamed to show my face. I loosened my sheema enough to eat without taking it off.

"You don't have to walk across the sea." He stabbed at his food with a piece of burned flatbread.

"So what do sailors do all day? Lounge around growing soft?" I poked him in the stomach, which was all muscle. I was stupidly pleased when he laughed. Before he could reply, Old Daud spoke up from beside the fire.

"Settle, children, and I will tell you a story." The story-teller had a voice deep like the desert night and quick like the fire. It was a good voice for stories.

"I wonder if he could set you straight on the moral of Atiyah and Sakhr," Jin whispered to me teasingly. I knew he was getting it wrong to annoy me.

"Maybe he ought to tell the one of the Foreign Man who pushed his luck," I whispered back.

"In the new days of the world, God looked down on the earth and decided to fill it. From his own body of fire he made immortal life. First the clever Djinn were crafted, then giant Rocs who soared through the skies from one mountaintop to the next, and wild Buraqi who raced from one side of the desert to the other, until the whole earth was full."

"I wonder if God could save me from having to hear this story again." A girl startled me, dropping down in the sand between me and Jin without warning. I already knew her: Yasmin, Parviz's daughter, the princess of the caravan.

Isra, her grandmother, walked past and reached over me to smack her on the back of the head, making Yasmin's braid flip over her shoulder. "You will be quiet and listen, Princess Big Mouth." That name worked, too, I supposed.

Yasmin stuck her tongue out at her grandmother's retreating back before leaning toward me. "Old Daud is telling the story for your benefit, you know." She lowered her voice. "It's a warning for the hired muscle about the dangers that creep in the dark." She waggled her fingers comically, which made the tin plate she was balancing on her knees almost tip over. She caught it before it could, rolling her eyes as she stuffed food in her mouth and talked around it. "The ones you're supposed to be keeping us safe from. Though it's been years since we saw a ghoul out here." *Same as Dustwalk*, I thought. I'd last seen a Nightmare when I was eight years old. "It's mortal men that cause the most trouble these days."

Isra raised her hand, threatening a slap from the other side of the fire. The caravan princess pulled a face but shut up for good, letting Old Daud lapse into the story.

Everybody knew the story of the First Mortal. But Yasmin wasn't wrong; Old Daud did seem to be giving me and Jin pointed looks as he told it. So I listened close as he told of a golden age when only First Beings roamed the earth. How, after time beyond counting had passed, the Destroyer of Worlds came from deep within the earth. She brought with her a huge black snake who swallowed the sun and turned the sky to endless night, and a thousand new creatures—the monsters she called children, but that First Beings named ghouls. And when the Destroyer of Worlds killed the first First Being, he exploded into the first star in the newly black sky. God had made the First Beings with endless life, so when they learned of death they were afraid. That was the dawn of the first war, and as First Beings fell, the night sky filled. The Djinn, the brightest of God's First Beings, feared death so much, they came together and gathered earth and water and used the wind to mold a being and set it alive with a spark of fire. They made the First Mortal. To do what they feared most, but what needed to be done in any war: die.

So the First Mortal took up steel, and with it he beheaded the huge snake who had swallowed God in his sun form. The sun was released from the monster's throat and the endless night ended.

The First Beings looked upon this mortal thing they had made and saw with awe that he wasn't afraid of death. He dared to fight because his destiny was to die. And where the Destroyer of Worlds had created fear, the First Mortal had bravery to meet it. The immortals had never had a need for it before. But mortals did.

So the First Beings made another mortal and another. They fashioned each in a duller image of an immortal thing—men instead of Djinn, horses instead of Buraqi, birds instead of Rocs. They worked until they had an army. And against the might of mortality, the Destroyer of Worlds finally fell. Her rule over the earth broke and the creatures she brought with her were left alone, stalking the desert night.

The story ended, the air full of the silent spell Old Daud's words had woven. Then the world rushed back in, the one the First Mortal had fought and died for, filled with idle camp chatter and the flicker of pipe smoke and Isra calling Yasmin away to scold her over the luridly bright khalat she'd just found among her other clothes.

"I'll take your watch," I offered as Yasmin joined her grandmother with a roll of her eyes and the camp settled around us. I felt alive. Filled up by the desert. Lit on fire. "I don't think I could sleep anyway."

"I'd rather stay up after that." Jin offered me a drink across the empty space between us. "He's got me half terrified I'm going to get eaten by a ghoul in my sleep."

"In Dustwalk they say that only happens to sinners." I took a swig from the flask and passed it back.

"And nonbelievers," Jin said. "Like me."

"You don't believe in God?"

"I've been a lot of places," Jin said. "And I've heard a lot of what people think is true. When everyone seems so very sure, it's hard to figure anyone is right."

I'd never thought about whether I believed in God. I believed in the stories in the Holy Books the same way I believed in the stories of the First Mortal or Rebel Prince Ahmed. It never mattered to me if they were true. They had enough truth of greater ideas, of heroes and sacrifice and the things everybody wanted to be.

"In Miraji you claim that God created the immortals, your Djinn, from fire, and they made the first mortals. In the Ionian Peninsula they say the immortals themselves are gods and they created us humans for their amusement. The Albish say that all things sprang straight from the river and from the trees, created by the heart of the world, immortal and mortal alike. The Gallan believe that First Beings and ghouls are no different—that they're both tools of the Destroyer of Worlds—and that some different god than yours created mankind to destroy them and purify the earth."

Immortals could be killed by iron. Same as ghouls.

But the notion of murdering a Djinni made everything in me rebel. The relationship between humans and immortals was complicated. There were a thousand stories about mortals tricking Djinn, finding their true names and using the names to trap them. But immortals were forces of nature. Creatures of God. As ancient as the world itself. And our short lives were nothing compared to their endless ones. Killing immortals was what the Destroyer of Worlds did. Humanity was created to save them.

"Is that what the Gallan are using our guns for?"

"Mostly they use them against other humans these days," he said. "They wiped out the First Beings in their country long ago. They're working on everywhere else now."

"Like Xicha." My eyes drifted to the open shirt collar where his tattoo was. I didn't realize until then that there'd been a part of me that was still angry at him for blowing up the factory in Dustwalk. Whether or not it hurt the Gallan, it crippled the whole of the Last County, too. And, sure, there were plenty of folks there who didn't deserve any better than starving to death. But there were also folks like Tamid who'd never learned to hate that place the way he should've. And my cousin Olia, who every once in a while caught my gaze behind Farrah's back and rolled her eyes with me. And my little cousin Nasima, who still hadn't caught on that she was supposed to be ashamed to be born a girl. Those people didn't deserve to starve.

Then again, Jin's country didn't deserve to get invaded the way Miraji had been.

Jin pulled up his collar. "The Gallan have been kept at bay for a thousand years now by their neighbors. When it used to be magic against swords, it was a fair fight. But the Gallan are armed with guns now, and magic is bleeding out of everywhere, no matter what you believe in."

"So what *do* you believe?" I asked.

"I believe money and guns get you a lot further in a war than magic these days."

"If that was true you'd be living rich in some city with a soft bed and five wives. Not blowing up factories in the dead end of nowhere, Xichian boy."

"Five wives?" He snorted into his flask. "I'm not sure I could keep up with that many." I didn't say anything. I'd figured out with Jin that if I gave him long enough usually he'd give me the truth. "I always figured the land creates its First Beings the way it creates its mortals. In the green forests and fields of the West, their magic grows from deep soil. In the frozen North it crawls and claws out of the ice. And here it burns from the sand. The world makes things for each place. Fish for the sea, Rocs for the mountain skies, and girls with sun in their skin and perfect aim for a desert that doesn't let weakness live." I'd never had anyone describe me like that before. His gaze flicked away too fast for me to fall into it. "Of course, my brother would tell you that the First Beings are all just manifestations on earth of one Creator God. That's what the new philosophers are saying."

"You've got a brother?" As soon as I said it I saw on his face that it was a slip. He hadn't meant to tell me that. But he couldn't take it back. "Where is he?"

Jin stood, brushing sand off his hands. "I think I'll take you up on that offer to cover my watch after all."

thirteen

The desert was changeless. For six weeks there was only sand and blue skies. The blisters on my feet turned bloody just in time for fresh ones. The restlessness I'd shoved into the bottom of my gut my whole life wasn't staying down so easy. I was on my way to Izman and I'd never felt more awake in my life.

At night, while the rest of the camp slept, I'd shed my sheema and breathe and sit some of Jin's watch with him until I was worn out enough to sleep before mine. He taught me words from other languages he'd learned sailing. After the first month I could threaten a man and insult his mother in Xichian, Albish, and Gallan. He showed me how he'd broken Dahmad's wrist in the wrestling pit, a move he'd learned from a Jarpoorian sailor in an Albish port. I asked him about his broken nose once. He told me a Mirajin girl had hit him, and his brother had set it for him. He did that sometimes, mention his brother, like he was forgetting to guard himself with me. But he talked freely about most everything else. He told me about the places he'd been, the foreign shores he'd sailed to and stories of all the things he'd done, until I was itching to see the Golden Palaces of Amonpour and feel the rock of a ship below my feet. The stories of Izman had belonged to my mother. But the world was a lot bigger than my mother ever told me. And it occurred to me once or twice that I could go anywhere in it.

I knew we were getting close to the end of the desert the first time I saw something other than sand dunes on the horizons.

"It's called the Dev's Valley," Jin told me as the camp settled down. We were on the outskirts of it. "It's a mess of mountains and canyons all the way down the western Mirajin border. They say it was carved into the land during the war against the Destroyer of Worlds. Before mankind."

"That's one hell of a battle." We were probably a two-day walk away. Two days wasn't so long. I looked up into the night. The sand rolled out in an endless ripple, turned blue by the starlight, so it was almost hard to tell where it met the sky except for the wild burst of stars overhead. "We've been walking for near two months now. The stars have moved."

"A captain on one of the ships I worked on used to be able to travel by the stars."

"But you need a broken compass." As always when I mentioned the compass, I got nothing from him except for the slightest twitch of his lip.

"You want me to take your watch?" I asked. It was a pattern we'd fallen into since the first night.

"You're unnatural." Jin ran his hands over his face. "This desert is enough to drain any man."

"Well, I'm not a man," I said. "And I was just trying to be nice, so—"

"No, wait." Jin's fingers laced with mine too quick to react, pulling me down to sit next to him. It sent a stupid wild jolt through me before he let me go just as fast. "I'm sorry, I'm just sick to death of the sand everywhere."

"I'm plenty used to it, I suppose." I stared out across the dunes. They looked like they went on forever, but the horizon felt closer with the mountains. "It gets deep into your soul after a while."

"It's in your skin, too." He reached out a hand, and before I could think, his palm was flat against my cheek, warm and a little bit rough. His thumb traced the length of my cheekbone. A cascade of sand went in its wake, falling away from skin where it was stuck and leaving a strange burning shiver behind.

"Amani." He didn't take his hand away from my face. "You're going to have to be careful when we get to Dassama. The city has been an encampment for Gallan soldiers for years now. It's got almost as many of them as it does Mirajin people in its walls."

"When am I not careful?" I tried for lightness, but in

truth I was all too aware of his hand on my face.

"You're never careful," Jin said wryly, his thumb tracing rough patterns on my cheek, his eyes following it. Like he was memorizing it. "Hell, right now if anyone from the caravan happened to look over, your cover would be blown." His hand ran along my jawline. I could feel his touch on my face leaving my breathing ragged.

"I'd say you're the one not being careful just now." He seemed to catch himself. His hand dropped away quickly. A cold ache spread out behind it. "Besides," I said, "you'll be with me. How much trouble can Atiyah possibly get into if she's got Sahkr?" Atiyah and Ziyah was a great love story. Atiyah and Sahkr was just our joke.

He didn't laugh. I'd gotten to know what silence meant from Jin. He was hiding something from me. Suddenly, how soon we'd be going our separate ways crept up on me. My aunt Safiyah might be blood, but Jin I knew. And I didn't want to leave him. He made the world bigger. I wanted to go to the countries he'd been to. And more than anything I wanted him to ask me to go with him. But we were running out of time together.

In the early light of morning, the mountains looked even closer. My stomach twisted in anticipation. The excitement of nearing Dassama, the end of the desert and the first civilization we'd seen in weeks, crept into the caravan as the day wore on. The normal stoic trudging through the sand turned restless. The younger kids dashed up and down the line of camels, already trying to talk anyone who would listen out of a few louzi so that they'd be able to buy themselves treats when we got to Dassama. Men and women were starting to pine loudly for a glass of something cool. Isra was berating Parviz loudly about the provisions. How it'd almost not been enough this time. How we were going to have to resupply as soon as we got into town. Yasmin was keeping her young cousins going with a game she called When I Get to the City.

"When I get to the city, I'm going to pull off my feet and get new ones that aren't so sore." Little Fahim drooped dramatically, letting his arms swing like a rag doll's.

"When I get there," his sister chimed in, pulling him up by the scruff of his shirt, "I'm going to eat a hundred yazdi cakes."

"One hundred!" Yasmin faked wide-eyed surprise. "How will you have room after eating a hundred dates and a hundred chickens?" She rattled off the list of foods the little girl had already promised to eat. I tried to stop my own stomach from growling in answer.

"What about you, Alidad?" Yasmin asked, trying to draw me into their game. "What are you going to do when we get to Dassama?"

Truth be told, all I wanted was to wash for so long that the dust from my skin would turn the baths to a miniature version of the Sand Sea. Only I couldn't do that without throwing away my secret.

But more than Dassama, Izman was preying on my mind as we got closer to the end of the desert.

My mother had talked about going to find her sister in Izman so often that it was like a prayer in our household, when my father wasn't there. But I didn't even know if I wanted it anymore. I didn't know if I'd ever wanted it or if my mother had just been wanting it enough for the two of us to keep us going all those years.

Hell, my aunt Safiya could be as bad as Aunt Farrah, and even if she wasn't, I wasn't so sure I wanted to turn myself over to anyone else who could claim a right to my life.

And I'd never see Jin again.

My eyes were latched to Jin's back up ahead when I realized that the front of the caravan train had come to a stop.

"What's happening?" Yasmin put her hand on Fahim's head, keeping him from going any farther.

A mutter ran back through the caravan train as folks raised their heads, straining to see up front, shielding their eyes against the dying sunset. They wanted to see, but a caravan ran on orders. Except for me.

I broke into a run for the front of the caravan, which had reached the top of a dune. Parviz was standing above me, Jin next to him, his sheema pulled down, as I climbed my way up the sand. The camels had dropped to their knees to rest, not understanding why we were stopping.

I broke over the top of the high dune next to them. At first I couldn't grasp it, either.

Where Dassama ought to have been, we were standing over ruins. Old, half-crumbled walls caught the setting sun, the last light casting shadows across them and stretching out across the sand. Then I realized they weren't shadows.

My mouth went dry.

"How," Jin said very carefully as I stepped up beside him, "does sand burn?"

• • •

THE CLOSER WE got, the worse it looked. Where the stone wasn't blackened, it had crumbled to ash. In places the sand itself was black or burned hard. We didn't speak as we drifted through what was left of the narrow streets and charred houses. This wasn't a fire. Fire was something that some folks survived, that you ran from and put out, smothered in sand.

Jin was the first to say what we were both thinking, too low for the rest of the caravan to hear. "No bodies."

"Bodies burn easier than stone." I kicked a rock, and what was left of it disintegrated. "No fire would catch like this unless the whole place was soaked in oil."

"A bomb," Jin said. It wasn't a question, but that didn't mean he was right.

"The pattern for it is wrong," I said.

Jin looked at me sideways. "How do you know that?"

"Come on, Xichian boy." I forced lightness. The wind dragging at my sheema tasted like ash and made me want to gag. "You telling me you never set off gunpowder when you were a kid just to blow things up?"

Jin snorted. "We didn't all grow up near a weapons factory."

I shrugged. "When a bomb goes off, it's always got a center. Here the buildings are burned on every side." Like something had crashed down from above and flooded the city with fire. Familiarity whispered in my ear, though I didn't know why. I rounded a ruined corner and pulled up short.

"And a bomb doesn't spare prayer houses, either."

In the middle of the destruction, a huge domed building was the only thing left whole in the city. Its walls were still a fresh gleaming white, the scorch marks stopping just short of it.

"What did this?" I whispered.

Jin just shook his head. "Something unnatural."

"We've got another problem." We'd wandered to the center of the town, and I nodded to the crumbled hunk of melted metal and stone in the middle of the square. "I'm thinking that used to be the well."

The fear that went through the caravan as they saw the same thing I had was unmistakable. No one knew the value of water like desert folks. "How much water do we have left?" Jin asked, raising his voice as he called to Parviz.

"A day's worth." Parviz looked grim. "Two, if we ration. It's a six-day walk to Saramotai." I recognized the name of the next Oasis town we were due at after stopping to re-supply in Dassama.

"It's only two days to Fahali, though," Jin said, "if we head west instead of north."

"That's off our path," Parviz replied too quickly.

"Better to die of thirst than take a detour, is it?" Jin's arms were crossed over his chest. His eyes were on his feet, but also far away. Like he had bigger things on his mind than us all dying of thirst. "Besides, I'm not hearing any other bright ideas."

Parviz glanced at his brother, a man named Tall Oman. They called him that to set him apart from the three other Omans in the caravan. Something silent passed between the two men. Tall Oman shook his head slightly. I glanced at Jin to see if he'd caught it, too, but he was lost in his own thoughts.

"Is there something we ought to know?" I asked. "About Fahali?"

"It's a dangerous city," Parviz said shortly.

"It's a dangerous desert," I said. He was hiding something, but I couldn't tell what. "Isn't that why you pay us?"

There was a moment of tense silence. Then Parviz nodded, his face pulled tight.

"Fahali, then. And we pray your aim is sharp, young Alidad."

fourteen

I could see the mountains from Fahali, like ragged teeth in the afternoon haze. Amonpour was across those mountains, on the other side of the Dev's Valley. And the border meant soldiers. We were stopped at the gates by the city guard, bored-looking Mirajin men in pale yellow, who flipped through our saddlebags lazily, chatting to Parviz as they did. Most of the caravan sank down to sit in the sand, leaning just inside the city walls while the bags were searched.

We'd walked with barely any rest since Dassama, only stopping in the darkest hours of the night when continuing might as well mean death by ghoul instead of by thirst. I remembered what Jin had said our first night in the desert: the desert didn't let weakness live.

And we were still alive. We were Mirajin and we survived. Even as my legs gave out below me, I'd never been prouder to be a desert girl, among the Camel's Knees.

A coin danced across Yasmin's knuckles absently, catching the sunlight. Worry danced across her face quicker than the sunlight off the coin and vanished just as fast. Her palm tightened around the half-louzi piece. Parviz's eyes veered away once too often as the guard rummaged through his belongings, his back too stiff. My hand drifted to my gun without really being sure what I was afraid of.

I looked around for Jin. I spotted him a good twenty paces away, pulling his hat low as he headed away from the caravan. My tiredness and my stiff legs forgotten, I pulled myself to my feet and dashed to catch up to him.

"Hey!" I shoved him in the shoulder, closing the distance a moment before he would've disappeared around a corner. In one movement, his hand was on my wrist, halfway to reaching for his gun before he realized it was me. He was jumpier than a barefoot beggar on hot sand.

"You ought to know better than to sneak up on a man like that, Bandit." He dropped my arm, trying for lightness. I didn't rise to the bait.

"And you ought to know better than to think you can sneak away from me." We were far enough from the Camel's Knees to not be overheard, but I kept my voice low all the same. "You're hiding something."

Jin laughed, though not like it was actually funny. Like he didn't even know where to start. When he pushed his hand through his hair his sheema fell back. I was seeing him unobstructed, in the light of day, for the first time in weeks. "There are a lot of things you don't know, Amani."

That was probably true. Jin didn't tell me much. There were just the moments when the walls he kept around himself cracked and I saw a hint of something through them, when he slipped and mentioned a brother, or a dead mother, but he closed those up fast enough.

"So what don't I know about Dassama?" The memory of the scorched sand hung between us uneasily, ending any attempt at a joke he might've tried to make. We'd both seen a whole city gone up in flames. And he'd barely said a handful of words to me since then. Like he was avoiding me.

"Amani—" He reached for me, his hand dropping away just in time to hide a gesture that didn't seem to belong to a brother in view of the caravan. I glanced behind me. They were still being searched at the gate. Colorful scarves unraveled in one of the guards' arms, making Isra scold him as she snatched them back off the ground.

"You don't have to carry on through the desert from here if you don't want to." My full attention came back to Jin. That wasn't what I'd been expecting. He was watching me close, gauging my reaction.

"How do you reckon?" I asked warily.

"There's a train. It runs from an outpost a few hours' walk outside Fahali. It goes straight to Izman. You could be drinking arak in the shade of the palace walls in fewer days than I have fingers, if you wanted."

A train. Like the one he'd pulled me off all those weeks

ago on the other side of the desert. A straight shot to the capital, after sixteen years of aiming for it, and he was offering it to me. And I'd never see Jin again. That was what he was really offering me: a way out of this. To turn my back on Dassama and what he knew and walk away to the life I'd always wanted. Or always figured I did.

"And if that's not what I want?" I had traitor eyes and there was no way he could mistake my meaning.

He took a deep breath. I couldn't tell whether it was relief or resignation. When he inhaled I could see the Xichian sun over his heart rise just above the horizon of his shirt collar. "I told you in Sazi that the Sultan was building weapons for the Gallan. But it wasn't just guns."

"What do you mean?" The factory outside of Dustwalk had made nothing but guns my whole life. Jin's jaw worked, like he was testing the words. I'd watched him cross paths with death and dodge it with a wry tilt of the hat a half dozen times now. This was something different. This was something more than just him in trouble.

"There were rumors of another weapon," he said finally. "Something they were making far down in the south. A bomb that could level whole cities like the hand of God itself. Whole countries even."

Whole countries like his. He'd told me other things about the Gallan: That they were building an empire at the borders of countries around them as their magic faded. A weapon like the one that had destroyed Dassama would let them swallow other countries whole.

"We thought it might just be something being spread to scare folks," Jin went on. "But in the end better safe than dead." He let out a long exhale, but my own breathing was feeling shallow. "So I was sent down to the end of civilization to see what I could find. And lo and behold there's a monster of a weapons factory. I figured even if there was no great leveler of civilizations, this was something. Something that might be able to cripple the Gallan for a little while, stem their supply of guns to their armies overseas. When I blew it up I thought any great weapon that could slaughter cities would go up with it. Judging by the burnt Oasis, Naguib got it out first. If the Sultan's made a weapon like this for the Gallan, they won't need a single bullet to bring the whole world to its knees."

I thought I understood fear. I'd grown up in Dustwalk. But that was a restless fear, the kind that made me want to run. This was the kind that crawled up from the bottom of your gut and told you there was no running. The kind that made you go still from it.

"And Dassama was—"

"A testing ground," he filled in grimly. "Commander Naguib must've taken the weapon up to Izman to hand it over. But they would've needed a testing site. Some place where the Gallan would be able to see it for themselves." And the Sultan had given them one of his own cities, with his own people, so they could test a bomb that would cripple the rest of the world. "Dassama was a large Gallan base, but rumor had it they were losing control of the city to the rebellion." I remembered the night we'd met in Deadshot. *A new dawn, a new desert.* The rebellion. The Sultan was allied with the Gallan. Holding his power depended on them. I'd never figured that the Rebel Prince might mean getting rid of the Gallan as well as the Sultan. I supposed the Gallan had.

"And you think the weapon is here?" I said. "In Fahali?"

"This is the only city within spitting distance of Dassama," Jin said. "Rumor has it the Gallan have doubled their numbers here in past months, searching for the Rebel Prince." He smiled, like at a private joke.

It'd be petty to yell at him about this. About not telling me. About turning around and walking away from the caravan without a word. "You're going to get us both killed if you go off looking for it on your own, you know. And if I was going to die on account of you, I'd rather have done it weeks ago before I had to do all this walking." So maybe I was a little petty.

"Amani, you are not a part of this if I—" Jin stopped abruptly. My eyes followed his behind me. I saw a flash of blue uniforms. It was all I needed to see.

Jin grabbed my hand as I moved to run, pulling me sideways instead, into a narrow side alley. The cool of the shade folded over me, and we both flattened ourselves in the shadows as the Gallan soldiers descended on the Camel's Knees.

"All caravans must submit to inspection." The Gallan soldier spoke Mirajin with a thick accent that came from the back of his throat and made it sound like he was gargling water while talking.

"We've already searched them." One of the Mirajin guards stepped forward. "They have nothing. We were about to release them, sir."

"We are to search again. Orders of General Dumas." The Gallan soldier waved his men forward even as the caravan drew back.

The city guard had moved through the caravan's bags like a lazy desert heat, but the Gallan soldiers tore through like a storm, only with more ill will. I stared as bags were ripped off of camels' sides, what was left of our supplies emptied into the street. Yasmin was forced to raise her hands above her head while the Gallan soldiers searched her slowly.

Then there was a shout. A young Gallan held up what was left of one of the saddlebags. He'd sliced into it with a knife, peeling the layers of leather apart, and he was holding what looked like a thin silk bag. He tipped it sideways and something fell out, scattering in the afternoon wind. It looked like fine blue thread, almost like hair. Jin swore.

"What is it?" I asked.

"Medicines." Jin said. "Only ones made from magic, not science." That couldn't be right. There were plenty of desperate charlatans across the desert who sold red water and claimed it was cure all Djinni blood, but nobody believed in that. But then, they didn't hide it in the linings of their saddlebags, either. "Magic'll cost anyone his head," Jin said grimly. "Figures that Parviz wanted to avoid the city."

I watched as Parviz was dragged forward and shoved to his knees in front of the soldier who'd spoken Mirajin. My hand flew to my gun at the same moment that the Gallan soldier pulled out his. My anger was sudden. They didn't belong in our desert. They didn't belong in my bloodline, either. I was a desert girl. I hated that half of me came from these foreigners.

I could shoot him.

The thought slid into my mind as neatly as a bullet slotted into a gun. It might not save Parviz, but I could try. Before I could move, Yasmin burst forward, shoving her way past the Mirajin guard. She flung herself between her father and the soldier, straight into the line of my shot. The soldier's gun didn't drop; it just stayed trained on Yasmin now instead of Parviz. His finger went to the trigger. Mine was already there.

"Stop." The Mirajin guard stepped forward. "You will not shoot him here."

"It is law that he be executed," the Gallan soldier said. "General Dumas's orders." He said the name again, as if it carried the weight of God's own command.

"It's law for smugglers to stand trial before execution," the Mirajin guard countered. "Prince Naguib's orders."

I felt Jin stiffen behind me at the name the same time as I did. Naguib was here. Commander Naguib, who had held a gun to my head and shot Tamid through the knee. Of all the people to save them. The pistol was reholstered.

I sagged back against the cool wall as the caravan was rounded up to be imprisoned. Jin and I stayed still in the mouth of the alley. When we couldn't hear footsteps anymore, his body relaxed against mine.

"You know, I never believed in fate until I met you," he said, tipping his head back against the wall with a deep sigh. "Then I started thinking coincidence didn't have near so cruel a sense of humor."

"You're a real charmer, anyone ever tell you that?"

"They have, actually, but usually they say it without rolling their eyes."

We leaned back in silence. A line of laundry drifted lazily above us in the afternoon heat as I took stock of the situation. We were stuck in a city with the Gallan, their great destroyer of cities, and Naguib, and now the caravan was gone. "We need to get out of here," I said.

"And what about everyone else, Bandit?" Every time he called me that it made something inside me pull toward him that I couldn't quite shake. "Planning to leave them all behind?"

I wasn't planning on leaving you behind. "I'm not planning anything," I said instead. "I haven't thought that far ahead." But now that I did think about it, Jin was right. I knew what most of the Camel's Knees would do if they were me. This was the desert. You took care of yourself and your own. The rest got left in the sand to die. Like Tamid.

"There's a train straight to Izman tomorrow," Jin said. "That's about as far ahead as you need to think."

"So come with me." The words were out too quick. "You're not going to find the bomb here without getting yourself killed. You've got to know that. And if we stay much longer, both of us are going to wind up dead."

Something between us seemed to still. I watched the slow rise and fall of his shoulders as he took a deep breath. Then a second one. A third. "All right."

"All right?" I'd been ready to argue and drag him out of here. But all the fight had gone out of him with those two words. "That's it? You're not going to smart-talk your way around me?"

"All right," Jin repeated. He spread his hands wide like he was surrendering, though the grim set of his mouth made it seem like he'd rather do anything but. "You're right. So what do you suggest we do?"

I was feeling bolder than I ever had. "We could just keep running, Jin. If we had to."

"You mean if I wanted to." His eyes searched mine, and for one second they looked as dark and focused as they had in the few moments after he'd kissed me on the train. My eyes were probably as wild as that second, too. The last time we'd really stood this close. On the edge of living or dying. Of wanting and needing.

"Tell me we couldn't do it." Jin interrupted my thoughts. "Tell me that the two of us together, we couldn't get every one of the Camel's Knees out of the city alive if we really tried. Hell, tell me you couldn't do it on your own if you set your stubborn head to it." A small smile was creeping back. "Tell me that and we'll walk away. Right now. Go and save ourselves and leave them to die. All you've got to do is say the word. Tell me that that's how you want your story to go and we'll write it straight across the sand to the sea. Just say it."

My story.

I'd spent my life dreaming of my own story that could start when I finally reached Izman. A story written in far-off places I didn't know how to dream about yet. And on my way there, I'd slough off the desert until there was nothing left of it to mark the pages.

Only Jin was right. I was a desert girl. Even in Izman I would still be the same Blue-Eyed Bandit with a hanged mother, who left her friend dying.

He didn't need me to answer, not really. I gave myself away too easily. Or maybe he just knew me too well. "Any ideas, Bandit?"

And that easily we were a team again.

I tilted my head back. Between two windows, laundry drifted lazily in the hot desert wind. "Some."

• • •

I WAS DRESSED as a girl for the first time since I'd left Dustwalk. The plain blue khalat we'd stolen off a clothesline was too tight around my arms with my boy's clothes on underneath.

"I'd almost forgotten you were a girl under there." Jin looked me over, hands hooked above his head. He still looked rumpled from sleep. Exhaustion had gotten the better of us while we waited for the cover of dark, and we'd both fallen asleep slumped inside an alleyway narrow enough to hide us. I'd woken with a stiff spine and Jin's arm slung across me like he was trying to keep me from running out on him in his sleep again. But there was no chance of that. I was done leaving people behind.

"Did you want to be the girl?" I asked, readjusting the

red sheema I'd wrapped around my waist like a sash.

"You make a prettier girl than I do." He winked at me, and I rolled my eyes at him.

The plan was simple. I was going to walk into the city barracks and walk back out with information on where the prison was. The city barracks housed the Mirajin guard most of the time, but it seemed like half of them were camping in tents while the Gallan army housed their soldiers. Once we knew where they were we'd be able to work on getting the Camel's Knees out. If anyone questioned me I was to say I was there to get water, just like the stream of women going in and out all day.

As it turned out, rumors were running freer than the pumps in Fahali. The Camel's Knees weren't the only caravan to turn up lips cracked and gasping out news of Dassama. The city's supplies were stretched thin under the weight of the extra people, caravans and soldiers alike. Water was being rationed, and half the wells and pumps were closed. But not the one in the barracks.

"I'll be nearby if you get in trouble. Just stay in sight." He nodded above at a rooftop with a decent overview of the barracks—decent enough that a good shot might be able to hit a soldier on the inside. I was the better shot. But he was right: I also made the better girl. Which meant I was counting on Jin to cover me.

It was a short walk to the army barracks, but the streets were busy in the cool just before dusk. I kept my eyes low as I fought my way through the crowds in the last of the setting sun. I'd near forgotten what it felt like to be a girl in Miraji. I was inconspicuous, but not the way I'd been as a boy. Not because I was the same as everyone else. Because I didn't matter.

Nobody in Miraji had ever thought enough of a girl to imagine I might be a spy.

The barracks were four long, low buildings painted in white around a dusty square. Besides the prison there'd be sleeping quarters, kitchens, storage, and the stables. That's what Jin had told me, at least. All I had to do was figure out which one was the prison and get back out.

I tried to look like I was keeping my eyes on my feet as I walked through the dusty yard. There were soldiers practicing with guns and various targets. One of the Gallan soldiers had a gun with a sharp end like I'd never seen before. He fired at a cloth figure of a man before ramming forward, driving the sharp tip through the dummy's stomach.

In the middle of the square was the water pump with three Gallan soldiers stationed at it, taking coin from anyone who wanted to use it. A line of women holding pails on their hips snaked out from the pump. They all kept their eyes low, like they were trying not to be noticed by all the armed men around them. I didn't have a bucket. I just had to hope nobody noticed, or there'd be more questions than I was fit to answer.

The girl at the front of the line was about my age and dressed in a dusty pink khalat. A small child was hanging off the hem, sucking her fist. The girl in pink's hands were empty of coin, but she was begging, her eyes red from crying. I heard a sliver of her conversation as I passed. Her family, they were thirsty, she was saying. Thirsty and poor. She couldn't pay the new tax on water, but she was begging for their pity. The soldier's eyes swept her with the same look the parched women were given the water pump.

Two Gallan soldiers leaned in and said something to each other in their ugly foreign language. Then one of them with pale eyes like mine and unnaturally yellow hair gestured to the girl to follow him. The girl knelt down and pried the child from her khalat, handing her the bucket. I was too far away now but I guessed she was telling the little girl to stay put. The little girl took a staggering step to follow all the same, but one of the other women in line grabbed her, holding her back. Even holding the child, she spat at the girl in pink.

"Foreigner's whore!" she called, loud enough for me to hear. The girl in pink shrank away.

I thought of my mother. Anger spurred me toward them before I could think better of it. I didn't have a plan, I didn't even have a weapon, but I'd figure that out on the way.

I was five steps behind them when two figures I recognized emerged from a doorway, making me stop short. Commander Naguib was wearing a golden Mirajin uniform with twice as many buttons as when I'd seen him in Dustwalk the first time. He looked like he was trying to stand straight enough to make it fit him right. The Gallan next to him, on the other hand, seemed like he was born in his uniform. He was old enough to have been Naguib's father, and a head taller. Red tassels hung off his uniform, but instead of making him look like a cushion, they reminded me of scars. The soldier dropped the crying girl's arm and snapped into a salute of his commanding officer. "General Dumas, sir."

So this was the Gallan general. The one whose name they spoke like it carried the weight of the law. Who'd moved half an army here to hunt the Rebel Prince. Who'd had a whole desert town razed as a testing site for a weapon to conquer the world.

I might be inconspicuous as a woman, but Naguib was bound to recognize me. I turned away quickly, eyes searching for an escape. There was a doorway to my right. Holy words were etched into the wood in a deep scrawl. That could only mean one thing: a prayer house. The Gallan did not worship the same god, Jin had told me that. The door came open under my hand and I plunged through blindly, slamming the door behind me.

The sound of praying greeted me, mingled with sobbing.

The last of the day's light was trickling in between the lattice of the windows. It was uneven where the wood had rotted away. Where the light hit the floor I could see that the tiles had been smashed to dust. As my eyes adjusted to the dark I realized the praying was coming from a girl, sprawled on her knees, her hands shackled to the wall. Her face was pressed to the ground, hidden behind matted hair that looked almost red-tinted in the dying sunlight. Like dye. Or blood.

Something else shifted in the gloom. And then a golden army uniform stepped into the light. I pulled back, toward the door, but it was too late. He'd seen me.

"Here to pray?" the soldier asked, a tinge of sarcasm in his voice. Something rattled on his wrists. More chains. This wasn't a prayer house after all, not anymore at least. It was part of the prison. "We don't have a Holy Father, but you're welcome to join us all the same."

For one stupid moment I could've sworn the words came from Tamid. I stumbled back to a hundred dusty days kneeling side by side with Tamid, saying holy words. Then I found my footing in the present, where Tamid was dead. It was just the accent, I realized. It was tainted with something that sounded like the Last County. But there was something else familiar about it, something that wasn't quite Dustwalk but that I knew all the same. Finally his face caught the light, with its unnaturally pale eyes, and the memory came fully formed.

"I know you," I said. From the other side of the desert, in my uncle's shop, when Jin hid below the counter and Commander Naguib stepped inside. *This desert is full of sin.* The smart-talking scrawny kid with eyes like mine who'd flanked his commander.

"And I know you." He frowned as he dropped his hands, the manacles rattling over the sound of the girl's praying. His sallow face twisted in thought before he hit on it. "You're the girl from the shop."

"So is this where smart-talking your commander lands you?" I asked. I couldn't help myself.

"No." His accent seemed to get thicker from talking to me, and I heard my own dropping back into the Last County lilt. "I'm just special."

"You've got a mighty fine opinion of yourself." The girl's praying got louder. "And what about her?"

"She's special, too," the soldier said.

I supposed they must've made Commander Naguib angier than most to warrant being locked away here instead of with the rest of the criminals. "And where would you two be if you weren't special?" I asked.

The young soldier looked straight through me. "You wouldn't be trying to find the prison, now would you?"

I ran my tongue over my dry lips nervously. I shouldn't trust him. He was a soldier. But he was a prisoner, too. And that ought to mean we were on the same side. Or at least that we had the same enemy.

"If I helped you get out of here, would you tell me where it is?" I touched the manacles on his hands. His wrists felt feverish. I'd promised Jin I wouldn't do anything stupid. But if we were getting the caravan out, we might as well get everyone else out, too. Jin could pick a lock. He'd told me that in the desert. One of those times he'd started to talk about something he'd learned along with his brother before cutting himself off.

"And where would I go?" he asked.

"I don't know," I admitted. We were both an awfully long way from home. "Wherever you wanted."

A gunshot from outside made me jump. Then everything went quiet again. Everything but the girl's praying.

"Amani." My name in the young soldier's mouth caught me off guard. "That's you, isn't it?"

"How do you know that?"

"Your cousin talked about you a whole lot. The pretty one with the dark hair." Shira, selling me out on the train. Who they must've brought along to find me and, through me, Jin.

"What happened to her?" I asked. She'd tried to get me killed. I shouldn't care. "Is she alive?"

"She wasn't as useful as she made herself out to be to the commander. Though maybe it was more that you weren't where you ought to be. She got left with the Sultan in Izman." The Sultan had once beaten a woman he'd loved to death. What'd happen to a girl who meant nothing to anyone in Izman?

"I'm Noorsham," he said. "Since you didn't ask and all." And what would happen to this poor scrawny kid from the end of the desert with too smart a mouth to be a soldier?

Voices came from the other side of the door. The girl's praying doubled. I stood up sharply.

"You ought to hide," Noorsham said, his blue eyes locked on mine seriously.

Heart pounding, I rushed away from the lamplight. There was no light at the back of the huge prayer-house-turned-prison. I pressed myself into the shadows just as the door opened. Naguib and General Dumas entered. Jin had said he didn't believe in fate until he met me, and I was starting to think he was right. The only thing between me and getting caught was a thin veil of darkness and Noorsham not selling me out.

But Naguib and General Dumas paid no mind to Noorsham. They stopped in front of the praying girl instead.

"This is her?" General Dumas's Mirajin was cleaner than the soldier's who'd arrested the Camel's Knees, like it'd been worn smooth by years of practice. His eyes flicked to Noorsham, "And this one?"

"Just a soldier who cannot obey a simple order," Naguib said. Even I knew disobeying a direct order meant execution in the army. If I didn't get Noorsham out, he'd be dead at dawn.

"Disobedient soldiers are a failing of their commander," General Dumas said. Naguib's jaw twitched. "It means they do not respect you." The general drew his gun. The girl's head was still pressed to the ground. General Dumas grabbed her hair, yanking her up. Her prayer turned to a scream of pain.

"Please," she begged. "I didn't mean to do it."

"Unlock her fetters," the Gallan general ordered. Naguib bristled at the command, but the general either didn't notice or didn't care. Naguib did as he'd been told, turning the lock on the girl's manacles.

The moment the manacles dropped away something happened to the girl. The features in her face started shifting. Her chin changed to a longer point, her nose flattened itself, her eyes pushed further back into her head before dropping again. She was frantically going from one face to another, like she was shuffling through a deck, trying to find the right card to play to save herself. Was she a Skinwalker? She sure as hell wasn't human.

The general watched with disinterest before he finally pressed the gun to her forehead. Her shape-changing stopped instantly, and she was frozen as a girl with round cheeks and a high brow, her hair still wrapped painfully around the Gallan general's fist.

I felt helpless. Standing in the dark, invisible, as someone else was about to die in front of me. The same way I had when Tamid was held across from me, a gun to his leg.

The prayer for the dead echoed loudly off the walls. It reached its crescendo as she called out for forgiveness of her sins. I squeezed my eyes shut.

Then a gunshot. I felt it down to my gut.

The praying stopped abruptly. I bit down on my thumb, trying not to scream.

"You will have her body burned." The general's voice swirled out of the dark. "And tell any who asks we have taken her prisoner."

When I opened my eyes again she was slumped on the ground, motionless, blood pooling around her ruined forehead. Noorsham had drawn away against a wall, as far as his chains would go, and was staring at the body, too.

"Why?" Naguib said. His voice was flat for once—it had lost that clipped edge. "She's already dead. What's the point in pretending?"

"It is one of the games we play, young prince. Your father and I." The Gallan general holstered his pistol. "I was there, the night of the coup, you know. The night your father took the throne. I was only a young soldier then. But I stood behind my general as your father made an agreement with him, and I know what was said better than most. Even my king, perhaps. I know that in public, the Sultan agreed to our authority, but he did not agree for us to strip your country of its sinful demon worship you call religion. But I also know what went unspoken but understood."

Naguib took a breath like he was going to respond, but the general barreled on, seeming to gather momentum as he spoke.

"My mother, too, lay with a demon, much as your father's wife did—the mother of that rebel son he cannot seem to control. My mother gave birth to this squalling and green creature instead of a baby. My father did as he should do. He had my mother bound in iron and thrown into the sea to drown. The baby he gave to me to deal with. It looked like it came from the ground. So I returned it to the ground. It was still screaming when I shoveled dirt over it."

I saw Naguib's throat constrict, as if he were swallowing his reply.

"When that demon child was born in the Sultan's palace, I admired your father for taking it upon himself to kill his wife by his own hand, following Gallan law. I remember thinking we had made the right choice in this man who saw eye-to-eye with Gallan values, though not all of your country agreed. And so, to keep the peasants quiet, we pretend these children of demons will be tolerated, and quietly, they are handed over to us and forgotten about. But your city guard tried to hide this prisoner from us and deliver her to you instead."

"The city guard is unused to such a large Gallan presence here. They do not know your ways." Naguib sounded like a kid quibbling with a parent.

"This desert is wavering," the Gallan general ignored him. "Your rebel brother's foothold is getting stronger. And Dassama is a great loss to us."

"He's not my brother," Naguib spat. "My father has rejected him."

"You are a greater insult to him as a brother than he is to you," General Dumas snapped. "Rumor in Izman is that your father speaks often of how he wishes his faithful sons were as strong and clever as his dissident one. Do you think I do not know that you scorned him by coming here on your demon-breed sand horses?"

Sand horses. He meant Buraqi. My heart jumped.

One Buraqi was all it had taken to distract Dustwalk enough for Jin to slip out and blow up the factory. If there was more than one, that could be one hell of a distraction.

"There is no law—" Naguib began.

"No, just the games we play," General Dumas interrupted him. He took a step forward, and Naguib faltered back. "I earned my first rank because I killed three of your uncles the night of your father's coup—men who had supported the sinful ways of magic and demons like your grandfather. I am very good at disposing of princes. I am here to find and kill your brother, but I decide who my enemies are, young prince."

"My father—"

"Your father has more sons than there are hours in the day. I wonder whether he would even notice you were gone?"

General Dumas turned on his heel and walked away. Naguib lingered, and he and Noorsham both watched the general go. When his steps had faded. Naguib spoke again, to Noorsham, too low for me to hear. And then Naguib was gone, too.

I leaned against the wall for a long time, shaking, the last of the light fading around us.

"Amani?" Noorsham called into the dark. I didn't have much time. Jin would try to come after me soon.

"Noorsham." I stepped out from the shadows. I could just make him out in the lamplight leaking through the cracks of the door from the yard outside. He looked scared. "Tell me where the prison and the stables are, and I'll get you out of this."

• ● •

I WONDERED IF Jin could see me on my rooftop perch from his. It was dark now, and even the light of a full moon wasn't enough to make out a single form plastered on a roof above the barracks with a gun. He'd told me not to do anything stupid. But it was damned stupid of them to leave a window open in the stables. And I'd be damned stupid if I didn't take advantage of it.

I gripped the edge of the roof and eased myself off slowly, my foot looking for purchase on the windowsill. More than once, I'd climbed in and out of Tamid's window with a bruised-up back to trade him one of my hoarded books for some of his pain pills. I could hang on to the edge of the roof the same way I used to hang off Tamid's window ledge and do just fine. Or at least have about the same chance of cracking my skull open as I did then.

The window was barely wide enough for a body. I had to slide through it like I was trying to thread a needle with a piece of wool. Stone scraped across my hips.

I took a breath and let go.

For one wild second all I could see was the stars and all I could think of was the foolishness of immortal things who'd never seen death and so didn't know to fear it.

The windowsill scraped across my back, taking skin with it. My elbow cracked against stone a second before my feet hit the ground hard enough to buckle every joint I had.

I let out a string of profanities in Mirajin and every language Jin had taught me to curse in as I dragged myself to my feet. There were a dozen stalls facing each other on either side of me, wooden doors with iron bolts.

The air in the stables felt like the desert sky before a sandstorm. I could feel it down to my bones. Dozens of bodies shifted audibly, penned into their stalls, magic chafing against iron. As I stood to my full height, I could see them now, heads peering out over the doors of the stalls curiously.

Buraqi.

I'd never seen this many immortal creatures in my whole life, let alone in one place; all but a handful of the two dozen stalls were full. But I supposed since they lived forever, the Sultans of Miraji had had plenty of time to stock the palace stables over the years. I wondered if any of them were the Buraqi from legends. The ones ridden by hero princes into battle or across the desert to save a beloved before night fell.

The iron bolt on the first stall door slid back with the sort of clang that ought to have woken the dead. Instead it seemed like everything stilled all around me. I took a deep breath, my fingers pressing against the cold iron. I pushed the door open before I could lose my nerve.

The head that rose to look at me was the color of sun at high noon over a sand dune. I stepped forward carefully. I was raised a horse trader's niece; I'd learned to take a shoe off a horse almost as young as I learned to shoot a gun. Even in the dark, the familiar work came to my hand easily. The Buraqi shook its head restlessly as the fourth shoe dropped to the ground. Might take a while to peel the taste of iron from its skin and shake off its mortal shape, but I didn't have time to wait. I was on to the next stall already, to a Buraqi the color of cool dawn light over dusty mountains. The next one was the endless dark of the desert at night.

All the Buraqi were moving now. Starting to raise their heads beyond the iron doors of their stalls. Starting to shift from flesh to sand and back again, like they were gathering themselves up into a hurricane while I crawled like the heat on a windless day until they were all freed.

Buraqi might be immortal creatures, but that didn't mean they liked gunshots any more than a regular horse. I pressed myself against the wall as I raised the barrel of my gun skyward and fired.

The Buraqi exploded from their stalls, shattering them in their wake. I flinched, squeezing my eyes shut as flesh, sand, and wind churned around me. They were so far from mortal now, more like desert storms in the shape of horses, and nature had torn down more walls than men's hands ever would. Hoofbeats rang around the stables, making my teeth clatter. And then a noise like an explosion. When I opened my eyes the wall into the barracks had collapsed.

I raced through debris into the chaos I had created. The Buraqi had torn into the training ground, taking half of it with them—most of one wall had already caved in and what was left looked like it had a mind to follow. Soldiers in every color of uniform, and some out of uniform, were pouring out. The Gallan were drawing guns, but the Mirajin knew better. There was no fighting a sandstorm with pistols. A man with a blue shirt half buttoned raised a pistol, taking aim, only to disappear below the hooves of one of the Buraqi. Soon, human screams joined the Buraqi's.

The Buraqi were beasts of the desert, and they'd make their way back into the sand. Sure enough, even as I watched, two of them ripped through another wall, bursting free into the streets. In the chaos I noticed more people pouring into the yard now. Women and children, folks in desert clothes. I recognized Yasmin first; she was frantically pumping water into a huge leather skin hanging from the camel, trying to resupply before the desert.

Noorsham. I'd near forgotten him in the chaos. I turned

toward the prayer house and slammed straight into Jin.

"What did I say about not causing any trouble?" There was a laughing glint in Jin's eyes and he was holding me off balance, close enough that he could tug and I'd fall straight into him.

"It worked, didn't it?" I fired back.

"No arguing with that." He let go of one of my arms. "And now we've got to run while we've still got a distraction." He eyed the path of destruction created by the Buraqi. "I'd say now's the time."

"No." I went to tug him the other way. "There was a soldier. I promised I'd help him."

Even as I pulled toward the prayer house, a Buraqi tore across my path, narrowly missing trampling me. Jin yanked me back. "Amani, we don't have time. We need to go now while we've got a shot or we might not get out at all."

I hesitated. I couldn't leave behind another stupid desert kid too weak to survive the desert. Not when I could save this one.

"Amani," Jin said again. "You're damn good at keeping yourself alive. Don't lose that now." He was right. Noorsham wasn't Tamid. I was too late.

I ran.

The streets were fast flooding with men and women from the caravan crowding each other for space, camels groaning, folks from Fahali shouting as they ran for safety.

We plunged in with the rest. One second I was staring into a terrified face, the next I was shoved against a wall. One second Jin was there, then his hand was torn from mine. And then I was alone, running in a crush of strangers. I stripped off my khalat as I went, turning myself back into a boy.

Gunshots sounded far behind us. I took a corner hard, my hands busy with tying my sheema, and I stumbled and went down. Hands were there, on my shoulders, pulling me to my feet. I looked back to see a man I didn't know, keeping me from getting trampled.

I didn't even have time to thank him before the crowd swallowed him and forced me on down the streets.

Open gates. The sight made my heart take off faster than the Buraqi had. My legs picked up speed, pumping twice as fast, carrying me forward like I was running on the winds and the sand, too. Forward. Forward. Out of the walls. Out of the trap. A shout of pure relief and joy and life on my lips.

And then all I could see was the sand and I forgot about everything. About fear. About bombs. About Jin. The desert reached out for us all with huge open arms. The churning mass that was chaos in the streets became order in the sand, welcoming us home.

fifteen

We had no choice except to walk through the dark. There were dangers in the desert night, but there were threats behind us in Fahali, too. And we needed to be far away from them by the time dawn came. Not even Commander Naguib would be stupid enough to follow us through the desert in the dark.

Night in the desert was different when it wasn't on the edge of the campfire. When there was no laughter and music and storytelling from the caravan to eclipse the sounds that came from the dark. There were things that made noises underneath the sand in the desert night. Things that screamed from the mountains. Now we could hear them all.

The Camel's Knees huddled close together. The only

noise that came from them was the clink of the tack on the beasts and the sound of mumbled praying. Yasmin's face looked pale in the light of the lamp swinging from the back of the nearest camel. One of her little cousins had fallen asleep with his head on her shoulder.

"Three hours until dawn," Jin said, checking the sky.

I nodded as he dropped back to hold up the rear of the caravan while I stayed in front. I knew we'd been walking for a long time. Distance had swallowed Fahali behind us. The night seemed much bigger than it ever had. And I felt a lot smaller than I ever had.

I heard a sound then and stopped walking. There was something out there. I turned slowly, peering into the dim glow offered by the moon and the handful of oil lamps that hung from the camels we'd been able to take with us, casting them in small pools of light.

I saw it a second before it sprang. The ghoul unfurled from a viscous leathery ball into spindly limbs and filmy black wings, its huge gaping mouth opened in a screech as it leapt.

I fired. A few of the caravan folks cried out and ducked instinctively at the noise.

My bullet caught it square in the chest. Black guts scattered across the sand. The thing screeched again. And this time, from the deep of the night, a hundred identical voices screeched back.

Yasmin turned the body over with her toe as the caravan silently stared. Frozen in shock.

"A Nightmare," Yasmin confirmed.

I hadn't seen a Nightmare since I was a kid. One had crawled into the house I grew up in while we slept. My mother had put a kitchen knife through it before it got to anyone. It'd barely put up a fight. But that one was alone and injured and desperate. This one was in its own territory, where they traveled in packs.

I could see them now as my eyes adjusted to the dark. Scuttling through the sand, their sinewy wings rippling through the blackness. They fed on fear instead of flesh and blood. One venomous bite sent victims into an uneasy sleep, and a second drew out the fear that bled from the first bite. Some said they drained the soul itself. Most folks didn't wake up from a Nightmare bite.

I checked the handful of bullets in my pocket.

"Everybody stay close to the light," I called down the caravan. Ghouls couldn't hunt in the day. Firelight wasn't exactly the same, but it was the closest we had. "This doesn't change anything. We keep walking, and—"

"Skinwalker!" The voice belonged to Tall Oman. My gun swung up, ready to face the new monster, tracking Tall Oman's pointed finger.

Only it was me he was pointing at.

My sheema, badly tied after the escape from Fahali, had fallen away when I shot, and now my hair was tumbling down to my shoulders, my face on show.

Tall Oman came at me in long, angry strides. Jin was in front of me in a blink. His hand caught Tall Oman in the chest three steps before he reached me, a warning gesture that he could easily turn more painful if he wanted. "Rethink your next move, my friend."

"He's a Skinwalker," Tall Oman spat, though he had the sense not to strain any farther against Jin's grip. "He changed his shape."

"No." Parviz held up a lamp so he could see me clearer. "She's a liar."

"Well, I didn't so much lie as trick you." It was a relief to speak in my own voice, even if it was strained by false lightness. "The difference being you can blame yourselves as well as me." I wasn't shaking anymore. I refused to shake, no matter that the whole caravan was looking at me like I was some abomination.

It was Isra who whispered too loudly to Jin, "So I guess she's not your brother, then?" She treated me to a once-over. "And here I was thinking you might be worth marrying to young Yasmin. Should've been suspicious when you listened to her so close. No man does that."

Parviz sized me up the same way he had back in Massil. I didn't know what he saw. The same kid with the gun, maybe, except with a chest and some hips, and not so much a kid. "And I'm supposed to trust a girl to keep us alive?"

"Father, she saved us from the gallows in Fahali," Yasmin snorted, but she was silenced with one raised hand.

"Saved us to drag us out into the desert at night." Parviz waved at the Nightmares stalking us in the dark. "And look where we are now. We would be safe in the daylight if it weren't for you." That one stung. After almost two months of being trusted, this was all it took.

"No, you're here because you decided you valued money over your own lives," Jin interrupted. "And now Amani is your best chance at staying alive. So I'd listen to the girl with the gun if I were you."

"I'm planning on surviving the night." I slammed the chamber of the gun shut. In this desert I could never seem to escape being seen as powerless, so long as I wasn't a man. "Everybody stay in the light and grab hold of any iron you've got. If something moves, we'll shoot it." But I'd lost any authority with my gender.

The caravan looked to Parviz, whose eyes traveled between me and Jin. "Do as she says," he ordered finally, spurring the caravan into movement. And then, turning back to me, he added, "Get us to dawn alive and I won't cut your pay."

The Nightmares were wary but hungry. They kept out of the circle of the light, but every time they spotted a shadow they leapt into the air in a spread of wings that blotted out the stars. A gunshot would go off and they would fall thrashing into the sand.

I was mostly shooting blind. Nightmares were as black as the night around us. They looked like part of the sand until they launched themselves, the torchlight catching them a second before it was too late.

But I was never too late. And I didn't miss.

I fired one shot after another, falling into a hypnotic daze as my mind surrendered to my hands and the trigger. The night was screams, and the smell of gunpowder, and my gun snapping shut with a fresh round in the chamber.

I fired again, two shots in a row. A pair of Nightmares went down and my gun clicked empty. I was reaching for fresh bullets before the last one was done twitching. My fingers scraped over three bullets. Only three.

I came back to myself all at once.

My hands shook a little as I loaded them into the gun. The sky was the color of a healing wound. Somewhere across the horizon, the sun was taking its sweet time. I didn't know if I could make three bullets last.

A Nightmare unstitched itself from the shadows two feet away, and I fired before my eyes could focus.

Two bullets now. One more dead Nightmare. Dozens more crawling in the sand. I knuckled my eyes tiredly.

"You all right?" Jin's hand was on my shoulder, but his eyes were still on the desert. The faint glow on the horizon sent light and shadow playing across his jaw.

"I'm alive," I said. "You seem to be, too."

"You know, there's a saying at sea: Red sky in the morning, sailors take warning."

I glanced at the horizon. "Yeah, well, it's a little late for a warning. We could've used that yesterday." I cracked my fingers; my hands were sore from clenching the gun so tight. "How many bullets do you have left?"

Jin just shook his head, spreading empty hands wide. I opened the chamber of my gun. My tired fingers fumbled for the bullet.

"No." Jin shook his head. "You're the better shot."

"One bullet each. It's only fair. You cover the back, I'll take the front." Jin hesitated only a second. Then he took it and flicked open the chamber of his gun as I trained my own pistol on the desert, covering long enough for him to reload and drop back. The sun was almost up now.

Two of them leapt at once. I aimed for the second. And hesitated. The first was racing across the sand, straight for Yasmin. She yelped. Jin shoved her out of the way, firing before I could take aim. And he missed.

The Nightmare latched onto Jin's chest. Its teeth sank straight into his heart.

I fired without thinking what would happen if I missed the beast and hit the boy, or about how it was too late to save him anyway. My last bullet caught the Nightmare in the head and the beast tumbled off Jin in a roll of thrashing wings, dying in the sand as the sun broke the horizon.

The desert came alive with the noise of screaming and scurrying as the Nightmares burrowed back into the earth.

I rushed to Jin, my useless gun by my side.

"Hey, hey." I tapped his face so that I didn't have to look at the huge black puncture wound in his chest and the blood and venom mixing just below his tattoo. He must have had a shot of venom straight to his heart. I was sure mine was pumping fast enough for the both of us.

My hands were shaking so hard, I couldn't find a pulse. His eyes were closed, his body sprawled, gun still in his hand like he was a fallen soldier. Finally I saw his chest rise and fall ever so slightly, his breathing shallow.

A shadow made long by the early morning light fell over us. I squinted up at Parviz.

"Help me." I wasn't much for begging, but I might as well so long as I was already on my knees. I didn't have any lower to go.

"He's as good as dead unless he gets treated properly," Parviz said, taking in Jin's worth now that he was injured. His pulse was beating too slowly against my knuckles. "We're days from civilization."

I tried to remember how long it took for Nightmare venom to get through the whole body. A night? A day? Less?

Parviz scraped his knuckles across his beard. "We're wasting sunlight."

He was right. I moved to put my weight below Jin's shoulder, to lug him to his feet. "Help me get him to a camel."

Parviz frowned, like I might be simple. I supposed he thought I was, since I wasn't a man any longer. "He's as good as dead. The dead are just more weight."

"Jin's not dead yet." I couldn't help but feel they'd help me if they still thought I was a boy. "And everyone here would be if it weren't for him."

"And we'll all drink to him in gratitude when we get to safety." Parviz didn't waver. "But until then we are mighty low on water, and it's a waste of it to try to help a boy who isn't going to live to see another dawn. You can stay with him and die, too, or you can come with us. You'd best decide quick, though."

He was right. Jin was as good as dead anyway. And I'd sworn I wasn't going to die in this desert, not on anyone's account. I'd told Jin once that he wasn't worth dying for. Not when I was so close to Izman.

It would be so easy.

No. It was Jin. It would be impossible. I'd been dreading Dassama because I didn't want to take a separate path. I wanted to stay with Jin more than I wanted Izman. I liked what life felt like with him in the desert. Like we were equals. Like we fit together. Too tangled to pull apart so easily.

I thought of the ruins of Dassama. If Jin died there'd be no one to take news of what the Gallan were doing to his people. The desert didn't give mercy and it didn't deserve any. It left the weak for dead if it didn't outright kill them.

But not Jin, who belonged to some other country. Who didn't belong to this desert at all—at least not enough to die with it. Or whatever stupid thing he was trying to do. Who didn't deserve to get left behind by a desert girl for her own life.

Like Tamid had. Like Noorsham.

"You can go to civilization or go to hell, for all I care." And it felt like the sand was stretching around my feet until that was all there was in the world, until Izman crept farther and farther away. "I'm not leaving him for dead."

sixteen

I pulled the knife out of Jin's belt. There was mercy and then there was a coward's escape, and the cowards had walked on. I pressed the knife against the wound and black venom oozed out across the blade. I wiped it on my shirt before laying it back against his skin. I did it again and again until my neck burned from the sun and more blood oozed out than black.

"Jin!" I slapped him hard across the face. His eyes squeezed shut tighter, so I hit him again. This time his eyes opened. "Jin!" I grabbed both his shoulders. "Don't you dare fall back asleep."

His eyes cracked open just far enough to see me. "Where . . ." he started weakly.

"They walked on." I sat back. We needed to follow the

Camel's Knees' tracks to civilization. Find help. Some medicine.

"And you're still here?" Jin squinted at me, then started to laugh halfheartedly. "Either I'm dreaming or I'm dead."

I had to keep him talking. "Dream about me often?"

"Dreams. Nightmares. Not sure." Jin's hand reached up like he wanted to check if I really was an illusion. I grabbed it as it grazed my jaw and swung it round my shoulder.

"Come on, dream yourself to your feet." I braced my shoulder under his arm and heaved him up.

Jin said something to me in Xichian and then laughed like it was the funniest thing he'd ever heard. Oh, well—he might not be lucid, but he was upright. And when I put one foot in front of the other, he followed.

We'd been walking for a little while when the babbling started. Words in other languages. Names I didn't know. One I did. *Sakhr.* Our old joke churned out by his mind made sick with the venom. I tried to convince him not to talk, but he was too far gone in some delusion. And so long as I kept him walking, I didn't have it in me to worry about anything else.

The sun was straight above us when I realized we weren't following the caravan's tracks in the sand anymore. I spun around, confused. Had we gotten off course? Had they blown away already? The sun had risen to our right this morning. I wasn't sure if we were still headed north—or anywhere at all.

"We're lost."

Jin was sitting with his head between his knees. He struggled to pull something that glinted in the sun from his pocket. The broken compass.

"Here." He pressed the compass into my hand. "We're not lost."

He was delirious if he thought a faulty compass would do us any good. Something inside me was cracking. At this rate, we were both going to die. In the desert, lost meant dead. If the things in the dark didn't get you, the sun did.

"Jin." I dropped down next to him, trying to keep him awake. "Jin, this compass doesn't point north. If we follow it, where is it going to take us?"

I could tell Jin was struggling to stay lucid, his body fighting against the Nightmare venom. "To help. We're not far."

"Not far from what?" I pushed. But Jin's only answer was something in Xichian I didn't understand. He was done making sense. I sagged onto the sand, holding the compass. The arrow pointed straight west now. Into the Dev's Valley. In the haze of the desert heat I could see the place the sand ended: a sheer drop down a cliff face. What the hell; it didn't matter what direction we died in.

It was a hell of a lot harder than it looked getting down into the canyon than it had looked from the top. And it'd looked impossible from there. Jin could still walk, but he leaned more heavily on me with every step.

I had a mean slice on my arm from skidding on some loose rocks near the top of the valley. One cracked rib from where I'd slammed into a rock nearer the bottom.

There were a few others in between that I hadn't had time to worry about yet. The rest of my body was just a dull ache under Jin's weight.

At least there was water at the bottom.

The Dev's Valley ran like a wound deep into the skin of the desert, a shallow river like an exposed vein at the bottom. I sat Jin down as I plunged my hands into the water and scrubbed blood before sticking my face in, too, and gulping as fast as I could.

I gathered a handful of water. "Jin." His head was tipped back, eyes squeezed shut against something he didn't want to see, except it was inside his head. "Jin." I pressed the water to his mouth and forced him to drink.

I sat back with my legs in the water and pulled out the compass. I'd managed not to smash it, at least. It pointed straight into the dusty canyon maze, but it didn't say how far I had to go, and Jin wasn't in any kind of state to tell me. Only one way to find out.

I was just lugging Jin back to his feet when I heard it, echoing through the canyon walls: the sound of hoofbeats on stone. Someone was coming out of the canyon. I hesitated for only a second before heading for cover. We moved painfully slowly, Jin's weight pressing down on my spine. I half led, half dragged him into the dusty maze. I could hear the hoofbeats getting louder with every step. We were going too slowly. We needed to get to cover before whoever it was spotted us. We reached the mouth of one of the paths into the canyon just as a soldier in Gallan blue emerged from another.

My whole body rebelled against the sight of him as I remembered the Gallan in Fahali. The general with his gun to the girl's head. But there was nothing I could do now except watch with bated breath from our place hidden in the shadows of the canyon, while the soldier dismounted, dropping to his knees to drink.

"Amani—" Jin had finally opened his eyes. They were clear for a moment. "He can't find us, if they do—"

I clapped my hand over his mouth as the soldier raised his head, looking in our direction. "He won't find us," I promised, quietly as I could.

We waited in silence while the soldier finished at the river before he mounted again. From the top of his horse, he pulled out something hanging around his neck that shined silver and pressed one end of it to his mouth. A sharp whistle blast echoed off the canyon walls. He waited while it went silent. And then another one answered. When that went silent, a third answered.

A search party. For us, or for something else. "They're not going to find us," I repeated, so quiet I wasn't sure if it was for Jin or if it was a prayer. "They won't find us."

• • •

WE'D BEEN WALKING a few hours when I needed to rest. I leaned against the rock face, letting Jin slide to the ground, trying to catch my breath. We'd had to double back twice already when the path dead ended. I clutched the compass to my chest. I was still following the needle, but I had to get my head to stop spinning. And every step brought more chance the next one would lead me to the Gallan soldiers.

The sun was getting low when I ran into another dead end. Except none of the other dead ends had looked like this.

The wall of the canyon was painted bright—almost violent—colors, climbing one on top of another, from the dusty ground all the way up to where I couldn't see anymore: A girl with yellow hair turning into an animal. An immense red Djinni raging against roiling water. A blue-skinned man surrounded by demons. A battle that might be able to split the earth open right where we stood and leave a mark the size of this valley. And wedged between a dancing girl with snakes for hair and a demon brandishing a severed head was a painted door. I checked the compass; sure enough, it pointed stright ahead.

I was raised on stories of Djinn and their world, of secret palaces in the clouds, homes that could be summoned from the sand. Doors to their kingdoms that could only be opened by whispering a secret word into the lock.

I traced the line of the door with my finger. Solid stone by the looks of it. Solid stone until the right password was whispered to it. Like in the stories.

Or else I was a deluded girl with a bad habit of putting too much stock in the stories my mother told me.

"Jin." I shook his shoulders. My voice was scratchy with thirst. "Jin, wake up. I need you to wake up. I need the password."

"Lost?" I jumped at the voice. The Gallan soldier, the one we'd seen, was standing a few feet away, leaning on the other side of the valley in the shade, looking smug.

I might've been afraid if I wasn't already so desperate. "How did you find us?" My voice sounded scratchy.

"On your feet, before I have to shoot you," he commanded, but I didn't see a gun. And he was speaking perfect Mirajin.

Something was wrong here.

"Why don't you come make me?" He was hovering in the shadows. Then I noticed the fresh blood smeared along his jawline. "Or are you afraid of daylight, Skinwalker?"

The change on his face was instantaneous. It became a person's face without any humanity in it. The Skinwalker bared its sharp teeth in the soldier's face—the face belonging to its last kill, I realized. I watched in horror as it sauntered over until it was at the very edge of the shadows cast by the canyon walls. "Well, it would have been nice to feed on you now." Its tongue flicked out, long and black between sharp teeth. "I am *starving*. Even after eating that foreigner's flesh. And you look so tasty. But I suppose I can wait a few hours."

"You can wait until you're dead. I'll be gone by night." I slung Jin's arm back over my aching shoulder. If there was one thing that could keep me going, it was a Skinwalker.

"And where will you go, blue-eyed girl?" The Skinwalker had a hungry smile. "You're trapped." My eyes flicked back the way I'd come. In the time I'd been sitting, the sun had crept along the side just enough to cast the opening of the valley into shadow.

Jin and I were standing in the last patch of safe sunlight.

• • •

"OPEN." I BANGED my hand against the door. "Unlock. Let me in." The rock surface of the painted door wouldn't budge. I didn't figure the password would be obvious, but I wasn't going to die for not trying.

"I think I'll keep you alive for a while." The Skinwalker was pacing back and forth along the shadow border. "That way, you can watch me eat your flesh with those pretty eyes and I'll listen to you scream." The Skinwalker grinned with the dead Gallan soldier's mouth, only it was full of fangs. It wanted my attention. It was practically on top of me now, the shadows so close I had to pull my elbow against my stomach. The light would burn it. But it could be patient with the light shrinking every second.

I was running out of time.

I sagged against the stone. We were going to die here. We'd escaped Dustwalk, jumped off a train, crossed a desert, and survived Fahali and the Nightmares, and now this was where my story came to an end. In a dusty canyon at the hands of a hungry ghoul.

Stories. The memory flickered tiredly in my mind.

Sakhr.

Jin had gotten the name wrong. The name of the Djinni used to summon help, to open doors into his kingdom.

And then he'd gotten it wrong again. He'd said it as he rambled incoherently from the Nightmare venom in the desert.

I leaned in close to the door. I felt stupid, but there was no one to see me except a Skinwalker who wanted to eat me whole, and I didn't care much what it thought. I pressed my mouth to the painted keyhole and whispered the name. "Sakhr." And I held my breath.

Nothing happened. The last of my hope fled as I sagged back against the door.

The sun betrayed me in a flash. One second we were in the last of the light, the next the shade touched me. The Skinwalker's hand came with it. Long talons scraped across my arm, blood blossoming in five long trails across my skin.

Its teeth went for my neck. I remembered what Jin had taught me: I didn't try to break free. I bore my weight into the monster. Its teeth scraped through flesh and blood, tearing my shoulder open. Agony tore through my whole body as we toppled to the ground together.

I shoved it off me and stumbled back into the painted wall. My blood smeared across the shape of a girl riding a leopard. Of all the unimportant things to notice before dying.

The rattling shriek of stone grating against stone filled my ears. In an open stone archway where the painted door had been stood the most polished-looking girl I'd ever seen. Like she was born pretty, but she'd been scrubbed and groomed until she was as close to perfect as any living thing could get. Her face was all desert planes and dunes, but her dark eyes weren't soft. Strands of black hair caught in her eyelashes as she stared the scene down. Her eyebrows raised as she saw Jin, unconscious in the sand next to me. Her eyes went to the Skinwalker next. She reached behind her and a pair of scimitars hissed as she drew them across her body. "You have blood on your claws." The Skinwalker sprang for her.

She didn't move like Jin, or like any of the soldiers I'd ever seen. She moved like a storm someone had given steel to. She sidestepped the ghoul like it was nothing, her right sword slicing across its arm. The monster snarled and rounded on her just in time to get her left sword straight through its stomach and her right sword through the neck. The eyes in the stolen face went wide. For a second my heart swelled—it looked so human. Then its fanged mouth fell open.

She yanked the blades out, black with ghoul blood. The thing slumped to the ground, dead.

"You must be the one who said the password," she said.

I opened my mouth to answer.

I had a second to realize I'd lost a lot of blood before everything went dark.

seventeen

I came awake staring at stars.

I squeezed my eyes shut again and then reopened them. The stars were stitched into the tent above me, yellow cloth constellations in the lamplight. I moved to prop myself up and my arm rebelled in pain, making my head spin. I felt like death. Which was a privilege of being alive, at least.

It took a second for my head to steady. My arm was bandaged from wrist to shoulder. The bandages smelled of honey and something I didn't recognize.

Next to me Jin was lying still under a heavy blanket pulled up to his elbows. His bare chest was slick with sweat. Fresh bandages were wrapped around him, so I couldn't see the wound anymore. But his chest was rising and falling with shallow breathing, and that was enough to make my own breathing ease. He was alive. We were both alive. The rush of relief that followed was enough to lift me onto my elbows to get a proper look around.

In the corner sat a stranger. A boy about Jin's age, with a round face, arms crossed over his chest, curly black hair falling into his eyes as his chin flopped forward in sleep.

I sat up slowly, careful not to wake him. The fact that I was bandaged and not bound and gagged seemed like a good sign. But just because they'd fixed me up didn't mean I ought to trust them—whoever they were.

My shirt had been replaced, but my sheema was still tied around my middle, and between it and my body was the compass. My heart raced in relief as I pulled it out.

My eyes dropped to a small pile of bottles and bandages in the corner, and among them, a knife that looked like it was for medicine. There was dried blood on it. I snatched it up. I needed to find out where I was. And I wasn't going unarmed.

The sleeping boy was an easy guard to slip. Sunlight hit my face violently through the tent flap, blinding me the second I pushed outside.

Somebody had painted the world while I slept.

I'd thought green was the color of dusty scrub that fought its way up between stones—not this color that boasted its existence, unafraid, to the desert. Behind me the huge dusty gold of the cliff face loomed over the camp, but the sand surrendered quickly enough as it crept away from the walls. We were overlooking an oasis, a burst of color and life, scattered with people. At a glance I guessed it was about the size of Dustwalk, a hundred or so souls. Only comparing this place to Dustwalk was like comparing a Buraqi to a donkey. And at the center of it all rose a gold-and-red tower that was high enough to scratch the blue off the sky.

My legs decided to walk instead of surrendering me to the ground at the last second. I held the compass close to my body with one hand; the other one clutched the knife. I didn't know how much use it'd be. I was light-headed, either from loss of blood or from the overwhelming strangeness of this place. My legs moved half on their own. In a few steps, the burning sand turned cool as I stepped into the shade of the oasis.

I passed below trees hanging heavy with oranges and pomegranates and some fruits I didn't even recognize. They sprang up everywhere, around pools so clear and deep, I felt if I got close enough I might see the beating heart of the earth in them.

The compass needle pointed straight through the oasis. Tents of every color were scattered among the trees, propped against trunks for support or hanging from tree branches.

And the people. Everybody I saw was dressed in colors that looked like they'd been born back when the world was new. A few folks were gathered around a pool, washing clothes and chattering; they didn't look up when I passed. The girl who had killed the Skinwalker was leading a half dozen men and women with wooden blades through what looked like army drills. I almost stepped on two boys, younger than me by the looks of it, who were tinkering with something that looked like a bomb. They both looked up at me.

"You're going to want to go the long way around," one of them said.

"We'd rather only blow our own hands off." As the other one spoke, I realized it wasn't a boy at all. She was a girl, hair cropped close to her skull, and so skinny she'd have to stand up twice to cast a shadow, but a girl all the same. Neither of them seemed to have even a bit of worry about me being a stranger. Maybe having a magic door just saved you a whole lot of suspicion. I took the long, long way around to be safe, even if I wasn't sure where I was headed.

I stepped out of the trees and into a large clearing of sand. Facing me was the biggest tent by far. It was twice the height of a man and it looked like it could hold half the camp—more like a pavilion than a place to sleep. The canvas was red, with a huge blue sun stitched into the canopy.

Identical to Jin's tattoo.

As I moved closer, I saw that a lone figure stood in the tent. He should've looked small under the high canopy, but somehow he seemed to fill the space as easily as the sunlight. He was bent over a table, so all I could see was the crown of his head. His hands were planted on either side of a huge map. Other papers were held down by stones and empty cups and weapons.

And one beat-up brass compass.

The sun caught the knife in my hand, sending a flash of light across the tent. The boy looked up, startled, his eyes going straight to me.

He didn't look at me like I really looked—a strange girl hovering in the opening of the pavilion, dusty, bruised, bloody, hair caked with sand. And a tongue suddenly unable to talk. He looked at me like I had every right and reason to be standing there.

"You're hurt." His brow furrowed with concern. For a second I didn't understand, and then I realized I was bleeding through the bandages.

Then his eyes swung to the knife in my other hand. I did the only thing I could think of. I held up the compass like a peace offering. "I've got this."

"Ah." Understanding dawned on his face. "You're the one Shazad brought in with my brother."

He said something else, but I only heard one thing.

Brother.

The word bounced around my head, looking for another meaning than the one I knew.

Then he said something else, but one word stuck itself in my head and didn't let anything else through.

Brother.

My head scrambled looking for another explanation, but there was only one person he could mean.

Jin was his brother.

"Who are you?" I asked, even though I already half guessed.

An uncertain smile flicked over his face, like he wasn't sure if I was joking. His smile looked nothing like Jin's. "I'm Ahmed."

He didn't say his full name. He didn't say he was Prince Ahmed Al-Oman Bin Izman. The Rebel Prince and rightful heir of Miraji. Prince. Stepped out of campfire stories. Who inspired cries to revolution across the desert.

I had no idea what I'd expected of the Rebel Prince, but it wasn't that he would look just like every other desert boy I'd ever known. He was young. Black hair, skin dark from the sun, a strong square jaw, clean-shaven. Standing in a pavilion crowned in the sun with the commanding air of a Sultan twice his age. His sun. Not the sun of some foreign country tattooed on Jin's heart. The sun of the rebellion. Of his brother's rebellion.

A new dawn. A new desert.

Which meant Jin was a prince, too.

He'd told me about breaking his nose and his brother setting it. About how he'd been born in Izman but was from Xicha.

He'd never told me he was a prince.

I'd kissed a prince.

I felt the barrel of a gun press into the side of my neck, interrupting the spiral of my thoughts. "Drop the knife," a girl's voice said. "You owe me that much for saving your life."

The instinct to fight reared its head, but my body was too tired to obey it. I uncurled my fingers so the knife planted straight at my feet. The gun moved away from my neck as the girl—the same one who'd killed the Skinwalker—walked around to face me, still aiming the gun at me. I remembered Ahmed had called her Shazad. She raised her voice. "Bahi, I found her."

"Oh, thank God and every First Being." A third figure dashed into the tent. It was the curly-haired boy who'd been dozing when I woke up. "I swear I only fell asleep for a second." He wagged a finger at me like a scolding mother. "It's not very polite to sneak away from someone after he's saved your life."

"Not the first time I've done that," I admitted. My mind was still racing, but having a gun pointed at you had a way of making a girl focus.

"Not the first time a girl has snuck out on you while you were sleeping, either," Shazad muttered at Bahi, low enough that I was the only one who heard. I hadn't noticed when she'd been slaying the Skinwalker, but her accent was as northern and sharp as Commander Naguib's, and it made me want to pick the knife back up.

"Are you going to shoot me or not?" My own accent scraped bumpily against hers as I stared down the barrel of the gun. "Seems like a waste of your saving my life."

Shazad raised an eyebrow at me appraisingly, then lowered the weapon.

"Wow," the curly-haired boy, Bahi, said to me. "I've never seen her give up so easily. She must like you."

Shazad ignored him, "She knew the password," she said simply. "Jin must trust her."

Sakhr, I remembered.

"The door didn't open, though," I argued.

"It only opens from the inside," Shazad said. "Any mortal who knows the true name of the Djinni who built this place can speak his name to request entry. It alerts us on the inside. We found the story of this place in an old book, along with the Djinni's true name. Lucky for us, it turned out to be true when we had to flee Izman."

True names had power. Shazad said, "So who let you lot in?"

"There are other ways in, if you're able to fly." Or willing to climb. I looked at the tops of the cliffs that surrounded us. If you knew the path, you could probably make your way in over the top of the canyon. How long until the Gallan from Fahali found their way in?

"Forgive us—" Ahmed paused expectantly.

"Amani," I supplied.

"Amani." He stepped around the table. "You're tired. Would you like to sit and eat something and—"

"Bahi!" A new voice made everyone's head turn. The girl who rushed in was younger than I was. Her hair was a dark purple, spreading in soft waves framing a round face earnest with panic. "Something's happening to my brother. Jin's babbling in his sleep."

There was that word again. *Brother.*

She looked even less like Jin than the Rebel Prince.

"That's normal," Bahi said. "The Nightmare venom'll be burning out of his system."

"You're sure?" The purple-haired girl's voice was thin with tears.

"Delila." The prince reached out for her comfortingly. For his sister, I realized.

"You're the Djinni's daughter," I blurted. My head was spinning, trying to remember what was real and what was only something I'd heard around campfires. "From the story."

Delila was momentarily distracted from her worry. She brushed her violent purple hair back behind her shoulders, like she could hide it.

"Expecting fangs and scales?" Prince Ahmed smiled like it was a joke, but there was a tinge of wariness there, too.

"Wings and horns, actually," I half joked. That was what they'd said the prince's monster sister looked like in Dustwalk. The younger girl's eyes dashed to the ground, embarrassed. The air shifted around her head, like heat in the desert. The tinges of purple disappeared and her hair was as pure black as her brother's. She fiddled with it self-consciously. I was suddenly sorry for having said anything at all.

"I'll go check on him anyway." Bahi scratched his neck, looking awkward in the tension. As he did, I saw blue ink etched into his palm in a perfect circle thick with lacing symbols.

My heart sank.

"You're a Holy Man." Back in Dustwalk, we stitched up our own gunshot wounds and missing fingers. You had to be missing a pair of limbs or a bucket of blood before it warranted the Holy Father's intervention. We only called him when everything but prayer was hopeless—to heal in part, but also to bargain at the doors of death. The presence of a Holy Man was never a good sign. It was a last resort.

The thought must've shown on my face. "Don't worry." Bahi held up his other hand. It was blank. The matching tattoo that ought to have been there was missing. "I'm not a very good one."

He put his marked hand on Delila's shoulder, leading her out as he leaned in conspiratorially, speaking in her ear. He said something that made her laugh through her worry. I wished I knew what. I could use some words that would unknot the worry in my gut. If I'd dragged Jin halfway across the desert to die, I was going to kill him.

"What happened to him?" Prince Ahmed's accent was neater than mine, but softer than Commander Naguib's. *Naguib.* He was the Sultan's son, too. He was Jin's brother just as much as Prince Ahmed was.

Jin had pointed his gun at Naguib's face and hadn't pulled the trigger. It was a sin to kill your own blood.

"Is there anyone else related to Jin I ought to know about before answering that?" If ever there was a time to watch my smart mouth. It wasn't even them I was angry at.

But Shazad snorted a laugh. An unpolished, undignified laugh that didn't match the rest of her, and that didn't seem to be *at* me either. "Not that we're aware of. But you can never be sure with the Sultan and his women."

But Ahmed caught the edge in my words. "You didn't know he was my brother." It wasn't a question.

"I didn't even know he was part of the rebellion." Humiliation burned inside me. Ahmed and Shazad were both looking at me, waiting for me to say something that might explain why anyone would drag someone she didn't even know through the desert. I wasn't sure how to explain how the two of us got so tangled up.

"Jin blew up a factory." That seemed like the right place to start, only it wasn't, really. "That was after we burned down a building," I added. "But that was sort of an accident." Shazad's face lit up with a smile. Like she'd just decided something about me and liked it. Then it all came tumbling out.

Shazad's smile faded as I got to Dassama, but she didn't interrupt as I rushed through the past few days. Fahali. Our escape. The Nightmares.

"We need to plan." By the time I finished, Shazad was tapping the map that was spread out in front of the prince, pinpointing Fahali. "The Gallan and the Sultan are getting closer. And now they're looking for us—with a weapon that can wipe out whole cities." She turned to me. "What kind of range do you think this thing has?"

"Not enough to blast the whole canyon." I looked at the jagged line of ink across the paper that showed the hugeness of the Dev's Valley. Shazad's finger rested on Fahali. There was a tiny x scratched at the other edge of her finger, marking the rebel camp. Less than a finger's width apart didn't seem far enough to be safe to me. "Enough that they don't need to be precise. Or get through your magic door." I hesitated. "And the thing is, there wasn't a single bit of shrapnel in Dassama."

"What does that mean?" Ahmed asked, looking down at the map. Surveying the country he'd already won once and was fighting for all over again.

"No shrapnel means it's not a single-use bomb," Shazad said, catching on quicker than the prince. "This is something new. Something they can use over and over again."

"Which means they don't have to know exactly where we are, because they don't need to get us on the first try." A look of perfect understanding passed between Ahmed and Shazad and right over me.

"We need Imin," Ahmed said.

The girl who followed Shazad back into the tent moments later seemed completely unremarkable. She looked so average that it was hard to pick out anything to notice about her at all. Except that she had yellow eyes.

"We need a spy," Ahmed said to the girl, Imin. "We need you to infiltrate the Gallan army in Fahali and send word if they get too close to us."

"Fine." The girl shrugged sullenly. Even as she did her face started shifting. Her lips narrowed, her skin paled, her shoulders widened, and her chest flatted. In a few blinks she was someone else entirely. A man with a whole new face. A Gallan face.

The only things that didn't change were her—his— pale yellow eyes and her clothes. I thought of the red haired girl in Fahali, right before she got shot.

"I don't like it." Shazad surveyed their spy. "Your eyes . . ." Imin rolled them expressively at Shazad. "We ought to send Delila."

"No." Ahmed shook his head. "An illusion is too risky. Sending a Demdji into a Gallan camp is like sending a lamb into the lion's den as it is. Illusions slip; shape-shifting doesn't."

"At least Delila can hide her mark," Shazad muttered.

"It has to be Imin." Ahmed's tone didn't leave room to argue.

Finally Shazad conceded with a nod. "There's a dead ghoul in the canyon in Gallan uniform. Help yourself. You're to report back by Shihabian." She turned to go, nodding at me to follow. "And try not to get killed."

eighteen

I followed Shazad out of the pavilion, blinded again by the golden light and bright colors. "How did she do that?" I asked as I caught up with her, glancing back at Imin. "Is she . . . That's not a Skinwalker, is it?"

"No, amazingly we don't all want to be murdered in our sleep. Imin is a Demdji, like Delila," Shazad said, as if that were an answer. She tossed open the flap to a tent that was smaller than the prince's but tall enough to stand in. It was organized with exacting precision: a neatly made bed, a stack of books, a trunk, and a line of weapons on the ground. Shazad flung open the trunk. "Here." She pulled out a plain white shirt and a brown shalvar. "These ought to fit you. You're covered in blood."

"What's a Demdji?" I asked, figuring a second too late I ought to have said thank you.

"You've never heard of Demdji?" She let the trunk fall shut.

"I was born a long way from you." Somewhere where princes and shape-shifting women lived only in stories told round campfires.

"Children born of Djinn and mortal women." Shazad sat herself on the trunk. "There are a dozen or so in camp. Ahmed practically collects them now."

"Can they all change their shape?" The wound in my arm twinged at the memory of the Skinwalker in the canyon. I pulled off my blood-soaked shirt.

"No, it depends," Shazad explained. "Djinn are things of the desert, naturals at illusion and manipulation. So that's what their children inherit: illusions, deceit, power from desert heat and winds. Delila can create images that look real but are empty to the touch, all air. Imin can change her—or his, depending on the day—shape to look like anyone. There's a pair of twins who change shape, too, only instead of changing into people, they become animals. Another one crawls inside your mind and twists until you see what she wants you to, like sun madness. In the holy texts they call it the Djinni's gift. Some say it's a protection to balance out the Djinni's mark."

"The mark?" I felt ignorant as she talked on about all these things like I should understand them.

"Imin's golden eyes, Delila's purple hair." Shazad scraped her own dark hair off her face. "Some of them can get away as human in the great wide world. When we were still in Izman, Delila used to hide her hair with dark henna, or she'd cast an illusion over it. But then there are the ones who can't hide." The ones who got bullets to the heads. "The Gallan will kill them because they think all First Beings are against their invented god."

I remembered the girl from the Gallan camp. I'd thought it was blood in her hair. It might've just been that it was red. The Djinni's mark.

"Half of Miraji would go after them to get something from them. Like a finger, for its supposed healing powers. Ask Bahi if you want theology. Most folks would call it—"

"Desert magic." So this really was where the stories came to life. Heroes and monsters come to fight and die for the Rebel Prince.

Jin and I had talked about those stories. About the Rebel Prince. And then Jin had lied to me until I was just some silly girl barging into something I couldn't begin to be prepared for.

• • •

SHAZAD WAS ABOUT my size. Except a lifetime of eating proper meals made her more filled out in all the areas that helped me look like a boy when I needed to. I tugged at the clothes she'd loaned me uncomfortably as I crossed the camp, trying to retrace my steps from that morning.

I met Bahi just outside the tent with the canopy of stars where I'd woken up. He was ducking out. He caught me tugging at the chest of the shirt, wet hair dripping down my back, making it stick to me. Shazad had showed me where I could wash, a small pool shielded from view of the camp, before leaving me to do . . . whatever it was she did here. I had nowhere else to go and nothing else I was meant to be doing.

"Why're you wearing Shazad's clothes?" Bahi asked, looking me over.

"Why do you know Shazad's clothes on sight?" I countered without thinking.

Bahi scratched the back of his neck, pulling a face. He looked like a kid caught doing something wrong. "She's sort of hard not to look at," he admitted. "Don't tell her I said that. I'm fairly sure she knows about five different ways to kill me without actually having to touch me. And if I'm dead there'll be no one to take care of your prince."

"He's not mine," I said defensively. And then, because I couldn't help it, "How is he?"

"You got him here in time." Bahi ran the hand with the tattoo on it through his hair. "Now we just have to wait."

"Can I see him?"

"I don't see why not." Bahi shrugged, gesturing behind himself.

The heat hit me like a wall as soon as I pulled back the tent flap. Jin was lying as I'd left him, still as the dead.

Only his brother sat next to him. Prince Ahmed's shirt was loose at the collar, and I could see the echo of Jin's sun tattooed on his own chest in the dim light from the lamp. He looked up at the sound of the tent flap falling shut behind me. "Your Majesty." The words tripped out, unnatural. "I'm sorry, I should—"

"No, please, stay." I stopped my retreat. I wasn't sure

how to refuse a prince. I sat down across from Ahmed on the other side.

I stilled. Ahmed brought the present rushing back in. Jin wasn't just some foreign boy with a traitor smile; he was the Sultan's son and I was far out of my place sitting with this pair of prodigal princes.

"Is Jin even his real name?" I asked when the silence had stretched too long.

"Yes," Ahmed said. "But it's not his full name. Our father named him Ajinahd Al-Oman Bin Izman. Lien, his mother, was the one who nicknamed him Jin."

Nearly two months and he hadn't even told me his real name.

Ahmed was watching me. "You think he doesn't trust you. But that's not true."

I scoffed.

"The compass." Out of the corner of my eye, I saw the battered brass thing in his hands. I thought of the tattoo on Jin's back. The compass. On the other side of the sun. Like his heart beat between the two. "It's of Gamanix make. While the Albish and the Gallan war over magic and mortality, the Gamanix balance the two. A little bit of science, a little bit of magic. Each compass is twinned with another. That compass is our lifeline. In the six years since we got them, I've never let mine out of my sight. I would have lost Jin a dozen times if not for this. My brother may have little regard for his own safety, but if he trusted you with his family, there's no way he could trust you more.

"It was Jin's mother who got us out of the palace alive, you know." I didn't know that. Just like I didn't really know anything real about Jin. But he didn't seem to need me to answer him. I wasn't even sure he was talking to me. "Lien and my mother were like sisters. They came into my father's harem near the same time, and Jin and I were born hours apart. I was early and Jin was late. I was fifth of my father's sons. He was sixth. We were born early enough in our father's reign that we were treated well, but not so early that he took more notice of us than our mothers liked. Lien called it fate. Jin doesn't believe in fate.

"I don't have a single memory of my mother's face. I was too young when she died." The Sultan's pretty young wife from the story. The one who was beaten to death for giving birth to Delila. She'd been a few words in the tale of the Rebel Prince to me. But she'd been flesh and blood to Ahmed. "All my memories of Miraji are of my brother. The night Delila was born, Jin was sick. Lien and my mother had been planning an escape ever since my mother learned she was carrying a Djinni's child. It wasn't safe to move Jin—he was running a fever—but it wasn't safe for Delila to stay. So Lien had to risk it. I remember little bits from that night. Clinging to Lien's skirts while she peeled off a sultan's ransom in gold bracelets to pay for a ship to Xicha.

"But those things belong to a dream. What I remember better than anything is sitting on a bunk with my hand on my brother's heartbeat as he burned up on an unsteady ship taking us away from home and Lien making me pray for Jin to make it through the night alive while she rocked my sister to try to stop her screaming." He swallowed, his throat bobbing. "I've lost count of how many prayers I've sent up for my brother to keep him alive since then. He has had more than his share of brushes with death for one life."

"Some folks are just better at putting themselves in the line of fire," I said. "Your Majesty."

"Please, call me Ahmed. All you need to do is look around to see that my majesty is very much in question." He looked nothing like his brother in that moment. Jin always smiled at me like we were both about to be in big trouble and he loved it. The prince smiled like he was forgiving you for it. "My brother may have little regard for his own safety, but most of the time, when he's stepped into the line of fire, it's been to put himself between death and Delila or me. I've never seen him flirt so carelessly with death for anyone other than us before. Until you."

I didn't know what to say to that. I focused on Jin instead of the Rebel Prince. His foreign features were the one familiar thing in this uncanny place full of purple-haired princesses and golden-eyed shape-shifters, even though he might as well have become a stranger all over again the moment Ahmed called him *brother*.

"Winning your throne, your kingdom . . ." I began. "Is it worth all these people dying?" *Is it worth his life?* "The Sultan killed *your* mother, the Sultim stole *your* throne—that's nothing to do with anyone else. You want to know who killed *my* mother? Your country." I didn't mean it to come out sounding like a taunt. But I wanted to hear him say it. That he really can save this desert.

"I'm not here for power." Prince Ahmed was calm, as if I hadn't just thrown his mother's murder in his face. Somehow it didn't come out cocky. "I've seen the way my father rules like a man afraid to lose even a scrap of his power to another. He thinks that's the only way, and that's why we are poor and occupied and weak. I never planned to come back to Miraji to take my father's seat.

"We went everywhere before coming here. We saw the Ionian Peninsula, where they have a council of men and women, chosen from among their people, poor and rich alike, so that they can be heard equally. We went to Amonpour, where their trade and their industry make them wealthy and full instead of poor and starving. We went to Albis, where women can inherit land and hold jobs and are treated as equal to men in all things. And Espa, where on one particular drunken evening we thought do-ing this"—the prince pulled aside his collar so I could see the whole of his sun tattoo, identical to Jin's—"was a good idea. It's a Xichian symbol for luck and fortune. Appropriate when you're living job to job, ship to ship, like we were then. I didn't exactly plan on it becoming the symbol for a whole revolution.

"The people of this desert should have a country that belongs to them, not to one man. Everybody in this coun-try lives like they're lit with fire at birth. There's so much greatness in Miraji, and so many terrible things being done by my father and by the Gallan. This country's people deserve better. Shazad deserves a country where her mind isn't wasted because she's a woman. The Demdji shouldn't fear for their lives just because my father has allied with a country that burns those touched with magic. My mother deserved better than being beaten to death for rebelling against a life she didn't choose for herself. We could make Miraji the greatest country in the world.

"My father made it the way it is, a warring, violent place, half in the hands of the Gallan king. And my brother Kadir is like him. With him as Sultim, we will keep living under foreign empires who come in and bleed the sands dry. Or we could change everything."

Prince Ahmed's face came alive when he was talking about the desert. And the more he talked, the harder it was not to believe him. I finally understood the crazy kid in the pistol pit the night I met Jin. That these ideas could make men shout for rebellion even when it meant they would hang for it.

nineteen

Dark fell in the oasis earlier than I thought it would. I hadn't noticed when we'd been crossing the desert, but now it struck me that Shihabian really must be close. At twilight, the colorful world turned to a softer version of itself. Campfires burned among the trees. Each was surrounded by a little pocket of people, sharing food, laughing. I thought of Dustwalk at dinnertime. Everybody shut up inside their houses, jealously guarding every scrap they had. Here the food was laid out on a big carpet in the middle of the camp, with a stack of mismatched plates.

Shazad and I sat down by one of the small fires. Shazad helped herself to two plates, piling flatbread and fruit on one and handing it to me.

"Where do all these people come from?" I asked Shazad

in between bites. I hadn't realized how hungry I was until I started eating.

Shazad looked around at the hundred or so rebels, as if the question surprised her. "A little bit of everywhere. There were only a dozen of us when we fled Izman after the Sultim trials. But in the last year, the cause has gotten bigger. More people have joined. A few were turned out of their houses or arrested for supporting Ahmed a little too loudly. Some we broke out of prison. Farrouk and Fazia are orphans from Izman." She gestured to the pair I'd seen tinkering with the bomb that morning, now building some kind of structure out of bread. "We hired them to make an explosive device on a mission a few months back and the Sultan's army identified them, so they're refugees now. Fairly useful to have around, although I worry one day they'll blow this whole place sky-high."

"What about you?" I asked.

"I'm a girl who could've done just about anything if I'd been born a boy." Shazad took a bite of her food. "But I was born a girl, so I'm doing this. My mother thinks it's an elaborate stall tactic to avoid getting married." I'd seen Shazad kill a Skinwalker. Watched her that afternoon run a dozen of the rebels through sword drills with the kind of command that could march a whole army across the desert. If she couldn't carve out a place for herself in Izman, what hope was I going to have?

"She's too modest." Bahi dropped down next to Shazad by the fire, folding his legs over the pillow. He was balancing a plate on his knees. "Shazad was born to greatness. Her father is General Hamad."

I gave them both a blank look.

"He's been the Sultan's chief general for two decades," Bahi bragged for her. "He had a strong daughter and a weak son. Being a man of unconventional strategies, he trained his daughter to follow in his footsteps."

"My brother's not weak, he's sick," Shazad said.

"Most people," Bahi said with a bold smile that was all teeth and no humor, "would have killed their son trying to turn him strong. Like my father tried to do with me."

Shazad saved me from having to answer. "Bahi's father is a captain in the army. He reports to my father, which is why Bahi and I have known each other since we were six years old."

"And we've been friends that long because I'm so charming," Bahi said.

"You're marginally less of an ass than the rest of your brothers," Shazad conceded. "Captain Reza"—there was scorn in Shazad's tone and Bahi snapped a fake salute—"has six sons, so he thought he could spare a few. Much as he enjoyed gloating to his superior officer that he has six strong sons, where my father had only one."

"And you," I said.

"Captain Reza never counted me."

"His mistake," Bahi put in.

"Does your father know . . ." I wasn't sure how to put it. "That you're turning against him?" I probably shouldn't have put it like that.

"I'm not against my father." Shazad smiled fondly. "I'm against the Sultan. My father turned against him a while ago, too. He's the one who told us about the rumors of the weapon being made down in the Last County. So highly secretive, the Sultan didn't even tell him—but he has other ways of obtaining information."

That made me sit up. Rumor in Dustwalk was that Ahmed's rebellion was just a band of idealistic fools in the desert. But the rebels had had enough of a hold on Dassama that it'd been worth destroying. And the general was high-ranking in court. If *he* was loyal to Ahmed . . .

"You're saying you've got allies in the Sultan's court?"

Shazad was easily the most beautiful girl I'd ever met, and when she smiled with all her teeth she looked like the most dangerous one, too. "A few. The stories would have you believe that Ahmed appeared in Izman on the day of the Sultim trials like magic. Same way they'd have you believe that he disappeared from the palace the night of Delila's birth in a poof of Demdji smoke. But campfire stories are never the whole story." I remembered what Ahmed had told me, as we kept watch over Jin in the sick tent. That his mother and Jin's had plotted their escape. But Jin's mother wasn't even in the popular story. Neither was Jin, for that matter. "Ahmed came back to Izman half a year before the Sultim trials, on a trading ship. He fell in with an intellectual crowd. A lot of very clever, very idealistic boys, including my brother, who sat around and talked about philosophies and how to make Miraji better. Many of them are children of people in the Sultan's court."

She took a bite of her food. "One night, I found my brother and Ahmed and three of their idiot friends in stocks in the middle of Izman because they'd been preaching that women ought to have the right to refuse a marriage." That struck down to the bone. "Fortunately, being General Hamad's daughter gets you a long way when dealing with soldiers. I dressed them down for arresting their general's only son, and they were rushing to unlock the rest of them. They had no idea they'd accidentally arrested the prodigal Prince Ahmed, or I doubt even being the general's daughter would've done much. Ahmed was renting rooms in the Izman slums under a false name then." I figured there was a reason things like that didn't make it into the stories. No one wanted to imagine their hero prince sleeping in a flea-infested bed. "I dragged my brother home, and Ahmed followed us. When we got there I dressed him down about almost getting my brother killed. And the next thing I knew, we were shouting about Ataullah's philosophy on the role of the ruler in the state, and then I was agreeing to train him for the Sultim trials."

"I was locked away in the Holy Order at the time," Bahi said with his mouth full. "Or I would have talked some sense into her."

"Would you like to tell her what you actually did when you got kicked out, or shall I?" Shazad took a bite of flatbread.

Bahi was suddenly very intent on his food. "I don't recall."

Shazad didn't miss a beat. "He got very drunk and turned up to serenade me outside my father's house."

I snorted a laugh. "What song?" I couldn't help but ask.

"I don't remember," Bahi muttered again.

"'Rumi and the Princess,' I think?" Shazad caught my eye, the spark of a laugh there.

"No." Bahi looked up defensively. "It was 'The Djinni

and the Dev' and it was beautiful." He puffed out his chest as Shazad's spark exploded into a real laugh. It was contagious, and soon I was laughing, too. Bahi started to call for a drink, saying he'd sing it for us once he had some liquor in him.

Truth be told I already felt drunk.

The night and the colors and the laughter and the sense of power and certainty in what they were doing made my head spin. This revolution was a legend in the making. The kind of tale that sprawled out long before me and far beyond my reach. The sort of epic that was told over and over to explain how the world was never the same after this handful of people lived and fought and won or died trying. And after it happened, the story seemed somehow inevitable. Like the world was waiting to be changed, needing to be saved, and the players in the tale were all plucked out of their lives and moved into places exactly where they needed to be, like pieces on a board, just to make this story come true. But it was wilder and more terrifying and intoxicating, and more uncertain, than I'd ever thought. And I could be part of it. If I wanted to. It was getting way too late to rip myself out of this story now, or to rip it out of me.

"Where the hell have you been, holy boy?" The new voice startled me out of my daydream. I stared at the speaker. I'd thought Delila and Imin were sights to see, but the girl who dropped uninvited next to our fire was made of gold. Everything from the tips of her fingernails to her eyelids looked like she'd been cast out of metal instead of born, except her hair was as black as mine and her eyes were dark. Another Demdji. "Can you deal with this?" She stretched out her arm toward him; it was caked in blood and burn marks.

Bahi hissed through his teeth as he took it. "What happened?"

"There was a small explosion," the golden girl said drily.

"The burns aren't that bad," Bahi said. "It's hard to burn the daughter of a First Being made of pure fire."

"When did you get back, Hala?" Shazad asked. Hala didn't answer; she just gestured sarcastically to her bloody traveling clothes in a way that seemed to suggest Shazad was stupid for not realizing she was fresh into camp.

"We were too late," she said. "She'd already been arrested. I thought she'd have longer. Shape-shifters are usually better at hiding. Imin lasted for two weeks, remember? But apparently this one is stupid. Rumor is they're holding her for trial in Fahali. I've just come for backup. I say we leave tonight, slip in, and scramble their minds before they can hang her."

"You mean the girl with the red hair." I interrupted, before I could think not to. For the first time Hala seemed to notice me. "That's who you were looking for in Fahali. A Demdji." The word still tasted strange. "She had red hair and a face that changed."

"You! You saw her!" Hala's golden face glowed eagerly in the firelight as she leaned forward, and I knew we were talking about the same person.

The next words that fell out of my mouth stopped her short. "The Gallan shot her in the head."

The cheery mood that'd been around the campfire a

moment before was extinguished. "So how come you're still alive?" Hala's golden face hardened.

Something in her voice said she expected me to grovel. To stumble over myself to explain how I dared to have survived when the person she'd been out to save hadn't. "Because they didn't shoot me in the head," I answered.

Her sneer reminded me of an ivory and gold comb Tamid's mother used to have. She waved a hand, like she was urging me to go on. I noticed she had only eight fingers. Two were missing on her left hand that I could've sworn were there before. She noticed me noticing, and a second later her hand was whole again.

"It's rude to stare." A black bug crawled out of the sand, over my boot, and up my body. "And it's rude to leave someone for dead to save your own skin." I swatted at it, but it just exploded into ten black bugs, and then each of them into ten more until I was crawling with them, my hands slapping at my skin until it was red and painful.

"Hala, whatever you're doing, stop it," Shazad ordered. I'd been wrong. Her voice wasn't sharp; it was clean, like a good cut. The bugs vanished.

Shazad had said something about a Demdji who could crawl into folks' minds. I guessed I'd just met her. I already hated her.

"Where I come from, people take care of their own." Hala picked at her nails as if she hadn't just twisted my mind around.

"She was," Jin said behind me.

twenty

J in was awake, leaning heavily on Ahmed's shoulder, standing on the outskirts of the light from the fire. He looked drained and tired, but he was alive. And he was looking at me. I reacted to him instinctively, my body pulling me forward like it was on a string tied to him. Like the swing of the compass needle twinned with another.

But before I could stand, there was a squeal from the other side of camp. Delila rushed forward and flung herself into Jin's arms, babbling in a foreign language I guessed was Xichian. She started crying into his shirt. Soon all the camp was on its feet, people crowding around him. Asking questions, welcoming him back.

"Easy there," Bahi called. "I've only just got him back on

his feet." Eventually folks started to trickle back to their campfires and their food, leaving Jin and Ahmed facing our small circle. Jin turned to Shazad.

"General," Jin said. His voice was thick with disuse, but the way he said it sounded so painfully familiar. *Bandit*, I heard him saying in the desert.

"Don't call me that." Shazad embraced him with one arm, more careful of the bandages than Delila had been. "What happened to 'I'll just go and take a look around. I'll be back in no time'?"

The laugh made its way round the small circle that was left around Jin as I sat on the outside. I hunted through my feelings for something to say here, in this place I didn't belong, to Jin, who'd just become a stranger all over again. These people had stood side by side planning a revolution since the days I was shooting tin cans off the fence behind my uncle's house.

"Better late than dead," Hala said. She didn't embrace him. But as the firelight danced over her golden skin, making it look molten, I saw that some of the hardness was gone from her now.

"Yes, and you have me to thank for that," Bahi added with his mouth full. Even on his feet, he was still shoveling food into his mouth while talking. "Not that anyone has thanked me yet."

"I thought Holy Fathers were meant to do their work for the grace of God, not the thanks of mortals." Jin was careful not to catch my eye as he addressed Bahi.

"Well, it's a good thing I failed my training, then, isn't

it?" Bahi gestured dramatically with the food in his hand, flicking crumbs onto Delila.

"You were bound to keep someone alive eventually," Shazad said. "And Amani's the one who dragged you here." I wanted to hug Shazad and curse at the same time. Finally, Jin didn't have any choice but to meet my eyes at the mention of my name.

Two months in the desert hung between us. All the things he'd told me and the ones he hadn't. The secrets and lies. The understanding that I hadn't left him this time. That in two months I'd gone from the girl who'd drugged him and left him facedown on a table just to make a break for it to the one who'd dragged him through enemy soldiers and killer ghouls to save him.

"Well." Hala draped herself carelessly over Delila's shoulders. "At least one of us was successful in bringing home a Demdji." The new word was still so strange, it took me a moment to realize Hala was gesturing to . . . me. The circle went silent.

"Demdji?" I was confused.

Ahmed's expression faltered. He said something to Jin in Xichian. Jin answered back with a shake of his head without looking at me.

"Just because I don't speak your language doesn't give you the right to talk about me in it." My voice rose higher than I meant it to. I was shouting in the presence of the prince. Two princes.

"Amani," Ahmed said gently. "Maybe you'd like to sit."

The plate that Shazad had given me had toppled off my

knees and to the ground. I'd stood up without realizing it, without knowing what I meant to do, but sure as hell that I needed both legs planted to do it.

"Maybe I wouldn't." I caught Jin's mouth twitching up at the corner and my anger rose. "Lying," I said, looking only at him, "is a sin."

Jin finally spoke to me. "I was going to hell long before I met you." There was something like regret in his voice.

"You don't know that I'm—"

Jin cut me off. "Don't fool yourself, Blue-Eyed Bandit." His voice was flat, a stranger's, resigned. "I knew you were a Demdji before I knew you weren't a boy. All I had to see was your eyes."

Traitor's eyes.

Delila's hair. Imin's eyes. Hala's skin.

The Djinni's mark.

"I realized you didn't know when you told me about your mother's husband. You called him your father. Demdji who know what they are don't do that." I looked at the two Demdji next to him. Delila was chewing her lip, looking uneasy, while on her shoulder Hala looked like she might be about to clap her hands at my discomfort.

"Plenty of Gallan soldiers have eyes like mine," I argued.

"Northerners have eyes like pale water. Yours are different. Yours are the color of fire when it burns too hot. And it's more than that." Now that Jin had stopped ignoring me, all his attention was mine. "You know the stories better than I do: Djinn can't tell lies. Neither can their children. I'd bet my life no lie has ever crossed your tongue."

My laugh was short and violent. Shazad took a step toward me, but I pulled back. "You calling me honest?"

"No, you're a great deceiver. But you're no liar."

I remembered something Jin had said in the shop in Dustwalk. *You're a good liar. For someone who doesn't lie.*

"At the shop, I hid you from Naguib—"

"You didn't lie to him." The world narrowed to Jin and me and the memory of that day. "Not *once*. You told him it was a quiet day. You said there weren't many foreigners in Dustwalk. Misleading truths, but still truths. You tricked him. Just like you did with the caravan. Just like you did when you told me I could call you Oman." I thought about how easily Jin had trusted my word. Of how easily he'd given up on finding the weapon in Fahali when I'd said. "Djinn are powerful, deceitful things."

"So what's your excuse?" I lashed out, but Jin didn't even flinch.

"I can keep going if you want."

"Jin." Ahmed's warning sounded far off.

"The sand and the sun don't drain you the way they do us mere mortals. You belong to them." I remembered one of our last nights in the desert. *You're unnatural,* he'd said to me. "You pick up languages *like that*." He snapped his fingers, and I realized he'd spoken the last two words in Xichian. All the nights in the desert when he'd fed me stories of far-off places and scraps of their language. Testing me.

"Stop it." I could barely speak the words. What was it Shazad had said about the Demdji? That they—we—were useful. Was that why Jin had saved me in the first place? Dragged me across the desert, not as an ally, not because we needed each other to stay alive, but because he knew his brother could use me?

I stepped closer, the circle around him parting for me nervously. Until I was close enough that I could've kissed him again. That kiss was a trick, too. Mine. I was a creature of deceit, but I wasn't the liar here. "Why should I believe anything you say?"

"Go on, then." His mouth twitched up. "Prove me wrong; tell me a lie. Tell me your name is Oman, straight out this time. Tell me you're a boy named Alidad. Tell me you are not a Demdji."

"Why should I?" I could feel my tongue fighting against the words he dared me to say.

"Because you can't." Victory was marked all over him as he watched me struggle.

My hand lashed out. His face cracked sideways and my palm stung. And before anyone could say anything more to me, I ran.

● ● ●

"SO ARE YOU planning on stealing all our guns, or do you think maybe you only need one per hand?" I whirled around. Ahmed was watching me from the mouth of the small cave in the canyon wall. I could just make him out.

I'd decided to leave. I'd decided that before my hand had even stopped stinging from hitting Jin. But I wasn't going unarmed. I wedged the fourth pistol between the sheema I'd tied around my middle like a sash, since I didn't have a belt, and my hip bone. "Maybe your armory ought to be better guarded if you don't want folks helping themselves."

"Not a consideration we've really needed to have before you," Ahmed said.

"Well, you ought to think of that next time your brother brings ignorant strays home." I pushed by him and started walking. Ahmed followed me.

"Am I a prisoner?" I turned to face him when we'd walked a few steps.

"No." Ahmed clasped his hands behind his back. "Though Jin did say we'd better send someone after you so that when you collapsed from sheer stubborn exhaustion, we could bring you back before you died."

"He has so much faith in me." I didn't try to keep the bitterness from my voice as I fiddled with the pistol at my waist.

"He does," Ahmed said. "He thought you'd have made it much farther than this by now, for one thing."

I flicked the hammer of the pistol restlessly. He wasn't wrong. I was exhausted. And wounded. And hungry. And miles from anywhere else I could go. Even farther from anywhere I wanted to be. But before Jin woke up, before the word *Demdji* spun out of Hala's mouth and landed on me, I'd wanted to stay.

"Why?" My voice cracked a little, and I cleared my throat.

"Well," Ahmed said, "from what I understand, you walked a long way here. Jin figured you'd at least make it past the point of no return . . ."

I caught myself before I laughed. I could almost pretend he was just another boy from the Last County, except with a better accent. "Why didn't he tell me?"

"You'd have to ask Jin for his own reasons for not telling you. But if you want honesty from me . . ." Ahmed sighed. He looked older than eighteen. "The Demdji are an asset, Amani. Don't get me wrong; every man and woman in this rebellion is. But Imin is the best spy I have. And Hala has saved more people than maybe even Shazad has. My sister is the reason I didn't die at the end of the Sultim trials. The twins can take animal form and can cover distances in a matter of days that would take a normal man weeks. In a war, you take what best serves your cause."

I wished it were Jin trying to convince me. He'd be so much easier to argue with. But Ahmed's logic couldn't be bickered against so easily. And that just left me as the problem.

"I can't . . ." I faltered on the words. "I can't do what your other Demdji can. I reckon I would've noticed by now if my face changed or I could make illusions walk through the air. I thought I might stay and . . . do what Shazad does." Though now I said it out loud, it seemed stupid, too. Shazad might be wholly human, but I'd seen her kill a Skinwalker without breaking a sweat. Without a gun, I was just a girl. Not a Demdji. "I didn't figure I'd stay to make bugs crawl out of people's skin or turn my-self into another person."

"If you choose to go, you can," Ahmed said. "It's danger-ous in Miraji for a Demdji, but you seem to have handled yourself just fine so far." I thought of the girl the Gallan general had shot through the head in Fahali. She had been like me. I remembered Jin warning me to be care-ful. Warning me against Izman. "But if you decide to stay, there are a half dozen other Demdji who could help you figure out what your power is, whatever it is that you *can* do that can help this rebellion. If you still want to."

If I wanted to.

If I wanted to be part of this story. This riddle.

Truth be told, it was more than a want.

twenty-one

There were three pomegranates hanging from the branch. And then there were two and then four. I glanced over at Delila, who smiled sweetly. "See, it's not that hard."

It'd been a week since Jin woke up and Ahmed promised they could help me unearth my powers. A week of meditating with Bahi and of Delila instructing me that the way she cast illusions was that she just *did*. Somehow she thought a demonstration would help.

"This is useless." It didn't help. "We don't even know that my gift is with illusions."

"It is the most common Demdji gift," Bahi offered philosophically from the sidelines.

"Just try," Delila said.

"Yes," Hala put in, looking on. "Make one disappear and you'll be on par with the street performers in Izman."

I stared at the tree. I wasn't sure what I was reaching for. Hala said it came from her mind. Delila seemed to think she pulled her power out of her chest. I couldn't find anything in either one. The whicker of horses nearby unraveled whatever attention I'd had. I glanced over my shoulder. It was the party Ahmed had sent out three days before. A raid on a mountain outpost to bring back more guns.

I'd asked to go with them. I knew guns. Ahmed had said no. That it wasn't worth it sending out a Demdji before she had her powers in check. Just like he had the time before that. I was starting to wonder what the point of staying was if I wasn't any use at all.

As I watched their saddlebags, clinking heavy with guns, the frustration that had been rising in me whipped itself into a frenzy. I couldn't manage to change my shape or my face, or climb into anyone's head, or conjure images out of the air. Folks in camp had started taking bets on how long it would take me to figure out my powers. Or maybe I didn't have any, the whispers had started to suggest.

As I stared, one of the three pomegranates split open, spilling angry black ooze. I knew it was Hala's work. My gun sprang into my hand on instinct. I aimed with easy certainty and pulled the trigger. The pomegranate exploded in a violent burst of seeds and red juices, Hala's illusion disappearing with it.

"There," I said, holstering the gun. "Now there are two."

A laugh made me turn my head. I realized Jin had been watching. He was passing by us, carrying a stack of firewood toward the center of camp on one shoulder. He'd recovered quickly from the Nightmare bite. I'd seen him training at hand-to-hand combat with Shazad yesterday. She still beat him. Badly. But he held his own for a while.

Fresh humiliation burned my neck as Jin saluted me and I turned away. We'd been doing a dance all week where Jin pretended nothing was wrong between us, and I pretended he didn't exist.

Like he thought it didn't matter that he'd tricked me to get me here. That he'd pulled me off that train to keep me from going to Izman, not to keep me safe. That he'd convinced me the best way to get there was the caravan, preying on my ignorance about my own country. That I'd gone along with it because I was stupid enough to think we really were a team.

I brushed the thought off. It was petty of me to hate him. This was a war. He'd done what he needed to do. Even if I turned out not to be all that helpful.

"Do you know that you cast illusions while you sleep?" I asked Delila. It came out sharper than I meant it to. "I'm not going to become some all-powerful Demdji overnight just by focusing."

"We should take a break in any case," Bahi interjected before Delila could reply. "It's only a few hours until dark, and tonight is Shihabian."

Hala glanced at the sky. The sun was getting low. Something that wasn't a sneer flickered over her face for once. Delila saw it, too. She dropped a hand on Hala's shoulder.

"Imin is on her way back," Delila said. My mind fell back to my first day in camp, when Imin had been sent out shaped like a Gallan soldier. She was meant to be back by Shihabian.

"How do you know that?" I asked Delila. The more time I spent in camp, the more worried I'd gotten about the Gallan in Fahali. The oasis was like nowhere I'd ever been, and if everyone here from all over Miraji was to be believed, it was like nowhere else that existed. All it would take to destroy it would be the Gallan and their weapon.

Delila looked faintly embarrassed. "It's something I picked up when I was little. When my brothers started taking work on ships and sailing away, leaving me behind, I never knew when they were coming back. So every morning I opened my mouth to make sure I could say that they were still alive, they were safe, they were coming home. Then I'd try to say that today would be the day that they'd dock. And if I couldn't say it, then it wasn't the truth and it wouldn't happen. Imin is on her way back." She said it with the confidence of a prophecy.

We couldn't speak anything if it wasn't the truth; what if it could work the other way? I'd done it once before, I realized, with the Gallan soldier. Told him that he wouldn't find us in the canyon. And he hadn't. But the Skinwalker had. "What would happen if I just declared that tomorrow my powers will show up? Or if I said—"

Delila's eyes went wide and Bahi's hand was over my

mouth whip-quick. The one with the tattoo on it. It smelled of oils and smoke, like the inside of a prayer house. For once he looked serious. "Demdji shouldn't make truths of things that aren't. You can never predict how they're going to turn out."

"No," Hala added, sounding bitter. "You might say Ahmed will win the Sultim trials but neglect to say that he will take the throne. For instance. And if you'd just left it alone, then he'd have been a great Sultan and ruled until he was old and gray."

The look on her face was the kind that only came from experience. I thought of all the stories I knew of men making foolish demands and wishes of Djinn that were granted to them in some misshapen way that robbed them of their happiness. The Gallan soldier hadn't found us in the canyon. He'd been eaten alive instead. Bahi paused, like he was making sure I understood, before taking his hand away from my mouth.

When I looked at Hala, she was staring at her feet. No wonder she hadn't forgiven me for the red-haired Demdji. She'd been holding a grudge against herself for a year now. And just because she'd tried to cheat the universe into Ahmed becoming Sultan by saying that he would. "I reckon I would've done the same thing."

Hala treated me to an image of my hands catching fire, the agony of it searing through me before it vanished. Whatever sympathy I felt vaporized. "Yes, but you didn't. I did. And if I hadn't, we might never have needed a war and people might not have needed to die."

And without another word, Hala stormed off.

Bahi clapped his hands together. "You know, I think now would be a great time for that break."

• • •

DELILA AND I made our way slowly back into camp, through the preparations for Shihabian. Folks were stringing lanterns between the trees, and the whole of the camp was rich with the smell of roasting meats and cooking bread. Even when I'd dreamed of Izman, I'd never imagined a place like this. Everyone seemed to fit easily into their roles, working with one singular purpose: putting Ahmed on the throne. To make the rest of Miraji like this tiny part of the world.

"How come Jin didn't compete in the Sultim trials?" I asked, breaking the uneasy silence that had fallen between us since Hala's outburst. "Tradition claims the twelve eldest princes are to compete."

"Ahmed is the fifth born, and Jin is sixth, so he had the right. If he'd come forward as another surviving son." Which meant he'd chosen not to. That Ahmed had decided to step up and claim his chance at his birthright and Jin hadn't. But then, the stories didn't mention Jin at all. Not the disappearance of another son on the night that Ahmed and Delila's mother was beaten to death, let alone his return.

"Why are you asking me and not my brother?" Delila had been chewing on her thumbnail nervously. She pulled it out of her mouth self-consciously.

Because I'm avoiding him. "Your brother has a bad habit of not telling me things straight."

"They fought about it," she admitted finally. "Shazad said it would be a tactical advantage to have an ally in the trials to watch Ahmed's back. Hala said no one would believe either one of them if we suddenly started claiming it was raining returned princes. Jin said no one would believe him because he didn't look a thing like the Sultan. Bahi said it would distract from Ahmed's impact. Then Shazad said the Holy Order had given him too much of a flair for dramatics. And they went on and on," she said shyly. "But in the end, nobody's ever been able to make Jin do something he didn't want. And the truth was, he never wanted anything to do with Miraji." She reached up, plucking an orange from a tree as we passed under, and started peeling it, avoiding looking me in the eye. "Ahmed fell in love with Miraji the moment he came back. Like a piece of his soul he'd almost forgotten had been returned to him, he said. When Ahmed decided to stay behind, Jin never understood why. I didn't understand until I saw it myself. It just . . . feels like home. They fought when Ahmed decided to stay as well. Jin sailed away without him. He always figured that Ahmed would change his mind and go back out to sea. Then our mother, Lien—Jin's mother really, but mine, too." She looked uncomfortable, like she'd spent a long time fighting with that fact. "She died, and Jin and I came to Ahmed instead. It was only a few months before the Sultim trials. Jin had been waiting for Ahmed to change his mind, and in the meantime he'd built up this following in Izman. I thought Jin might break his nose when we finally tracked him down with the compass. Shazad broke Jin's nose first."

Jin had told me a girl broke his nose and his brother set it. I'd just figured on some lover's quarrel in a foreign port, not Shazad. Nice to know it wasn't all lies, though.

"He figured the best we could hope for was for Ahmed not to get killed in the Sultim trials. And then we'd leave and Ahmed would stop fighting." She gestured around herself at the camp. "He was wrong."

"So why does Jin stay?"

"Jin has fought for Ahmed since they were boys. He'd throw a punch whenever anyone would call Ahmed a . . ." She stumbled over the translation of the Xichian word. "It means 'dirty foreigner,' I suppose. He'll do the same now. I still don't think he's forgiven Ahmed for falling in love with something outside of our family, though. Well . . . it might be he's starting to now." That small shy smile was back on her face. I felt the back of my neck get hot.

"It's not . . ." I stumbled over the words. "Jin and I aren't . . ."

"If it were true," Delila singsonged in a little girl's voice, "you'd be able to say it." She laughed as she spun away from me, jumping over a small campfire, leaving me even more confused.

• ● •

IT WAS LATE afternoon, which meant Shazad would likely have finished training and be back in our tent. Or rather, her tent. I'd slept there the first night, too drained from the revelation of being a Demdji to put up much of a fight. And then I'd just stayed. She still hadn't kicked me out, and there was a small pile of her clothes that she had loaned me piling up in a heap on the floor on my side, dividing me from her militarily clean side. It was almost like home.

Stepping into the tent, I was greeted by a flying cloth bundle to the face.

"Catch," Shazad said too late. I picked it up off the floor. A bright swathe of gold cloth with deep red stitching unfurled between my fingers.

"What is it?" I asked.

"A rare occurrence for which it's traditional to wear your finest clothes." I realized Shazad was already dressed for Shihabian. It couldn't be natural to be as pulled together as she was. Her dark hair was piled in tight waves against her head, golden pins catching the dimming light, a khalat—so green it made the trees look dull—draped across her.

"I didn't think to grab my finest clothes while running for my life." I ran my hands across the fabric and imagined putting it on and turning into some phoenix creature from the stories, fire and gold.

"Well, in this case, your friend's finest clothes," Shazad said.

Friend. The simple word grabbed my attention. I'd been shedding friends since Tamid.

Shazad must've caught my hesitation. "I have other

khalats. If you don't like it," she added quickly, pushing a loose piece of hair back behind her ear like she was nervous, only that was impossible.

"Is Imin back yet?" I asked. No matter what Delila said, I was nervous about the yellow-eyed Demdji in the Gallan camp.

"No." Shazad became serious. "Not yet. I'm giving her until the end of Shihabian, and then tomorrow we're going to look for her." To make sure she hadn't wound up like the red-haired Demdji.

"Who's we?" I asked, starting to undress.

"Me and Jin, and you if you want."

My hands faltered on my buttons, Delila's words fresh in my mind. "I don't think I'm meant to leave camp before I figure out my powers." I didn't sound that convincing even to myself, and Shazad made a disbelieving noise at the back of her throat.

"However short our lives might turn out to be if this revolution fails, you can't avoid him forever, you know."

"Want to watch me try anyway?"

• • •

THE HOLY TIME of Shihabian started when the sun vanished, a reminder of the night when the Destroyer of Worlds came and brought darkness with her. Last year Tamid had spun me in place until I was dizzy, and we both laughed until we had to hold each other up, tipsy-turvy from drink and dancing. We celebrated until midnight, when the whole world would turn black in memory of the first night. And then, when the stars and the moon came back, we prayed until dawn.

But Dustwalk's celebrations had nothing on those at the Rebel camp. Lanterns were strung between the trees so thick, I could barely see the branches for the light. Figs plucked straight from the trees, cakes so sweet my fingers stuck together. The air smelled of oil and incense and smoke and food and the desert and being alive in the desert.

I was fiercely conscious of the way the silk and muslin of my borrowed khalat felt on my skin. The golden cloth draped and clung like nothing I'd ever owned. I'd cinched it at the waist. Shazad's figure was better filled out than mine, but I wasn't going to be mistaken for a boy in this, especially not when she opened the top three clasps at my throat. I'd put up a bit of a fight, but Shazad was a better born fighter than I was, and in the end I had to let her loose on me. I'd figured she'd try and fail to turn me into something as bright and polished as she was. Instead, when she'd held up the mirror, a wild thing stared back.

My hair was twisted and half-bound, coming apart in waves that kissed the edge of my jaw and my neck like I'd been caught in a sandstorm. She'd painted my lips red enough that I imagined I could taste blood. My eyes were so dark around the blue that I feared for anyone caught in their crosshairs.

I looked like something that belonged in a revolution.

The pair of us drifted from one fire to another, people

catching us to talk, sweeping me up in camp chatter as easily as Shazad. I ate honey cakes and washed them down with sweet wine. I spotted Jin across the campfire, playing some game or other with his sister and laughing as he lost.

There was a pair of cats by a fire. One blue, the other gray with a blue tuft on its head. I knelt down to scratch the blue one absently, and instead of a cat I found my hand on the stomach of a very naked, very blue boy.

"Happy Shihabian, General." The boy saluted Shazad, who barely bothered to look down as she stepped over him. I tried to keep my eyes on his face and off any other part of him.

"Izz," Shazad replied, nodding to the blue-skinned boy, "meet Amani. Amani, meet the twins. Or one of them. They just got back from doing a supply run for us this morning."

I flushed and looked away, catching Shazad looking too damn amused. The other cat turned into a boy, too. He was identical to Izz, but his skin was dark. Only his hair was the same pale blue as his brother's skin.

"And this is Maz." Shazad gestured.

Maz grinned. "The one and only."

I glanced from him to his twin. "Who taught you to count?"

The twins beamed at me. "So you're the new Demdji," Izz said, standing to inspect me with no mind to how bare he was. "We wanted to meet you."

"We were wondering if you might be our sister," Maz said. "On account of your eyes." He gestured to his hair, an unnatural blue, a few shades off from my eyes. If we'd both inherited it from our Djinn fathers, it might be that we shared one. The realization that I might suddenly have a brother after seventeen years unsettled me.

"I've always wanted a sister," Izz said brightly. "Have you met Imin? She and Hala had the same Djinni father, you know. Their mothers lived on the same street in Izman." So I was responsible for Hala's golden-eyed sister risking her life in the Gallan camp. It seemed I couldn't stop doing things to make her hate me.

"Amani's not our sister, though." Maz looked faintly disappointed as he said it. "Or else we wouldn't be able to say that she's not our sister."

"Still!" Izz said, perking up. "You might be able to change your shape like us. That would be just as good."

"Do you want a drink?" Shazad blessedly pulled me away from the naked twins.

The dancing started soon after. I'd never danced properly at Shihabian before. Not with Tamid's injured leg. I couldn't stand to leave him out. But my body loosened soon enough and was weaving through the sparks from the fire, from one partner to the next. As drink flowed more freely and people got sloppier, we spun more wildly. I careened round Shazad dancing with Bahi, and a pair of hands belonging to my next partner grabbed me, spinning me around to face him.

I was chest to chest with Jin. We both stopped, letting the dancing go on around us. I could feel the warmth of his hands through the delicate fabric of the khalat. After weeks of my being a boy around him, everything that made me a girl was in his hands. His eyes traveled over me slowly, resting for just a second on the red sheema tied around my waist. It was the one he'd given to me. All the way back in Sazi. "You look like you were born out of fire."

"Jin—" I started. I never finished. Midnight dropped like a cloak over the sky like it always did on Shihabian. One moment there were fires and lanterns and stars and moonlight, and then there was just blackness.

No matter that the Buraqi were fewer and the Djinn didn't live alongside men anymore, no matter how many factories rose up filled with iron and smoke: this was magic that didn't fade. It lived in the memory of the world itself. The first true dark, when matches wouldn't strike, tinder wouldn't catch, and stars hid. Jin's hands slipped away from me, and I felt even his presence fade. I couldn't follow him. Not in this kind of dark. All of us stood completely still where we'd stopped. Waiting for the light to come back.

A fire flared to my right. The stars were blinking back to life one by one. Still, no one spoke. The hours up to midnight were for festivities; now was a time for prayers and memories. My eyes darted around for Jin as the crowd shifted me toward the single fire like moths.

The storyteller was a young woman. She stood on a raised stone by the fire, Demdji gathered all around her, facing the rest of the camp.

"The world was created in light," the storyteller began, the traditional opening. Every story might be different, but it always began with the same words. "And then came the night. The Destroyer of Worlds came from the dark that existed only in the places the sun couldn't touch."

I spotted the back of Jin's head as he escaped the crowd. I followed, weaving my way through the people dropping into prayer, walking until the noise and light and illusions and laughter were far away and the edge of the desert opened.

"Blue-Eyed Bandit." I jumped at Jin's voice. I could just make him out now in the returning starlight.

He took a swig from the bottle dangling from his fingers, and for a wild second I thought he might be drinking up the courage to really face me this time.

"Want a drink?" He held out the bottle. "There was this girl once I knew from the Last County who could hold her drink even when I wound up head down on the table."

He meant at the Drunk Djinni, by the gutted-out mines of Sazi, when I was just the girl with the gun who could hold her drink and he was just a foreigner who couldn't hold the drugs I slipped in his. Instead of a Demdji and a prince. When I was still so certain of everything and he started lying to me.

"Then again," Jin said, taking another swig, "that girl didn't walk away from stories halfway through either."

In that moment, I did turn to fire. My hand sent the bottle flying to the ground, the sand guzzling the spilled liquor as it rolled. I realized I'd been expecting him to stop me, catch my arm before I could hit him.

"Stories and lies." I found my voice and swallowed

whatever else was snaking up my throat lest it come through as tears. "I'm not so fond of them as I used to be. But you know by now, all your lies to get me here were wasted. Haven't you heard what they're saying? That I'm the only Demdji in the world without powers?" He struggled through his drunken haze to focus on me. "Did you ever think about telling me what I was?"

All at once Jin filled my senses, the smell of liquor and heat and the sight of the distant planes of his face, of the tattoos just visible through his shirt.

"You want to talk about this? Now?"

"Why not?" I spread my arms wide, daring him. "Why don't you tell me what the plan was? If things had been different in Dassama, were you going to truss me up like a prisoner and drag me here? Or did you have different lies all ready?"

"I didn't make you come here." Jin's eyes bored into mine, but I wasn't backing down. He said I had traitor eyes. Let him see the betrayal there. Let him drown in it. "I didn't trick you and I didn't ask you to."

"What else was I meant to do? Leave you to die?"

"You might've."

"I wouldn't have."

"The truth is I had no idea what I was doing when it came to you, Amani. I tried to leave you in Dustwalk because I didn't want to drag you into my brother's war. I came back for you because I didn't want to see you die at the hands of my other brother. But either way, I was bound to wind up doing one or the other. Just depended on which one." His hand came up like he was going to reach for me but dropped to his side instead. "I was glad in Sazi when I saw you'd gone because it meant you'd escaped on your own path, and I was glad when you took the compass because it gave me a reason to go after you. And yes, I lied to keep you out of Izman because I was afraid someone would know what you were and you'd get snapped up and sold to the Sultan. And I steered you toward Dassama figuring there was a chance I might be able to deliver you to the sea and get you out of this country before it killed you." His face was so close now. I remembered what he said once, crossing the desert, that the sea was the color of my eyes.

"You don't have any right to decide that for me." I shoved him away from me, trying to tear him out of my space, out of my head.

"But *he* does?" Jin shouted, the moment breaking. "My brother says you're a Demdji and you think that will make your life matter, more than being the Blue-Eyed Bandit?"

I rounded on him, my hair catching in the air as it came loose from its braid. "You can't judge me for wanting to be more than just another worthless grain in this desert. Not when you were born so much more than this. Not when *you* were born powerful and important."

"Really?" Two of Jin's quick steps carried him across the sands so fast, it was almost violent. "I was born the same year as ten brothers and a dozen sisters. Being born doesn't make a single soul important. But you were important when I met you, that girl who dressed as a boy, who taught herself to shoot true, who dreamed and saved and wanted so badly. That girl was someone who had made herself matter. She was someone I liked. What the hell has happened since you came here that *she* is so worthless to you? What's happened that only my brother's approval and some power you never needed before can make you important? That's why I didn't want to bring you into this revolution, Amani. Because I didn't want to watch the Blue-Eyed Bandit get unmade by a prince without a kingdom."

I wanted so badly to tell him he was wrong, but my tongue turned to iron just at the thought. But that didn't mean he was in the right either. "And what are you doing fighting for this country if it's not for him? This country you don't understand and you resent for taking your family—"

"You're right." He cut me off. "I never understood this country. I never understood why he chose to leave everything else behind and stay for this. Not until I met you."

I felt like he'd pushed me, like I was falling and I needed him to reel those words back in to keep me standing straight.

"You *are* this country, Amani." He spoke more quietly now. "More alive than anything ought to be in this place. All fire and gunpowder, with one finger always on the trigger."

We stood close, anger pulsing between us. My heart was beating fast—or maybe that was his. We were breathing each other.

Just him and me.

There was more fire in me than I'd felt since I was told I was a Demdji. I opened and closed my hands, wanting to reach for him.

"Jin." Bahi's voice broke the moment. His face was graver than I'd ever seen it. "Ahmed is looking for you. There's news of Naguib's weapon."

• • •

"THE WEAPON IS on the move." Imin was gulping down water. She—he'd practically run from Fahali.

"You've seen it?" Shazad asked.

Imin shook his head. He was still wearing the shape of the Gallan soldier. Everyone from the inner circle stood around him, hanging on his every word: the prince, Shazad, Jin, Bahi, Hala. And then me. "Just rumors. Some accidental fires in Izman that they're trying to blame on us. And three ships anchored in port that burned down. But there was a missive this morning. To Fahali. Commander Naguib is coming as a representative of his father to negotiate the terms of the alliance with General Dumas."

"Well, that certainly sounds like 'We're bringing you a weapon to annihilate the rebellion' to me," Hala commented, putting a hand on her sister-brother's shoulder.

"Have they found us?"

"Not yet," Imin said. "But they were close."

"So we move the camp."

"And where do we go?" Bahi interjected. "If we go

north, we walk into Gallan hands. If we go west, we cross the border into Amonpour—if the mountain clans don't get us first. East, your father kills us, and south, the desert has the privilege of it. It was different when we first fled Izman, but the rebellion has grown since there were a dozen of us. You can't move a kingdom so lightly. Even a small one."

"He's right," Shazad acknowledged.

Ahmed's hand gripped the table. His knuckles were pale.

"So we intercept it," Jin said. He was tossing his compass from hand to hand. The needle swung frantically, pointing at Ahmed's. "Are they moving it by train?"

Imin nodded, blond Gallan curls falling into his face.

Ahmed didn't speak immediately. We all hung on to his silence. "They can't know we're looking," he said finally. It was Jin he spoke to, not his general, not the Demdji. His brother. "You make it look like you're common bandits raiding the trains for the money. Jin, you take—"

"I'll go." The words fell out of my mouth before I could think better of them.

Everybody looked at me.

My argument with Jin was still fresh. He was right. I was never going to be good for anything if I just waited for my Demdji powers. I'd been still too long.

"You're a risk," Ahmed said honestly. But it wasn't a no.

"I'd take that risk in a heartbeat," Jin said, looking at his brother. "I don't need her as a Demdji."

Shazad spoke up for me. "Amani is the best shot I've

ever seen and she can pass for human. She's been doing it her whole life."

"I can do this," I insisted.

Ahmed's eyes locked with mine, and for a moment he didn't look like anybody's brother or friend; he looked like a ruler. I straightened, trying to look like a worthy soldier.

He nodded. "You leave at dawn."

twenty-two

"**D**o you know why they call this Deadman's Ridge?" Bahi asked cheerfully. He'd been chattering ever since we landed, flown here on Izz's back while he was in the shape of a giant Roc, the open desert rushing below us. The blue-skinned Demdji was now curled up among the rocks as a large blue lizard. At least he wasn't trying to help set up camp as a naked boy.

"Is it because I'm going to kill you if you don't stop talking?" Shazad asked, chucking a piece of firewood at him.

"Sadly, the mapmakers didn't anticipate you, Shazad." Bahi slung his arm over her shoulder. We were perched on a mountain. Below us the desert spread out on all sides. Except to the north, where I could just make out what Jin told me was the sea. And directly below us, straight through the mountains, was the railway. "It's because so many workers died blasting the tunnels," Bahi explained. "They say their restless ghosts wander the rails."

"Another fine achievement of the Sultan's allegiance with the Gallan," Jin said, kicking a rock out of the way before laying out his bedroll. Jin called him the Sultan, I'd noticed. Where Ahmed called him their father, Jin never did.

"And you're telling us this *now*?" Hala shoved Bahi. "Right as we're about to blow out a tunnel?"

"Just trying to help everyone reflect on the situation." Bahi's good spirits were running a little too wild for my taste, given I could barely rein in my nerves.

The section of the railway that Deadman's Ridge overlooked ran from Izman, before the tracks sliced their way through the mountains to Fahali on the other side. And from there it was only a day's journey to Ahmed's camp.

We were going to make sure the weapon didn't make it that far. The train was due in two days' time. Tomorrow we'd rig the tunnel with explosives that would force the train to a stop, giving us time to board, pretending to be bandits. Hala would climb inside the heads of the passengers so they would see a dozen bandits, not just four of us, distracting the soldiers while we removed the weapon.

"Aren't Holy Fathers supposed to reflect in silence?" I asked, shaking out my bedroll.

Bahi's mood wasn't even dented. "I'm too young and good-looking to be a father, anyway."

"That's not what Sara says," Shazad muttered.

I wondered if Sara was the reason he'd failed as a Holy Father. He claimed he'd drunk too much before morning prayers once and the previous night's dinner wound up on the High Father's robes, but I'd heard a dozen stories of why Bahi hadn't finished his training.

"No one can prove that that baby is mine." Bahi sagged.

"He has your smart mouth," Shazad retorted.

"He's an infant," Bahi said. "Don't they just wail and scream?"

"Sounds like your son," I muttered.

Jin snorted.

"Ah, well." Bahi pulled a bottle of something out of his bag. "Here's to my son, then."

"Why do you have liquor?" Shazad massaged her temples, like she already had a hangover. In answer, he pulled out two more bottles.

"Medical reasons. It's in the scripture. Look it up. Ladies first." He held the bottle out to her. Bahi's face was pure victory as Shazad's fingers closed over his. He let his fingers linger just a second before he released them. I was starting to think I was right about him leaving the holy fold for a girl, only not one named Sara. I wondered if Shazad really hadn't noticed or if she was just pretending for his sake.

"You know I'm not allowed to drink," Shazad said, taking a deep swig.

"You're not allowed to drink?" I couldn't keep the skepticism out of my voice as she passed the bottle on to me. It was cheap stuff that burned on the way down.

"The general doesn't approve," Bahi interjected. I knew he meant her father, not her.

Shazad gave a mock salute, but her smile was too earnest to make me believe she didn't love her father. "He says a drunk soldier is a dead soldier."

"Clearly one time the general was wrong," Bahi said, pulling out a second bottle. "Or else he would've had a dead captain a thousand times over in my father."

Shazad started to retort something, but Bahi was already roping Izz, Jin, and Hala into some drinking game that seemed to involve flipping over a pair of coins and then slapping palms into rocks before taking a swig.

We might die here, I realized. They were just used to it. For the past year they'd all been throwing themselves into danger and near death over and over, just for the shot at a better world. I'd done that, too. I'd walked into the pistol pit with nothing but a good shot at death for the chance of finding a better place. But that'd just been for me. They were walking into danger for themselves and everybody else. The whole of Miraji. So that no one else died like they had in Dassama. So that no one had to live like I had in Dustwalk.

"Ladies!" Bahi called, pulling me out of my own head. "Won't you join us? So far, I'm winning."

"I thought the point was not to drink the most," Hala retorted.

"Clearly you and I have different definitions of winning." Bahi said.

"We were just giving you a head start." Shazad bumped

my shoulder with hers. "When you wake up and all your blood has turned to liquor, you will look back on that as your first mistake on the way to losing."

I laughed in spite of myself. After one bottle was empty, Bahi got up the bravery to re-create his drunken serenading under Shazad's window. We were drunk on anticipation and good old-fashioned liquor under stars that seemed to belong to us to rearrange at will.

And I realized that, scared as we were, I'd never been so happy as I was that night.

• ● •

THE NEXT MORNING something woke me before the sun. I lay very still, trying to figure whether it was just a memory from a dream I was already forgetting.

The camp was still asleep around me. The fire'd been doused. Shazad was on her side, one hand resting across her blade like she was expecting someone to come for her any second. On the other side of the fire pit, Hala was curled up, buried in her bedroll.

Izz would be on watch duty in the sky in the shape of a Roc, but Bahi and Jin's bedrolls were both empty. I got up, joints popping, and started toward the sunrise, pulling myself up onto the ridge that protected the camp. That was where I found them.

Bahi didn't have a prayer rug, but he was sprawled on his knees, his head down, his lips pressed to his hands. I stood very still. I could hear the words of morning prayers muttered like a whispered secret. It felt like witnessing something intimate. I stepped back, not wanting to intrude. I caught sight of Jin, crouched a few feet away on a narrow ledge, his back against the mountain, his hands dangling into the open space over the rails. I padded across the dusty stones of the ridge in bare feet.

"The hangover's not *that* bad." I heard the croak in my own voice as I went to sit next to him.

"As much as I would like to blame Bahi's cheap liquor, I can hold my drink." He ran a hand over his face. "I haven't slept well since I woke up from the Nightmare bite. When I close my eyes I see the camp burning if we don't intercept the weapon. My family burning. You burning."

I looked up at the last one. He let out a long exhale.

"You don't have to stay—you know that, don't you? You were right at Shihabian. You're here because I . . . because I got you involved in this. Because I wanted you to stay. But I don't want you to have to die. You could still go. To Izman. Or wherever you want. Get out of this." He was apologizing, only I wasn't mad anymore.

I stared out over the desert. It seemed endless, but the sun was rising to my left, which meant that somewhere, the way I was looking, was Dustwalk. "I reckon I'm where I'm supposed to be."

"You know, I sort of miss the girl who was ready to leave everyone else to save her own skin," Jin said. "She seemed less likely to die doing something stupid and heroic."

"I'm going to go ahead and take that as a compliment." I laughed, but then I stopped. The way I was staring, across the rails, I saw the glint of sunlight off something. "Is that—"

The sky came awake with a scream before I could finish.

We both looked up to see Izz circling the camp and then spiraling down, changing from bird to boy a few feet above the ground as he dropped into a crouch. I was on my feet, turning back toward camp, panic already racing in my chest. But Jin's hands were on my waist. He turned me around quick as a whip. His mouth came down hard and desperate over mine.

His hands burned across the bare skin at the bottom of my spine. His touch sparked along the edge of my clothes. I didn't know if being kissed by him set me alight or if it just turned the fire already in me loose.

He broke away before we were consumed, hands on my face. "Still feeling immortal, Bandit?"

We ran back to the camp. Shazad was already awake and armed. Izz had a wild look in his eyes. "There's a train coming."

Shazad shook her head like she was trying to clear out her mind. "There's no train scheduled before ours," she said, confirming what we were all thinking. I read it in Shazad's face the same moment I thought it.

"They put it on another train." I might as well spit it out. "The weapon is on this one."

• ● •

THERE WAS NO time to rig the tunnels, no time to stop the train so we could get on board. That's what they were counting on. No one talked as we perched on the ridge overlooking the tunnel, waiting for it to come through. At first all I could hear was everyone breathing into the silence, and then breaths mixing with the rattle of rails, and then nothing but the mountain rumbling below our feet as the train raced through the tunnel.

Waiting.

Waiting.

The train burst through in a blast of black smoke.

"Go!"

We half ran, half slid down the mountain and plunged into coal smoke. The black cloud invaded my lungs and my nose, blinded my eyes, so I went sprawling. I was back up and jumping before I had time to feel the sting of the skin stripped from my elbow.

One moment it was stone below my feet, the next it was air. The whole world was suspended.

My feet hit the roof of the train unsteadily and I slid, panic wrapping me up as I fell toward the edge. A hand was around mine, grabbing me. Jin hauled me back up. There was no room to thank him over the deafening noise of the train. I tightened my fingers around his for a moment.

Then we split, his hand tearing out of mine. Shazad and I bolted for the front of the train, Jin, Bahi, and Hala for the back. I didn't look down, not at the rails rushing below us, not at anything, until we were as close to the front as we could get without climbing into the engine.

I eased myself down first, toward the door that would

take us inside, clinging to the outside of the train as it tried to shake me off with every rattling movement, the air howling around my ears.

Shazad landed next to me with the grace of a cat. I checked the pistol on my belt as her hand closed over the handle of her blade.

Terror and excitement battled for my attention. Everything I was feeling was mirrored straight back at me from her eyes. We turned as one.

The door of the carriage burst open under our feet.

Rows of empty seats stared back at us. Dusty glass hurricane lights juddered quietly from the motion of the train. Shazad and I lowered our weapons. One of the windows was shattered, a table overturned.

Wordlessly, we moved forward, my finger on my trigger. My other hand rested on the spare gun on my other side.

We moved through the train together, one empty carriage at a time. Halfway, Shazad gave voice to the fear that had started to grow in my mind. "The others should've made it this far by now."

I flexed my grip around my gun and wished for something to shoot at.

When we wrenched open the next door, a gap an arm's-length wide stretched before the next carriage. Standing on one side of it, I thought it seemed as wide as the Dev's Valley.

I couldn't look down. I wouldn't look down. Not with the rails rushing by in a blur below. But we had to keep going. We needed to find the weapon before it found us.

"Step back," I told Shazad, storing my gun away. "I'll go first." She didn't have time to argue; I grabbed the door frame, swung myself backward, and flung my body forward.

The wind whistled in my ears, daring me to fall.

I crashed into the other carriage. The door didn't give. I stumbled; my arm lashed out. I was grappling through thin air as my heart threatened to drop into my stomach and take my whole body straight into the rails with it.

My hand closed around something solid and metal: a ladder to the left of the door. I heaved myself upright, shaking as I clung to the cold metal bar. All I could see were my hands and the metal. Shazad shouted something I couldn't hear over the wind.

I turned as far as I could to grab on to her hand. Her fingers were on the edge of my eyesight, stretching for me.

The door clattered open. All I saw was a golden uniform that looked like my death.

But Shazad was faster than death.

She dove across empty space. I caught the flash of a knife in her hand and then red across gold and white. If the soldier cried out before he went under the rails, it was lost in the drone of the train.

I didn't see him die. All I saw was Shazad landing too hard on her ankle.

Her foot giving out below her.

The wind grabbing her dark hair, tying it around her neck like a noose.

Her eyes catching mine as she fell toward the rails.

twenty-three

For the longest moment of my life, there was nothing but air between my fingers.

Then my hand clamped over Shazad's wrist. Relief engulfed me as her other arm swung up and her fingers latched onto my arm, like some greater force was drawing us together.

One of Shazad's feet caught on the narrow ledge, just enough for me to keep hold of her. Her weight battled between my grip and gravity as she tried to pull herself out of the dangerous backward lean that could turn into a fall if either of us loosened our grip.

My fingers shook with the will to not let go. She was shouting something that the wind carried away. "I can't hear you!" I screamed back.

"More of you?" There was another voice on the air, like something spiraling out of a dark dream. I'd forgotten about the open door and the uniforms behind it, my back exposed to them so they could put a knife through it any second. "We're practically invaded."

I knew this voice. Sharp and northern and threatening to put a bullet straight through Tamid's leg, holding me at gunpoint, speaking to the Gallan general in Fahali.

Commander Naguib's laugh swirled on the wind.

My eyes locked with Shazad's. I couldn't look away, not even a little bit, not without letting her slip. The rails rushed by below her scrabbling feet, her sheema loose and whipping violently in the air. My arm trembled, try-ing to pull her back to standing.

But Shazad could see everything. She could see behind me straight into the carriage. She just didn't have the gun.

"Someone drag them in," Naguib ordered lazily.

Shazad's eyes went to the gun on my hip and then over my shoulder. I knew exactly what she wanted me to do. I could pull my gun, swing around, and put a bullet straight into Naguib's head.

Only I couldn't do it without dropping her.

Let me go. Her lips shaped the words into the air.

She was willing to kill and die for this cause. Because if Commander Naguib didn't die, we were all dead. From somewhere deep inside me I saw Tamid's face. I wasn't that girl anymore, the one who left people.

My hand tightened on her wrist.

Arms grabbed my waist, dragging me backward, carrying Shazad with me as we were pulled into the safety of the carriage. Well, *safety* wasn't exactly the word.

Hands searched me for weapons. I pressed my forehead into the carpet, panting while they scoured my body. My legs were shaking so badly, I couldn't have stood or fought anyway. It took Shazad's hand on my elbow to help me up.

We were in one of the luxury private carriages. It was filled with neat uniforms and our own battered rebels. I counted about two dozen soldiers.

Two of them were holding Jin. He was on his knees and he looked like he was struggling not to slump onto the floor. But he gave me a weak, rueful smile, which I tried to return.

Hala had a gun to the back of her head, arms tied behind her. At first I didn't see Bahi, and for one stupid second I hoped he had been smart enough to get off the train. Then I recognized him, shirt red at the collar from the blood gushing out of his nose. He barely looked like himself.

And standing by the polished wooden bar like the host of some demented party was Naguib. "Well, this is a sorry little mission." His attention skimmed over me, then veered back. "And if it isn't the blue-eyed bitch. Not allied with the traitor, you said?"

"Circumstances have changed." I picked words Shazad would say, nice and sharp and clean, because if I used my own they might get me shot. "Nothing quite like a gun to the head to make you join the other side, *Commander.*"

"I'm sure." Naguib stepped away from the bar in that unnatural nervous gait. "And I'm sure my *brother* here was very persuasive." His foot lashed out into Jin's ribs on the last word, doubling him over onto the thick red carpet. I didn't react. I wouldn't give Naguib the satisfaction.

"You know"—he straightened his cuffs—"you might as well tell me where my other would-be usurper of a brother is now and spare yourself a lot of misery. After all, I have seven of you, and I only need one of you to talk. In fact, I only need one of you alive at all." He touched the pistol at his hip.

"You're obviously a very poor gambler," Shazad said. I reckoned it was her accent that made Naguib finally notice her.

"Shazad Al-Hamad?"

Shazad batted her eyes at him like we really were guests at a party. "You'll forgive me, have we met?"

His expression curdled. "Of course. I wouldn't expect the great general's only daughter to notice one of the Sultan's many sons. Though many of us noticed *you.*"

"I noticed the sons that mattered," Shazad replied coolly.

I watched the words slice through Naguib the commander, hitting the boy underneath. "Your father will hang for this, you realize. Which is fine with me, since my father has promised that I will be general when he's gone." Naguib reached for Shazad's face. "All thanks to you. But I think I'll deal with you—"

"If you hurt her you will burn in hell." Bahi's voice was thick from the blood clotting his nose. "If you don't believe me, the Demdji will tell you." I realized he meant me. "She can't tell a lie." Naguib's gaze went to me, finally seeming to take in my strange eyes.

"It's true." I spoke without hesitation. Bahi had warned me not to do it. Not to bend the universe by making truths. But now he was asking me to. For Shazad. To keep her alive and safe. "Touch her and you'll die screaming." The second the words fell out of my mouth, they were true. With Bahi's warning, I'd thought it would feel different. That power would surge out of me as I felt my words rearrange the universe to make Shazad safe. But that was the danger. They were just words. They slipped out easily. Like any other words. "Begging for your life."

Naguib's fingers stopped just short of Shazad's chin. Wary at whatever game we were playing.

Bahi caught my eye. "Lying is a sin, after all." Jin snorted.

A laugh burst from my lips, even with the gun to my neck.

"What would you know about sins?" A hollow voice spoke from a corner, cutting off my laughter and sending a slow cold finger down my spine. I squinted into the dark, where all I'd seen was piles of weapons and helmets.

Then one of the old-fashioned suits of armor moved.

The man was made of pure metal. Bronze chain mail hands rippled when his fingers flexed, bronze joints clicked when he walked. Even his face was a smooth mask of copper that caught the sun that blazed through the train windows.

I didn't like the way the soldiers gave him room, as if they were scared of him.

"Sit up straight, preacher boy." The metal lips didn't move when the man talked, but a hollow voice echoed inside the mask, tainted with an accent that sounded an awful lot like he was from the Last County. Bahi struggled to raise his bloody face until two guards forced him up against the wall, slumped and barely standing.

The bronze man reached out and took Bahi's hands, one of them tattooed, the other blank. The metal man tilted his head like a curious bird. As he did, I saw the sliver of skin at his neck. Not a metal man, then. A man dressed in metal.

"Noorsham," Naguib said, on the edge of giving an order.

Noorsham. And then I was standing back in Fahali. In the prayer-house-turned-prison. A boy with a slightly uneven smile chained up to a wall. *I'm special,* he'd told me.

Through the slits in the copper, all I could see was blue. Blue like the desert sky, like the oasis water. Blue like my own eyes.

"You are a traitor." Noorsham's voice was distant as he turned his burning blue gaze back on Bahi. So far removed from the desperate hopeful tone when he'd helped me. I strained against the soldier who held me. "Traitors should be returned to the arms of God. For judgment."

He raised one bronze hand and rested it flat against Bahi's forehead like he was blessing him.

Bahi smiled through bloody, swollen lips. "Sorry to disappoint. I think I've strayed too far to find my way—" And then he was screaming.

Shazad cried out his name.

Before I could move, heat rolled across the carriage in a violent, suffocating wave as I watched the hand against Bahi's forehead turn as bright as an ember. Bahi's skin sizzled and blackened as we all cried out.

The hold on my arms broke. I was two steps to Bahi before the heat was too much. I fell to my knees, gasping.

Bahi's skin turned black and then white. I watched helpless as he turned from a boy into ash.

We'd found our weapon.

twenty-four

The heat vanished. My skin felt fevered. My lungs burned.

I was on all fours, gasping for air, my heart going in time with the rattling of the train below me.

Bahi was dead. He'd died screaming, just like I'd said Commander Naguib would. I'd bent the universe and turned the harm away from Shazad straight onto Bahi. The carriage had gone still now, except for the chandelier above us, slightly singed, swinging frantically from side to side with the motion of the train.

Jin surged forward. One of the soldiers holding him shoved a knee into his spine, forcing him to the ground.

"Restrain him." Naguib was doing his best to sound bored, but there was a waver in his voice. His hair was stuck to his skin with sweat. Hala let out a small sob without moving. "Might I suggest my esteemed foreign brother is next?"

But Noorsham ignored his commander. "Amani." All his attention belonged to me. "You're still alive."

I didn't understand him at first, and then I realized my clothes were charred, blackened, and burned away in places. Only I wasn't. My skin was a Demdji's. Daughters of immortal things didn't burn easily. "I grew up in the desert." My voice shook. "I know heat."

"No." He reached down a metal hand, like he might touch my face. I could feel the heat radiating off it. "You're special, like me."

And it was true, right down to our accents and blue eyes. I couldn't tell him it wasn't. We were both Demdji; we weren't made for lies.

"I want to be alone with her." He raised his voice so Naguib could hear him.

"Like hell." Shazad was unraveled on the carriage floor. But with those two words I knew she still had some fight in her.

"Couldn't have said it better." Jin was struggling back to his knees. Naguib's boot connected with his side again.

"Nobody hurts them." I shouted as Naguib raised his foot again. He stopped, his boot hovering above his brother's ribs. He wasn't a commander with a prisoner then. He was a son who wasn't allowed to compete for his father's respect at the Sultim Trials. Who couldn't command his soldiers' respect and heard behind his back that his rebel brother was a better man than him. And he was taking it out on Jin. "I'll come with you. And while I'm gone, nobody hurts them." I turned back to the pair of blue eyes, set deep in the metal face. Were mine that unsettling to look at? "We got a deal?"

His eyes smiled, but the metal mouth never moved. I wondered if he'd grown up stupidly ignorant of what he was, just like me.

"You've got my word: no one will hurt them while you are gone."

He held out his hand again. It didn't matter that I was a Djinni's daughter; his metal glove still made my palm blister when I clasped it.

• • •

THEY SEARCHED ME twice before they left me alone with him, but they did it hastily. I got the feeling even the soldiers were dying to get away from their Demdji weapon. Then we were alone in the next carriage over, a large dining car. It looked almost exactly like the one I'd eaten in on the train out of Juniper City. Every motion of the train made the glasses clink like a manic chorus of bells. Noorsham sat in a bright red chair while I leaned against the door, as far away from him as I could get.

"You didn't come back," he said finally. "In Fahali. You didn't come back for me." He sounded younger than he had in front of Naguib. And for a moment, the terrifying bronze armor blurred back into the scrawny soldier boy on the floor of the prison.

"I meant to. I wanted to. I tried, but . . ." I was making excuses. A lot of excuses for a broken promise, made when I thought we were both just children of foreign men. Not a defective Demdji and a weapon of destruction. "I know," I said finally. "I'm sorry.

"How come you were locked up?" I asked.

"I wouldn't obey my commander's orders."

"The prayer house," I realized. "You wouldn't burn the prayer house in Dassama." He inclined his head slowly. "How come?" I remembered his disgust at Bahi. "Don't believe anyone holy enough to be at prayers could be a rebel?"

"I knew there wouldn't be any Gallan inside," he said simply.

"The Gallan." I shook my head in confusion. "Why would . . ." Dassama hadn't just been allied to Ahmed; it had been a major base for the Gallan army. The Sultan wasn't trying to burn out the rebellion on behalf of the Gallan. He wasn't using it as a testing site because it was rising in support of Ahmed. He was scouring the foreigners out of his desert. "You're not after us. You're after them."

"The Sultan told me that God was angry that we'd let faithless foreign powers into the desert. He said he needed me to return our land to our people. My fire could clean out the foreign armies, the ones that would harm us, control us, and take from us what isn't theirs."

Who marched in with their blue uniforms and took women and guns alike from this desert.

I thought of standing in the tent with Ahmed, scared

his father was coming for us. How stupid and naive. The Sultan didn't care about a handful of rebels wanting to make a better world. He was making a new world, too. One he didn't have to share.

Something flashed outside the window. Blue wings. A huge blue Roc. Izz circling above the train. He must've realized something was wrong by now.

Noorsham followed my eyes just as Izz flung himself upwards, darting over the top of the train and out of sight.

"You're from Sazi," I said, drawing Noorsham's attention back to me. I pushed myself away from the door and started pacing, keeping his eyes on me. Just because we told the truth didn't mean I couldn't fool him. "I can hear it in your accent. The mines." The pieces were starting to come together: the way the burnt city reminded me of something I couldn't put my finger on. Two great disasters separated by the desert. "It wasn't an accident. It was you."

"I destroyed the mines on the day I discovered my gift." He stood up with the same ponderous motions as a Holy Father. "The day I brought light and wrath down on the wicked."

"And Sazi was wicked, was it?" I traced my finger down the wood of the bar. So long as I was here, my friends stayed alive. So long as I was here, I could buy us some time. I just had to keep him talking. When I glanced out the window, Izz was gone. How long would it take him to figure out we were in trouble?

"You're from the Last County, too," he said. "How good were people where you were from?"

He wasn't wrong. "You've killed more people than anybody in the Last County ever did."

Noorsham spread his hands and the tightly woven chain mail caught the light. "I was chosen for greater things. This is my purpose."

I recoiled. *Greater things.* It sounded too close to things I'd said to Tamid about leaving Dustwalk. About there being another life out there. One that wasn't so small and pointless and short. The things I'd thought in the rebel camp. I could share an accent with someone who killed so gleefully, but I wasn't willing to share my words. "What'd they do to you, anyhow, the wicked folks of Sazi?"

For a second, even made of metal, he looked human. "Do you remember seven years ago, when the Gallan army came through?" His fingers tapped out a rhythm on the bar as he walked toward me.

"The Gallan army came through more than once," I said. I didn't dare move away from him.

"Don't you pretend you don't remember." His accent stumbled, and I heard the Last County thicker than ever. His tongue righted itself again. "This time was different."

"I remember," I admitted, even though I didn't want to. It was a drought year. The restlessness went bone deep, and there were more of the foreigners in their blue uniforms than usual. "My mama and I hid under the house for a whole day. She tried to make me think it was a game. But I was old enough to understand some of why."

Noorsham nodded. "My sister Rabia was old enough, too," he said. "And then when the army was gone, folks up on the mountain got together and tossed stones at her and all the other girls for lying with foreign men. Until they were lying dead. And my mama let them."

I had nothing to say to that.

"For years I waited for God to punish them. I prayed. I'd never figured the punishment would come from me." His words reminded me of the Holy Father's voice blistering through the masses on prayer days. I even used to hear the wild religious fervor on Tamid's tongue sometimes.

"I'd been out of the mines for a while. I was too sick to work. I tried to go, but my mama wouldn't let me and I didn't have any fight in me. When I came back all the other men were looking at me sideways. They kept asking after Suha, my other sister. By lunchtime one of them got drunk enough to tell me. While I'd been sick, we'd run low on money. And my mama had been afraid of starving to death, so she sold Suha as a whore to the men in the mine. The same ones who'd killed Rabia for lying with foreigners. And as I found out, I felt it all rush out of me, a light sent from a higher power, destroying them and leaving me whole."

Like hell.

Noorsham stopped pacing, a foot away from me. The unchangeable features of his bronze mask were calm. But one single bronze fist was clenched tightly in anger. I felt the anger with him. For the folks in Dustwalk who had hanged my mother. Who had hanged Dalala. Who would've let someone like Fazim or my uncle have me.

"After that, Prince Naguib found me. I had been huddled on the mountain, awaiting my next order from God, and he came. And he took me to our exalted Sultan, who explained to me that my fire was a gift. That it would kill the sinful and spare the worthy."

"Fire doesn't know good from evil any more than a bullet does." I couldn't stop myself.

He tilted his head, like a puzzled bird. "You're still alive," he said.

"That ought to be proof enough." I leaned back against the bar, hiding my shaking hands as I gripped the edge. "And I reckon you know it, too. Why else did they have you all chained up in Fahali? How come they've got you all trussed up in your armor now? I reckon you know as well as I do, being from the Last County, we put bronze in with the iron to make Buraqi obedient." The Gallan army that was hunting for the rebel camp was stationed in Dassama. They had meant to burn that, too. Only Noorsham wouldn't. So they had taken him back to Izman and they had made him bronze armor. "Seems like he thinks you need to be made to obey, too. You want to know what I think? Naguib's afraid of you." And I couldn't blame him. "He's just using you. You're a common weapon."

Noorsham's fingers twitched. "You sound real sure of yourself."

"Because I'm right." I grasped for something to say, some truth I could give him. There was no point telling him he was a Demdji, not a weapon of God. Or that he was fighting for the wrong side. He could say the same to me. He believed in the Sultan; I believed in the Rebel Prince.

Jin had told me once there was no arguing against belief. It was a foreign language to logic. And Djinni's daughter or not, I reckoned he could still burn me alive if he decided I was on the other side.

I needed to get out of here. I shoved myself off from the bar and paced to the window. I could still see Izz, flying high above. The window came open with a tug, letting cool air in.

"What are you doing?"

"I'm hot." I said, pulling my sheema free from my neck. I released my red sheema, stolen off a clothesline in Sazi, letting it whip out into the sand like a bloody flag. I prayed Izz would see it and understand.

"Is this a trick?" He sounded so young again.

"You don't have to let them use you." My voice took on a desperate note as I turned back to face him. "Prince Ahmed, if he were Sultan, he could expel the Gallan, too. Without killing so many people. He has people like us on his side, too. Only he doesn't use us to raze cities. We're not weapons; we're soldiers."

"I'm not a weapon," Noorsham said.

Maybe Jin was right. Maybe there was no arguing with belief. I looked out the window again. Izz was lower now, keeping pace with the train. "So how come," I asked, steadying myself against the bar, "you can't take the armor off?" His fingers flew to the clasp on the side of the mask that was welded shut just as Izz, in the shape of a giant Roc, flung himself at the train.

The train rocked sideways so hard, I thought we might

tip straight off the rails. I crashed into the bar, knocking the air straight out of me. I heard metal tear, and from the corner of my eye I saw a piece of the carriage wall ripped away in Izz's razor talons.

I bolted to the narrow opening, desert sprawled on all sides.

Then a shape in bright desert clothes launched herself into the sand. Shazad landed in a practiced roll, on her feet before she vanished from my sight, two soldiers following her out. A golden girl grappling with a soldier hit the sand next.

The door banged open. Naguib rushed in, coming to find Noorsham. I moved with the sort of speed that usually belonged to Shazad, reaching across the bar. My hand fastened around the neck of a bottle. I turned, swinging it, narrowly missing Naguib's face. He grabbed my wrist, wrenching it downward. I felt a shot of pain through my whole body and screamed. The bottle shattered against the ground, distracting him long enough for me to pull free.

Someone called my name. Jin was standing in the doorway. A huge hole torn in the train separated the two carriages, but damn him, was he thinking of coming for me?

"Go!" I shouted at him. "I'll be right behind." He knew better than to argue with me. He jumped as I started to run for the tear in the side of the carriage.

I wasn't far behind him, my arms bracing either side of the gap in the wall.

Noorsham.

I glanced backward. He'd been knocked sideways by the blow. There was a dent in the metal helmet he wore, but he was righting himself. I glimpsed through the gap that we were coming up on a canyon, where the rails crossed over the chasm.

I had to jump. Now. But I couldn't leave Noorsham. I couldn't leave him alive. I couldn't leave him here in Naguib's hands. I had to kill him. Or save him. Our blue eyes locked across the debris littering the carriage.

The noise inside me sounded like Bahi's scream, begging me to cross the carriage and rip off his mask, drag him away. But the valley was almost under us; I might have already waited too long.

If I went back they'd have me trapped and there wouldn't be time to jump.

If I jumped now, I might go over anyway.

I was damned either way.

I flung myself through the rip in the carriage. The wind caught me, tossed me. I hit the ground and my body exploded into a constellation of pain. Momentum carried me through the sand as easily as if it were air; I was in too much agony to fight it. My vision cleared just in time for me to see the canyon gape open to swallow me. My empty fingers scraped through the sand. I fought for purchase that wasn't there to stop my body. There was nothing to cling to but sand.

My legs went over, taking the rest of me with them.

twenty-five

My fingers caught on something. I felt a tug of falling in my stomach as I willed my injured hand to hold on. My body swung against the canyon wall and I heard my ribs connect with the sickening noise of bones breaking. I cried out, agony taking me over. For a moment all I could do was hang, eyes shut, breath shallow, telling myself not to look down. Willing my hand to hang on.

Only then I realized I didn't know what I was holding on to.

I was shaking so hard, I could barely move. It seemed like it took forever to open my eyes. I tipped my head back slowly, like any move might throw me off balance and send me hurtling to the bottom of the chasm.

I'd grabbed hold of the sand. Or rather, the sand had

grabbed hold of me. An arm made of sand had clamped around my wrist. It was holding on to my life.

I dropped my head, squeezing my eyes shut. Trying to remember how my lungs ought to work. How fast my heart ought to beat.

I'd seen dozens of things born from the sand and the wind and the spirits in the desert in my sixteen years. I'd heard every story, about immortals and ghouls alike that came from the sand. But this was something new. And it felt wholly foreign and entirely familiar at once.

This wasn't a creature from the sands. This was me.

I took a deep breath. My ribs stretched into an endless ache that wrapped around my whole body. I swung my left arm up, the motion ripping a cry out of me, catching the sand-arm by the wrist, trying to pretend I didn't feel grains of it slipping between my fingers.

Slow as the setting sun, it recoiled into the sand, dragging me up with it. My hand started slipping and a new sand-arm snaked out from the desert, grabbing me. And then another. A dozen hands held me, pulling at my clothes, my arms. Pulling me back to the desert.

And then I was up, lying flat on my stomach. I crawled away from the edge, my body shaking. I didn't know if it was pain or something greater waiting to crash into me. Something my body knew before my mind. I was blank. Watching without grasping it. Around me, a dozen arms of sand disintegrated. I flinched.

Nothing else moved. Not even me. Then I reached toward a heap of sand that had saved my life. I hadn't even touched it before it began to rise toward my palm, like the snakes in baskets called by charmers.

So this was the kind of Demdji I was.

A gun went off. The sand collapsed as I spun toward the sound. The world poured back in around me all at once. There were bodies in the sand already. I was just in time to see Shazad jab her elbow into a man's throat, whirling to catch him in the gut with a knife. A soldier came at her from the right.

"No!"

I wasn't empty anymore. I was furious. The sand lashed up, exploding between them, sending them both sprawling. I ran for Shazad as it settled.

She was finishing coughing up desert dust when I dropped to my knees next to her. When she saw me she starting hacking all over again. "I thought you were dead! I saw you go over," she got out between coughs. "I saw you fall."

To our right a gun went up. Without thinking, I flung out my hand; a wave of sand sent the soldier sprawling. Buried him. His gun skittered to my feet. I didn't pick it up. The rush made me feel dizzy and drunk and scared all at once. It was like I'd just grown another limb I wasn't fully in control of yet.

I clasped Shazad's hand, pulling her up. I was still shaking too hard to find words. When I turned, the sand at my feet turned with me—I knew it without looking. I *felt* it. Like I always had, without knowing that I was. The desert all around me, the sand like a living thing, calling to me, begging me to use it. To be part of it.

The fighting had stopped, but I couldn't.

"Amani." Shazad's grip slipped out of mine. The sand was moving underneath me, a swirl like a tiny sandstorm, and then it was getting bigger, rising, rising until it was all around me, pulling at my hair, my clothes, calling me into it, into the desert.

To drown in it.

I couldn't breathe. I couldn't control it. There was too much of it. I couldn't breathe.

A new hand closed over mine, and this time it was flesh and bone. Jin appeared through the sand, his sheema wrapped tightly around his face as he pushed his way through blindly. I saw he was holding something metallic a second before his arms went around me and he pulled me into his chest. He was saying something I couldn't hear over the storm. All I felt was his hand press into my arm. It was a bullet, cool and hard, the iron biting into my bare skin.

The cold of it cut through the heat in me.

The sand dropped away, spiraling down and down and down until it was back under my feet and I could hear Jin's heartbeat under my forehead, feel the pain of the bullet pressing into my flesh too hard, hear him whispering my name over and over again in my ear until I stopped shaking.

twenty-six

We finally stopped flying a few hours before dawn to
let Izz get some rest from carrying the four of us.
We were halfway between home and where we'd jumped off
the train. It was open empty desert on all sides, though I
could see the mountains of the Dev's Valley on the horizon.
We didn't unpack supplies or even build a fire. Everyone collapsed where they stood. Izz turned into a huge catlike beast
I'd never seen before and fell asleep. Shazad leaned against
him. Her eyes were red, even though I hadn't seen her crying.

Jin sat down next to me without a word. There was
something in his hands. The red sheema, I realized. The
one I'd let go out the window. He took my right arm, gently, without asking. My hand was swollen and tender,
but I'd almost stopped noticing the constant throbbing.

Sprained. Not broken. The place where my ribs had connected with the canyon wall had faded to a dull ache. I felt Bahi's absence like a badly stitched wound as Jin's hands worked, clumsy with exhaustion, binding my hand with my sheema. He tied it off, his fingers skimming over the cloth before he set my hand down gently.

"You all right?" he asked.

"It'll heal."

We both knew that wasn't what he'd been asking, but Jin let it pass anyway.

"Can you shoot left-handed?"

"If I have to," I said.

Jin held his pistol out to me. "Do you want it?" I stared at the gun in his hands, but I didn't snatch it up like I would've once. Yesterday. "You've worked it out, haven't you?"

"It's because of the iron." I took the gun by the leather handle, careful not to touch the metal. I thought of the way he'd pressed a bullet to my skin as the sand was rising. Just one touch and I was stripped powerless because of the thing that had shaped my whole life, with or against my will. It was like the Buraqi and the metal horseshoes: so long as I had iron against my skin, I couldn't touch my Demdji powers. "It's the reason I got through my whole life without knowing I was a Demdji. Because I'm from Dustwalk." *The girl who taught herself to shoot a gun. Until she could knock down a row of tin cans like they were nothing and the gun was everything.* "Because I'm the girl with the gun." And Noorsham was the boy from the iron mines. He said he'd been sick. Sick enough to leave the mines and stop inhaling iron dust for a little while, maybe. So that when he went back to work, he did it as a Demdji.

"From the town where even the water tastes like iron." And when they'd been afraid of Noorsham in Fahali, iron was what they'd chained him with. Jin's hand was clenching and unclenching around nothing. His knuckles were torn up, and the motion was making the scabs break all over again. That had to be painful.

"Bet you weren't counting on all this being so damn complicated when you abducted me from that godforsaken place."

"I didn't *abduct* you!" At least he'd stopped punishing his knuckles raw. He realized I was baiting him a moment too late. His shoulders eased. The cautious angry fragility wasn't something either of us could keep up long.

"You abducted me a little bit." It was like we were back with the Camel's Knees, except there was no more pretending about what I was.

I wasn't going to craft illusions out of the air or twist people's minds or change my shape. Those were the powers of Djinn in the stories where they tricked men and one another. Then there were the other stories. Massil and the sand that filled the sea in a fit of Djinni anger. The golden city of Habadden burned by the Djinn for its corruption. Just like Noorsham did. I wondered if I could bury the sea in sand, too.

"Noorsham's eyes are the same color as mine," I blurted out. I couldn't be the only one who'd put it all together. "He's about my age. He was born spitting distance from where I was." I couldn't be the only one thinking it. "Dustwalk to Sazi, that's only a few hours as the Buraqi rides. How far do you reckon that is as the Djinni walks? He's my brother, isn't he?"

"Amani. No matter what he is, he's not your family. Family and blood aren't the same thing."

"If that's true, how come you didn't shoot Naguib in Dustwalk?" The truth showed on his face, just long enough for me to read it. "I don't want my brother to have to die either, Jin." We understood each other. His brother and mine were both just the Sultan's weapons.

Jin put his hands on my face. "We don't have to do anything. He's after the Gallan. You don't have to stop him." I was so used to Jin's unwavering certainty. The hitch in his voice, the tentativeness of his hand on my face, this was unfamiliar ground. "We could retreat. Live to fight another day."

"We'd just be living to die another day." I leaned my forehead into his. "Noorsham—we have to stop him. If the Sultan has a weapon like that, it's only a matter of time before he cuts his way through the foreigners and comes for us, too. We might never get another chance." I wasn't even sure what I meant by "stop him." Kill him? Rescue him? Save him? "They're headed to the Gallan camp," I said, and the moment I did, I knew I was right. "They're going to kill them. We can get there first."

"I'm not that inclined to save any Gallan soldiers," Hala interrupted. "I've been a Demdji in an occupied country longer than you have. They all deserve to burn, if you ask me. We should take care of our own."

"And Fahali?" I looked around the group of tired, ragged rebels. "What about all the people there? They're headed back there to burn out the Gallan. A lot of desert folks will burn with them."

No one answered me.

"We need to sleep." Jin ran his hands over his face. I felt that exhaustion, too. It was soul deep. "Nobody makes smart decisions in the dark. We sleep and tomorrow we head back to camp. Tell Ahmed about the weapon. And then we decide."

• • •

TOMORROW WOULD BE too late. I knew that down in my gut as I lay between the desert and the stars, dead tired and too alive with thought to sleep.

Nobody made smart decisions in the dark, Jin said. A stupid decision in the dark was how I'd wound up dressed as a boy in Deadshot. I'd make it all over again if I had to. It hadn't even been a decision, really. And neither was this.

I was up before I knew for sure what I was thinking of doing. In the light of the embers I started to pack supplies. Enough for a day's walk across the desert.

"Running away like a thief in the night?" My gun leapt into my hand. Shazad was still leaning against the blue furred beast that was Izz, but her eyes were open now, watching me. I didn't know how long she'd been awake.

"You planning on stopping me?" We both knew she could and that I wasn't going to shoot. Still, I didn't drop my gun right away, even clumsy as it was in my left hand.

"He's my brother, Shazad. It's my responsibility. And I can warn them. Even if I can't do anything else, I can—"

"I don't want to stop you." Shazad pushed herself to sitting. "I'm just offended you didn't ask me to come with you."

"Is that the smart thing to do, General?" But I could feel the fire taking light in me again. The one that'd been trampled by fear and Bahi's loss. And I could see it in Shazad.

"No," Shazad admitted. She reached for her weapons and started buckling the scimitars over her shoulders. "The smart thing would be to let the Sultan wear himself out fighting his allies and hope that they catch on and kill him, leaving an empty throne for Ahmed." She tightened the buckle on her second sword. "But Naguib recognized me. So I don't have time to wait around for that. If we don't stop him, he'll send news to the Sultan—and my father, my mother, and my brother will all burn like Bahi. Then he will come for the rest of us. Besides"—she reached a hand for me and I clasped it, pulling her to her feet—"it's the right thing to do."

I might be tangled with Jin. But with Shazad it was simpler. We were tied together.

She turned to Jin now, sprawled by the fire, his hat pulled over his eyes. "I can tell you're awake. Are you coming with us?"

He sighed, tipping his hat backward. "Yeah, yeah. Just trying to get some sleep before going to near certain death."

"I think thieves in the night are meant to be quieter than this, you know," Hala muttered from her side of the campfire. "What exactly is your plan to get us all killed, General?"

"Simple. We get them to destroy each other." We all

stared at her, waiting. It seemed to take her a second to realize she was two steps ahead of the rest of us. "The Sultan might be aiming to drive out the Gallan, but he doesn't want open war. That's why he's trying to blame Noorsham's destruction on us. If the Gallan soldiers *see* Noorsham, see that he's the Sultan's weapon and not ours, then open war is what the Sultan will get. He'll lose his alliance with the Gallan. And that leaves us with just the Sultan to usurp, not a whole foreign army after us, too. All we have to do is kill Noorsham before he kills them."

"Or us," Hala pointed out. "So it's five of us against two armies and an insane Demdji superweapon."

I looked around the circle of faces in the dark. At Shihabian two days ago—God, was it only two days?—I'd felt like an imposter. Like a part that didn't quite fit in this rebellion, no matter how much I wanted to. Jin's foolish Blue-Eyed Bandit who gave up the city without knowing what she was giving it up for. The Demdji without powers who couldn't save anyone. But now, standing in this circle, I felt it, the thing that made them all stay and risk their lives. Being a link in the chain.

"Yeah, I guess it is," I said.

"There's an old expression," Shazad said. She might not want to be called General, but it was written all over her. She surveyed her small army: a shape-shifter, a gold-skinned girl, a foreign prince, and a blue-eyed bandit. "About fighting fire with fire. It never made much sense to me. But fighting fire with Demdji who don't burn so easily, that might work."

twenty-seven

Noorsham was impossible not to see first. Even from far away, I tracked his progress by the sun glinting off the brass helmet with the barrel of the rifle.

It was only half a day's walk from the railroad outpost to Fahali. We'd landed on the mountain just after dawn. It was close to noon now, the sun high over the scene. Every once in a while I could just make out Izz's shadow dashing across the mountain face as he circled slowly. Waiting for his chance.

I tracked the barrel of my gun along from Noorsham, through the soldiers. There were a few dozen of them. And there was Naguib.

My finger tightened on the trigger.

"Not even you can make that shot, Bandit." Jin's voice

in my ear eased my finger off the trigger. "He's still out of range." As soon as my finger was away from the metal of the trigger, the terrifying, dizzying sensation of having an entire desert at my fingertips, ready to rip out of control, rushed back. My powers were still too much of a liability, Shazad had declared in the end. I didn't know enough about what I was doing to be any kind of help as a Demdji just yet.

I let out a long breath. Just as I did, Noorsham's head swiveled, swinging up toward us. I could swear he looked straight at our hiding place. Next to me, Shazad sucked in a breath.

He couldn't see us, I reminded myself.

Hala was making sure of that. She lay on the rock next to me, eyes closed. I could see the strain in her face that holding on to every soldier's mind at once took. Fixing an illusion there so that all they saw when they looked to the cliffs above Fahali was an empty mountain.

As Noorsham's head tipped up I saw the flash of skin where the bronze mask didn't quite meet the armor at his throat. It was a harder shot than a glass bottle in a pistol pit at the other end of the desert. I was just praying it wasn't a shot I was going to have to take.

The plan was simple. Use Hala's illusions to draw Noorsham away from his little army and into revealing the Sultan's treachery to the Gallan. Then kill Noorsham and run, leaving Naguib and General Dumas to face each other.

Simple as saving an entire city of Mirajin and destroying a two-decade-old foreign treaty. Simple as murdering my brother. Killing Noorsham was the hard part. I was glad it belonged to Izz. I only had the gun in case he failed. In case I got a clear shot.

General Dumas had said it himself. He had a long history of killing folks with royal blood. It just wouldn't be the prince he'd thought.

Without Noorsham, Naguib had nothing to face the Gallan army with, a small rabble of Miraji soldiers against the general's troops. He would be killed, or captured. And one way or another, from the death of a Miraji prince or the betrayal of the Sultan, there would be war.

I only had the gun in case I got the chance to kill my brother.

No. I stopped that thought. Jin was right. Family and blood weren't the same. I might not want to see Noorsham die, but this was a war. What I wanted didn't matter.

My heart pounded between my backbone and the rock I was flattened against as Naguib's small army advanced toward Fahali.

Next to me, Jin was frowning at something in his hand. Craning over, I realized he was holding the beat-up brass compass. The needle was swinging frantically. The way I'd only seen it do once, when the two were close together for the first time.

"Why's it doing that?" I whispered. The army was close now, close enough that anything louder might carry down the canyon.

"It means Ahmed is on the move. Only there's no reason Ahmed ought to know what we're doing."

"Delila told him," I realized aloud. She'd told me how she used to lie awake at night, trying to say out loud that Jin was alive. That he was safe. That he would be home soon. That it would only come out if it were the truth. We were in enough trouble that one of those wasn't true. And Ahmed was coming to find us.

"We have to get out of here before Ahmed can reach us." Jin shoved the compass into his pocket. I had a sudden surge of resentment from nowhere. That he got to keep his brother alive while I was aiming a gun at mine.

"Hala," Shazad ordered. "Now."

"Oh, it's that easy, is it?" Hala said sarcastically. But she sucked in a breath all the same and then twisted three dozen minds to see the same thing.

We shared the illusion with all of Naguib's men that the gates of the city were swinging open, letting out a dozen men in Gallan uniforms. All I could see was the tops of their uniform caps as I craned over the edge of the canyon and watched them ride toward Naguib's army, their horses kicking up sand.

They weren't real. But they were enough to fool anyone who didn't know. To confuse the real Gallan soldiers. Who I could now see climbing onto the city's walls. Looking over the soldiers they thought were their allies, riding toward illusions.

Naguib leaned forward and said something to his weapon. Noorsham dismounted and started walking out to meet the Gallan soldiers. A safe enough distance that he wouldn't burn up his own side with the enemy.

Almost there. Another step. He raised his hands. *Almost. Almost.*

The heat struck like a physical blow. I could feel it, even perched above the illusion. I swayed back; everyone else did, too. The first thing I saw was the sand turning black at his feet. The second thing was the illusion of the Gallan soldiers screaming. Screaming like Bahi had screamed. Screams planted in Naguib's army's mind by Hala. Even as she filled the air with the smell of burning.

Noorsham advanced.

A few more steps. My heart hammered.

His hands were raised, like he was blessing them.

And another step.

The heat swept across the sand and hit the walls of the city. Hit the real Gallan soldiers. Suddenly the screams turned real. The smell of burning snagged the corner of Hala's attention. Not long, but enough. Enough for the illusion to waver.

One of the soldiers called something out, pointing straight at us, as our invisibility slipped. Guns swiveled toward us. I rolled away from the edge of the canyon a moment before the first bullet clipped the stone. I was on my feet, pistol back up.

High above, Izz screeched. The illusion vanished altogether, a second before Izz crashed down from the sky into Noorsham. The small bronze figure slammed into the ground as Izz transformed into a giant ape. I turned my head away. I didn't want to see Izz's fist crunch through copper and skull.

"Izz!" Hala's cry drew my eyes back.

Noorsham was rising to his feet. Izz was still on the sand, turned back to a boy. For a second I though he was dead, and then he rolled. My own skin stung at the sight of the angry red burn mark across his neck.

Noorsham raised his hand over Izz's head.

I shouted his name.

It was drowned out by another screech. A huge brown Roc with a blue tuft of feathers on his head crested the canyon.

Maz. And Ahmed riding on his back.

Maz dove straight for his brother. Noorsham was already raising his other hand toward him. The tips of his wings caught fire. *No!*

I was on my feet in a second, teetering at the edge of the drop from our mountain perch. Noorsham was in my sights now, and my finger was on the trigger.

The bullet hit him square in the breastplate. Noorsham stumbled back. His head reared up. Even this far away I could see his eyes, spots of blue behind the mask. He saw me.

He raised his hands like he was reaching out to a long-lost friend.

The blow of the heat carried me off my feet.

twenty-eight

$S$and was under my back and I was staring at the sky. The same color as my eyes, as Noorsham's eyes. He'd knocked me clean off the face of the mountain.

It was a twenty-foot drop. I ought to be dead. But I remembered sand surging up to catch me, just as I lost consciousness for a moment.

I dragged myself to my elbows, my whole body protesting. I could see Jin and Shazad craning over above me. Jin moved forward as if to jump off after me, but Ahmed pulled him away from the wall of the canyon as a bullet struck. Ahmed and Maz had landed safely. Why weren't they running? Why weren't they flying away? Were the twins too injured?

Another bullet hit near my elbow.

I rolled on instinct. My fingers scrambled for my own gun. I must've dropped it when I fell.

Naguib's small army was moving up the mountain, toward our rabble.

It wouldn't be a fair fight even without Demdji, but they had Noorsham. I could see him now. It would be a clear shot if I had a gun. But I didn't.

I shifted my sore fingers. The red sheema was still tied around my right hand like a brace. I unknotted it quickly, wrapping it around my neck. I felt the sand shift around me in response to my every move. I had no idea what I was doing. I'd spent the last sixteen years as the girl with the gun, not a Demdji. I saw what Hala did, creating new worlds in people's minds. Delila bending reality. Noorsham turning the world to fire.

Like it was second nature.

A gun felt like second nature to me; this didn't. But this was raw power that was part of me, not something I'd learned. Something ancient in me that tugged toward the sand. My father's bloodline that stretched back to a time before death.

Across the sands, my eyes met Noorsham's. He was extending one blazing hand toward my friends. He was going to burn them all alive.

I whipped my hands up, pouring every scrap of my energy and focus through them and into my newfound power. The sand roared up like a wall. It sliced behind Noorsham, cutting between him and the rest of Naguib's men. Between him and my people.

Exhilaration surged through me. I'd done it. My whole body was shaking. Sweat from the effort was streaking my face. My throat tasted like rising bile. Noorsham was right: I *was* like him. This was the sort of power that could level cities. That I couldn't control. That could slip away too easily and take revenge against a whole backward Last County town. That could fill the sea with sand out of spite.

I heaved the sand up higher, splitting Noorsham and me off from the army once and for all. We were on one side and Naguib and the rebels were on the other.

Now it was an even fight.

Noorsham raised his hands, and the ground at my feet blackened. I staggered backward. Beyond the wall of sand I heard a gunshot and a cry. I prayed that bullet had found one of Naguib's men.

Noorsham turned at the sound. Heat surged off him, striking the churning wall of sand. I flung my arms up, squeezing my eyes shut even as the sand turned to glass, peppering my arms, my scalp, my legs. When I looked up, my arms were bloody.

"Amani." Noorsham's voice sounded from deep inside the brass armor. "Why are you fighting me? It's not you I'm after. It's them." He spread his arms expansively, encompassing the Gallan soldiers and the rebellion.

"Them, and an entire city of your own people."

I had to lead him away from them. I took a staggering step backward, dragging the sandstorm wall with me, forcing Noorsham forward. Drawing him away from the fight. This came down to the two of us.

This was Demdji business. We took care of our own.

I felt searing pain across my leg where a bullet grazed my calf. I screamed as I dropped to my knees.

Just the touch of iron was enough.

My grip on the sand loosened. The storm separating us from the fight fell. I held my breath, trying to control it, but I'd lost it.

I could see the fight now. Rebels against Naguib's army. Half of Naguib's men were fighting invisible opponents, ones that existed only in their minds thanks to Hala. The twins shifted from one shape to another, huge leathery beasts to small birds, talons digging into a man's eyes. Shazad was fighting two men at once, her swords spinning in a blur that turned from steel to red in one motion. Jin and Ahmed were back-to-back, moving in sync as if they had spent their whole lives doing it. And I supposed they had.

They were holding their own. But Noorsham was already turning toward them, ready to level the battlefield. I reached for my power again. The barrel of a gun against my neck drew me up short. The kiss of iron turning me into a human again.

"You will put your hands on your head." I recognized General Dumas's heavily accented voice without having to look up.

I did as I was told for once in my life.

It was a matter of moments before I was surrounded by two dozen Gallan soldiers, armed and armored. Ready for battle.

My eyes were fixed on Noorsham. He was standing perfectly still a few paces away. His back was still blessedly turned to the battle raging between his army and my mismatched group of Demdji and rebels. His head was cocked like a curious bird as he watched me with the Gallan.

General Dumas walked a slow circle around me, the barrel of the pistol dragged along my head, never leaving my skin, until it was pointed squarely at my forehead. Until he was blocking my view of the fight. And of Noorsham.

He ripped the sheema from my neck and handed it to someone else. They tied it around my eyes. Blindfolding me.

The last thing I saw before the world disappeared was the general raising his gun to kill me.

I closed my eyes.

twenty-nine

A scream came instead of a gunshot.

I felt the cold metal of the gun leave my forehead. I grabbed the moment, flinging myself to one side in the sand. I ripped the sheema off my eyes as I moved. The sight that awaited me was horrifying and glorious all at once.

General Dumas was burning. Burning the way Bahi had. As he dropped to his knees I saw Noorsham behind him, one hand raised, like a Holy Father in the middle of a blessing. The Gallan soldiers turned their guns on him. Shots went off. Most bullets missed harmlessly, badly aimed in the frantic shooting. One or two hit his breast-plate, leaving a dent but nothing more.

The Gallan soldier nearest me wasn't rushing, though.

He was taking his time, taking his aim. I could see the line of the shot. I could see it would be a clean hit.

His finger squeezed the trigger even as I whipped my hand up. The sand below his feet exploded, throwing him off balance. His cry drew Noorsham's attention. A second later it turned to a scream of pain as the soldier burned.

One of the Gallan turned toward me, gun already halfway up. My hands moved on instinct, like they did with a gun. Like this was as familiar as the feeling of a trigger.

A body made out of sand surged up in answer. I twitched my fingers and its arms grabbed the soldier around the neck, yanking him down to the ground.

Another sand body formed itself and surged into the fight. A soldier fired, but the bullet passed harmlessly through its chest before the sand creature was on top of him, pulling the gun away. Then another sand creature, and another, until I had half a dozen of them clawing at the soldiers as Noorsham burned them one by one. I moved like a sandstorm, like I'd seen Shazad with a blade. Except the whole desert was my weapon, my feet spinning the sand moving with me. I dodged a blade and whipped my hand up, the sand scattering into the soldier's face.

And then everything was quiet.

I looked around. In the chaos, I realized the fight had brought us into the walls of Fahali. The Gallan soldiers were gone. It was just me and Noorsham left. We were facing each other down an empty city street, cleared by the fight. Folks had retreated inside their homes. I saw a flash of movement in one of the windows. Someone watching us.

The sun glinted off his armor. There was a dent near his heart where my last bullet had hit him. It might leave a bruise.

With the rush of the sand gone, everything went too still, too quiet.

"What now?" Noorsham asked. The lilt of his words was Last County. Everything about him ached with familiarity. Of the town I'd left. Of the desert heat that lived in my very skin. Of our eyes that looked like a clear desert sky on fire. Of the bloodline we shared, which remembered a sky without stars and an ancient war.

I could hear the sound of running feet. We weren't done here yet. Fahali was a border city. It had a large guard. Noorsham raised his hand, already starting to glow red.

"Noorsham! You don't want to do this." My heart was still rushing. He hesitated.

"Noorsham," a voice from above called. We both looked the same way at once. Naguib was standing over us. He stood by the city's gate. He'd extracted himself from the fight with the rebels to find his weapon. "You are not finished."

Two dozen more Gallan soldiers burst into the street, surrounding us, guns leveled, shouting in their guttural language. I reached for the sand. Their general was dead. He couldn't give them the order to shoot. But one of them would get trigger happy soon enough.

Naguib raised his hand. A bronze ring glinted there, the same stuff that Noorsham's armor was made of. There were words marked on it. Noorsham's true name, I realized. Like Atiyah'd had her Djinni lover's true name. Like all the stories where a greedy merchant or too-proud ruler sought to control some Djinni he chanced upon in the desert. The secrets the Djinn guarded jealously but that had a way of slipping out to the women they loved.

And it was my true name, too, I realized. Our father's name.

"Burn the city."

Noorsham's blue eyes turned back to me. I saw that we understood each other. He didn't want to kill me. He raised his hands toward me, like he wanted to embrace me or bless me or burn me. The slightest gesture scalded the air close to my face.

I knew what I needed to do. And I had one shot at it.

There was sand stuck to my hands. I shifted my fingers ever so slightly. I felt the sand answer even as the heat coming off Noorsham built, even against his will, even as he tried to hold it back. The barrels of the Gallan guns swung between me and Noorsham uncertainly. His fire was inching toward me. Toward my feet. I gathered the sand in my fingers into a bullet.

The world came into that familiar focus. Like I was a desperate girl standing in the pistol pit in Deadshot all over again.

I had one last shot.

I had good aim.

I moved in one motion, whipping my hand forward like a gunshot. The sand went with it. Not a violent, uncontrolled burst this time.

One clean bullet.

It hit Noorsham's face, sending him staggering back with a cry as the bullet burst back into dust and the heat faded.

I held my breath as Noorsham looked up. The lock on the side of the mask was loose. The force of the sand had knocked it open. I watched as Noorsham's hands came up to his face, shaking. The bronze mask that encircled his whole head came off.

He looked terribly young without it. As young as he had when he'd been just a blue-eyed, smart-mouthed boy from the shop in Dustwalk. A kid I'd figured was fragile and human and destined to die.

I'd been wrong on all counts.

"This city's not the one who ought to burn," he said, raising his hand toward Naguib.

The heat rolled off him in one angry wave, rocking everything in its path. The Gallan guns leveled on Noorsham. I pulled both my hands up, dragging the desert with them. Shielding him from the bullets as his fire crashed toward our enemy.

Naguib screamed.

thirty

I was born in the desert. The desert was part of me. That was all I remembered of the fight that followed. Chaos and sand and gunshots that didn't hit me. And when all my enemies were gone I slumped back against a wall, too tired to care if anyone wanted to shoot me or burn me alive.

"Amani." My eyes flew open. Jin was standing in the gates to Fahali. His face cleared as he saw me, and he ran toward me, relief written all over him. "Thank God."

"You don't believe in God," I said. It came out half a croak just as he closed the last of the space between us with a kiss.

A throat cleared behind us. We tore apart.

The twins were standing a few feet away with matching crossed arms. They looked a little singed, but otherwise no worse for wear. "Is that the congratulations we're going to get for surviving?" Maz asked. "Because I'm not sure how I feel about that."

Izz's hair stuck up. "I know how *I* feel about it."

"And I know how *I* feel about breaking both your noses." Shazad shoved Izz with one hand without breaking stride. Hala trailed in her wake, golden skin smeared red with blood. I realized the fighting was done. And we were all still alive. I wanted to cry in relief. Shazad sheathed her scimitar before reaching and pulling me into a hug. I collapsed into her gratefully.

As we broke apart, I realized we had an audience. The people of Fahali were crowding around us, gathering as the dust settled. Only they weren't looking at us. Every eye in the street was fixed on Ahmed.

He was standing just outside the city gates, with three Mirajin soldiers. Prisoners, I guessed, as they waited on their knees, heads bowed, for his verdict.

He really did carry himself like a prince. I saw it now. The smiling, friendly Ahmed who'd brushed off *"your majesty"* was gone. But he wasn't some golden ruler ready to climb onto a throne either. He looked like a legendary hero fresh from battle. Like a man who could lead this country.

"What happened?" I asked, leaning on Shazad. Everything was a blur after Naguib's death.

"The Gallan soldiers who survived retreated," Shazad answered in a low voice as we looked on. "I saw them riding north. When they report back to their king that the

Sultan tried to kill them, he won't have an alliance on his hands anymore. What was left of Naguib's army surrendered to us after he died. Everyone saw him burn."

"And Noorsham? I lost track of him in the fighting . . ."

"Then he's gone." Shazad's jaw tightened.

He'd gotten away. I tried to hide the relief on my face. Noorsham had killed Bahi. The boy who drunkenly serenaded her below a window and joined a rebellion for her. But he was still my brother. My brother, who had the power to destroy this whole desert if he chose to, was out there somewhere. And he knew my true name.

"I am not going to kill you." Ahmed was speaking to the Mirajin soldiers who had surrendered, his voice loud enough for those around him to hear. "Execution without trial is what the Gallan have done here for decades. And their influence on our desert will be ending soon." One of the three Mirajin soldiers glanced up, like he was just daring to hope he might get out of here with his life. "So I will release you on the condition that you carry a message to my father."

A rustle went through the crowd at "my father." If Ahmed noticed, he didn't let it show. "You will tell him Fahali is whole and it is under my protection. That I am laying claim to every city west of the middle mountains. My father cannot hold this whole country against its will without the Gallan alliance. And if he will not listen to the people's will, he will listen to mine. One way or another, I will take the throne of this nation one day. But until then, these are my people."

Everyone's attention was on Ahmed now as his eyes traveled between the three soldiers. They might flee Miraji before going back to the Sultan with Ahmed's words. But stories had a way of traveling in the desert. The Sultan would hear that the Rebel Prince had stood in the ashes of the battle of Fahali and laid claim to half his kingdom. "And if he comes after my people, I will bring war to his doorstep."

"A new dawn!" The cry burst out of the crowd before Ahmed had even fully finished speaking.

"A new desert!" A dozen voices called back, ragged and out of pace.

"A new dawn! A new desert!" The cry was taken up around Fahali, thousands of Mirajin voices together as one. Chanting for their prince, their hero, for all of us.

The sun was setting as we made our way out of the city and back into the Dev's Valley. When the story of this day reached the Sultan, no one would tell him we were a small rabble of tired and sorry-looking rebels. That we didn't look fit to fight the war that was coming. That half of us weren't sure if we could. He would only know that we had won and were still alive.

And tomorrow the sun would rise on the first day of a new desert.

ACKNOWLEDGMENTS

This is a book about a girl who went from going it alone to becoming part of something bigger than herself. I'm coming to realize that also describes the journey of having your first book published.

The very first person on this book's journey was my agent, Molly Ker Hawn. I don't think I'd ever heard Amani's name out loud until she said it the first time we met, and I will always remember that as the moment this book found someone else who knew it and believed in it. Since then, she has taken this book further than I ever imagined, and I am so grateful to her and the rest of the amazing Bent Agency team for continuing to support and guide me at every step.

I am ridiculously lucky that this book found its way to my editors, Kendra Levin and Alice Swan, who were so enthusiastic about this story and so smart in guiding it where it needed to go. So thank you for everything from taking a chance on me, to edit letters with Star Wars and Chekov references and a whole section entitled "sexytimes," to six-hour phone calls. But more than anything, thank you for being so endlessly patient with a debut author trying to figure it all out. I am very glad that this book found its home with Viking and Faber, and I'm completely indebted to the amazing teams both in the U.S. and the U.K. for all their work. A book goes through more people's hands than I ever knew, and probably even know now, and I am grateful to every single one of them.

To everyone who has acquired this book in another country, the fact that you will be translating my words into languages I can't even read blows me away. Thank you.

This book is already dedicated to my parents. If "show, don't tell" is a rule of writing, it's one my parents perfected in real life. I can't ever remember being told anything as clichéd as "We believe in you" or "We support you no matter what," but I also can't remember ever not knowing it.

I owe a debt to every person who has kept me sane as I moved from writer to author. The ways they helped me are mostly abstract, so I am reduced to having to thank them for the concrete things that came along with the moral support. So thank you to Rachel Rose Smith, for almond croissants, sleepovers on her floor, and just being one of the best people I know. Michella Domenici, for reading this book more than once through its changes and being an amazing sounding board and the first person to fangirl at me. Jon Andrews, for motivational pictures of Taylor Swift drawn on napkins. Amelia Hodgson, for spending an entire afternoon helping me brainstorm the middle. My little brother, Max, for putting up with me over Christmas while I tried to figure out that bomb thing, and for valiantly attempting to give me scientific advice that went over my head. Janet Hamilton-Davies, for engaging so naturally and completely with the fact that your niece had written a book in a way that only a teacher, who has spent a lifetime making sure young people around her are aware that they are capable, could. Nick Sims, for being amazingly understanding with a distracted employee trying to edit a book. Justine Caillaud, for making me WANTED posters and spending the last twenty-four years being creative with me. To the Sweet Sixteens, I'm only starting to understand what an amazing support network a debut group is and how much I need it. Thanks to everyone who is taking the trip into 2016 publication with me. And to all the amazing book bloggers for sharing the cover, for organizing chats, and just being so endlessly and tirelessly enthusiastic and positive about books on the internet and off. And thanks also to anyone who offered up any kind of support through this process, even if it seemed insignificant at the time—so for every time you told me I could do it when I wasn't sure, be it in the form of encouraging words, a silly text, or the gift of a notebook. Roisin Ellison, Tempe Nell, Catherine Parkes, Meredith Sykes, Olivia Bliss, Annik Vrana, Elisa Peccerillo, Anne Murphy, Sophie Cass, Heidi Heilig, Roshani Chokshi, Jessica Cluess, Harriet Reuter Hapgood, Kathryn Purdie, Stephanie Garber, Alexia Casale, and lots of other people I'm sure I'm omitting accidentally. Please pretend the music is playing me off as I scramble to remember everyone who has been there in this journey. But you know who you are, and I hope you know I am grateful.

The end of this book is about a girl finding her home and her place. And so finally, thank you to you, reader, for picking this book up and being the end of this book's journey.

TRAITOR
TO THE THRONE

Forget everything you thought you knew
about Miraji, about the rebellion, about Djinn
and Jin and the Blue-Eyed Bandit.
In *Traitor to the Throne*, the only certainty is
that everything will change . . .
Read on for a sneak peek.

two

I'd always liked this shirt. It was a shame about all the blood.

Most of it wasn't mine, at least. The shirt wasn't mine, either, for that matter—I'd borrowed it from Shazad and never bothered to give it back. Well, she probably wouldn't want it now.

"Stop!"

I was jerked to a halt. My hands were tied, and the rope chafed painfully along the raw skin of my wrists. I hissed a curse under my breath as I tilted my head back, finally looking up from my dusty boots to lock eyes with the glare of the desert sun.

The walls of Saramotai cast a mighty long shadow in the last of the light.

These walls were legendary. They had stood indifferent to one of the greatest battles of the First War, between the hero Attallah and the Destroyer of Worlds. They were so ancient they looked like they'd been built out of the bones of the desert itself. But the words slapped in sloppy white paint above the gates . . . those were new.

WELCOME TO THE FREE CITY

I could see where the paint had dripped between the cracks in the ancient stones before drying in the heat.

I had a few things to say about being dragged to a so-called Free City tied up like a goat on a spit, but even I knew I was better off not running my mouth just now.

"Declare yourself or I'll shoot!" someone called from the city wall. The words were a whole lot more impressive than the voice that came with them. I could hear the crack of youth on that last word. I squinted up through my sheema at the kid pointing a rifle at me from the top of the walls. He couldn't have been any older than thirteen. He was all limbs and joints. He didn't look like he could've held that gun right if his life depended on it. Which it probably did. This being Miraji and all.

"It's us, Ikar, you little idiot," the man holding me bellowed in my ear. I winced. Shouting really didn't seem necessary. "Now, open the gates right now or, God help me, I'm going to have your father beat you harder than one of his horseshoes until some brains go in."

"Hossam?" Ikar didn't lower the gun right away. He was

twitchy as all get-out. Which wasn't the best thing when he had one finger on the trigger of a rifle. "Who's that with you?" He waved his gun in my direction. I turned my body on instinct as the barrel swung wildly. He didn't look like he could hit the broadside of a barn if he was trying, but I wasn't ruling out that he might hit me by accident. If he did, better to get shot in the shoulder than the chest.

"This"—a hint of pride crept into Hossam's voice as he jerked my face up to the sunlight like I was a hunted carcass—"is the Blue-Eyed Bandit."

That name landed with more weight than it used to, drawing silence down behind it. On top of the wall Ikar stared. Even this far away I saw his jaw open, going slack for a moment, then close.

"Open the gates!" Ikar squawked finally, scrambling down. "Open the gates!"

The huge iron doors swung open painfully slow, fighting against the sand that had built up over the day. Hossam and the other men with us jostled me forward in a hurry as the ancient hinges groaned.

The gates didn't open all the way, only enough for one man to get through at a time. Even after thousands of years those gates looked as strong as they had at the dawn of humanity. They were iron through and through, as thick as the span of a man's arms, and operated by some system of weights and gears that no other city had been able to duplicate. There'd be no breaking these gates down. And everyone knew there was no climbing the walls of Saramotai.

Seemed like the only way into the city these days was by being dragged through the gates as a prisoner with a hand around your neck. Lucky me.

Saramotai was west of the middle mountains. Which meant it was ours. Or at least, it was supposed to be. After the battle at Fahali Ahmed had declared this territory as his. Most cities had sworn their allegiance quickly enough, as the Gallan occupiers who'd held this half of the desert for so long emptied out of the streets. Or we'd claimed their allegiance away from the Sultan easy enough.

Saramotai was another story.

Welcome to the Free City.

Saramotai had declared its own laws, taking rebellion one step further.

Ahmed talked a whole lot about equality and wealth for the poor. The people of Saramotai had decided the only way to create equality was to strike down those who were above them. That the only way to become rich was to take their wealth. So they'd turned against the rich under the guise of accepting Ahmed's rule.

But Ahmed knew a grab for power when he saw one. We didn't know all that much about Malik Al-Kizzam, the man who'd taken over Saramotai, except that he'd been a servant to the emir and now the emir was dead and Malik lived in the palace.

So we sent a few folks to find out more. And do something about it if we didn't like it.

They didn't come back.

That was a problem. Another problem was getting in after them.

And so here I was, my hands tied so tight behind my back I was losing feeling in them and a fresh wound on my collarbone where a knife had just barely missed my neck. Funny how being successful felt exactly the same as getting captured.

Hossam shoved me ahead of him through the narrow gap in the gates. I stumbled and went sprawling in the sand face-first, my elbow bashing into the iron gate painfully as I went down.

Son of a bitch, that hurt more than I thought it would.

A hiss of pain escaped through my teeth as I rolled over. Sand stuck to my hands where sweat had pooled under the ropes, clinging to my skin. Then Hossam grabbed me, yanking me to my feet. He hustled me inside, the gate clanging quickly behind us. It was almost like they were afraid of something.

A small crowd had already gathered inside the gate to gawk. Half were clutching guns. More than a few of those were pointed at me.

So my reputation really did precede me.

"Hossam." Someone pushed to the front. He was older than my captors, with serious eyes that took in my sorry state. He looked at me more level than the others. He would't be blinded by the same eagerness. "What happened?"

"We caught her in the mountains," Hossam crowed. "She tried to ambush us when we were on our way back from trading for the guns." Two of the other men with us dropped bags that were heavy with weapons on the ground proudly, as if to show off that I hadn't gotten in their way. The guns weren't of Mirajin make. Amonpourian. Stupid-looking things. Ornate and carved, made by hand instead of machine, and charged at twice what they were worth because someone had gone to the trouble of making them pretty. It didn't matter how pretty something was, it'd kill you just as dead. That, I'd learned from Shazad.

"Just her?" the man with the serious eyes asked. "On her own?" His gaze flicked to me. Like he might be able to suss out the truth just from looking at me. Whether a girl of seventeen would really think she could take on a half dozen grown men with nothing but a handful of bullets and think she could win. Whether the famous Blue-Eyed Bandit could really be *that* stupid.

I preferred "reckless."

But I kept my mouth shut. The more I talked, the more likely I was to say something that'd backfire on me. *Stay silent, look sullen, try not to get yourself killed.*

If all else fails, just stick with that last one.

"Are you really the Blue-Eyed Bandit?" Ikar blurted out, making everyone's head turn. He'd scrambled down from his watchpost on the wall to come gawk at me with the rest. He leaned forward eagerly across the barrel of his gun. If it went off now it'd take both his hands and part of his face with it. "Is it true what they say about you?"

Stay silent. Look sullen. Try not to get yourself killed. "Depends what they're saying, I suppose." Damn it. That didn't last so long. "And you shouldn't hold your gun like that."

Ikar shifted his grip absently, never taking his eyes off me. "They say that you can shoot a man's eye out fifty feet away in the pitch dark. That you walked through a hail of bullets in Iliaz, and walked out with the Sultan's secret war plans." I remembered Iliaz going a little differently. It ended with a bullet in me, for one. "That you seduced one of the Emir of Jalaz's wives while they were visiting Izman." Now, that was a new one. I'd heard the one about seducing the emir himself. But maybe the emir's wife liked women, too. Or maybe the story had twisted in the telling, since half the tales of the Blue-Eyed Bandit seemed to make out I was a man these days. I'd stopped wearing wraps to pretend I was a boy, but apparently I'd need to fill out a little more to convince some people that the bandit was a girl.

"You killed a hundred Gallan soldiers at Fahali," he pushed on, his words tripping over each other, undeterred by my silence. "And I heard you escaped from Malal on the back of a giant blue Roc, and flooded the prayer house behind you."

"You shouldn't believe everything you hear," I interjected as Ikar finally paused for breath, his eyes the size of two louzi pieces with excitement.

He sagged, disappointed. He was just a kid, as eager to believe all the stories as I had been when I was his age. Though he looked younger than I ever remembered being. He shouldn't be here, holding a gun like this. But then, this was what the desert did to us. It made us dreamers with weapons. I ran my tongue along my teeth. "And the prayer house in Malal was an accident . . . mostly."

A whisper went through the crowd. I'd be lying if I said

it didn't send a little thrill down my spine. And lying was a sin.

It'd been close to half a year since I'd stood in Fahali with Ahmed, Jin, Shazad, Hala, and the twins, Izz and Maz. Us against two armies and Noorsham, a Demdji turned into a weapon by the Sultan; a Demdji who also happened to be my brother.

Us against impossible odds and a devastatingly powerful Demdji. But we'd survived. And from there the story of the battle of Fahali had traveled across the desert faster even than the story of the Sultim trials had. I'd heard it told a dozen times by folks who didn't know the Rebellion was listening. Our exploits got greater and less plausible with every telling but the tale always ended the same way, with a sense that, while the storyteller might be done, the story wasn't. One way or another, the desert wasn't going to be the same after the battle of Fahali.

The legend of the Blue-Eyed Bandit had grown along with the tale of Fahali, until I was a story that I didn't wholly recognize. It claimed that the Blue-Eyed Bandit was a thief instead of a rebel. That I tricked my way into people's beds to get information for my Prince. That I'd killed my own brother on the battlefield. I hated that one the most. Maybe because there'd been a moment, finger on the trigger, where it was almost true. And I had let him escape. Which was almost as bad. He was out there somewhere with all of that power. And, unlike me, he didn't have any other Demdji to help him.

Sometimes, late at night, after the rest of the camp had

gone to sleep, I'd say out loud that he was alive. Just to know whether it was true or not. So far I could say it without hesitation. But I was scared that there would come a day when I wouldn't be able to anymore. That would mean they were a lie, and my brother had died, alone and scared, somewhere in this merciless, war-torn desert.

"If she's as dangerous as they say, we ought to kill her," someone called from the crowd. It was a man with a bright yellow military sash across his chest that looked like it'd been stitched back together from scraps. I noticed a few were wearing those. These must be the newly appointed guard of Saramotai, since they'd gone and killed the real guard. He was holding a gun. It was pointed at my stomach. Stomach wounds were no good. They killed you slowly.

"But if she's the Blue-Eyed Bandit, she's with the Rebel Prince." Someone else spoke up. "Doesn't that mean she's on our side?" Now, that was the million-fouza question.

"Funny way to treat someone on your side." I shifted my bound hands pointedly. A murmur went through the crowd. That was good; it meant they weren't as united as they looked from the outside of their impenetrable wall. "So if we're all friends here, how about you untie me and we can talk?"

"Nice try, Bandit." Hossam gripped me tighter. "We're not giving you a chance to get your hands on a gun. I've heard the stories of how you killed a dozen men with a single bullet." I was pretty sure that wasn't possible. Besides, I didn't need a gun to take down a dozen men.